The Distance Between High and Low

A Southern Gothic Novel

*by
Kaye Park Hinckley*

Copyright © 2019 Kaye Park Hinckley
Prytania Publishing
All rights reserved.

OTHER BOOKS

A HUNGER IN THE HEART

BIRDS OF A FEATHER

MARY'S MOUNTAIN

THE WIND THAT SHAKES THE CORN
2018 INDEPENDENT PRESS AWARD

SHE WHO SEES BEYOND

BRIDGE-MAN BURNING
SEQUEL TO A HUNGER IN THE HEART

THE GHOSTS OF FAITHFUL
POETS & WRITERS MAGAZINE MAUREEN EGAN AWARD, FIRST RUNNER-UP

FOR

MY MOTHER AND MY GRANDMOTHER

*The redeeming things are not happiness and pleasure
but the deeper satisfactions that come out of struggle.*
-- F. Scott Fitzgerald, *The Great Gatsby*

*Not till we know the high things
shall we know how lovely they are.*
-- G.K. Chesterton, *William Blake*

Voices

Lizzie

Downstairs, in the old Highlow, Alabama house where I was born, the doorbell is being rung by guest after guest coming to Pearl's annual Christmas Open House. Conversations disrupted by sporadic laughter ascend the dark staircase to what was, years ago, my brother's room. The conversations are muffled by the closed mahogany door, and by my brother's still-present voice, a voice I hear on turned-back pages. Some pages pronounce history. Some expose hearts. Once, I seemed a trespasser here; now I am home, holding a suitcase of memories.

Like siblings at odds with each other, a paper poster of the first Russian satellite, Sputnik, used to hang on that wall, and beside it, a poster of Explorer, the first satellite launched by the United States in the Space Race between the two countries. My brother, Peck, kept his diary in the drawer of that yellow pine table, until I found it. Afterwards, he hid it in the closet across the room, beneath his National Geographic Magazines. The closet was his sanctum. He sat on its carpeted floor with the door closed, only a tiny light above him, and filled pages with a story of distance, when our father was sought, but could not be found.

Through the window, there is a Confederate Rose bush. It has no blooms now, only broad leaves that quiver in the night wind. Above it, the milk-colored moonlight lays a shadow on the swaying tops of trees. Caught behind a single pine, the moonlight divides like the wide wings of an osprey—that bird my brother hungered for--to fly down over the grass, mount the ancient, brick wall, and flutters inside, fondling the faces of my sleeping twins; a girl and a boy. Almost as if Peck intended it.

Peck and I were twins, too. In the darkest of watery wombs, we waited for the voice of our father, and heard silence. So, we placed our arms around each other, and I felt the beating of his heart, its tiny, sweet pulsations thumping against my skin. Wound together, my brother belonged to me, and I to him, for our breath was the same breath. Our loss was the same loss. I loved him then. I love him now. I will always love him. He died too soon.

Back Then

Saturday Morning in Highlow

The Breakfast Club plays low on the radio and I'm in the kitchen with my grandmother, Pearl. We sit in chairs beside the enameled, white table. My right foot is in her lap. Her tiny hand is around my ankle to keep it from moving while she tweezes a piece of glass from my heel. "Hold still, Lizzie!" she orders, always in control.

Around us are boundaries are kept spotless. Ordered counters, perfectly cornered, support high lacquered cupboards enclosing a myriad of functional things. Bright turquoise walls, like burnished canvases, snatch low sprays of sunlight from a single great window to collect our sapphire shadows. But in the back yard, our world of diversion, there is disorder. The stems of plants no longer hold their spent blooms. The branches of fertile pear trees slump. Fallen fruit scatters decay in the grass, delivering its fetid odor through the screened door and into the black and white tiled kitchen.

Just inside the screen, my twin brother, Peck, watches us. His jaw set tight, his green eyes guilty over the moment of frustration when he shattered a glass Coca Cola bottle on Pearl's concrete driveway. I haven't told Pearl that he did it, and won't. That's just the way it is between Peck and me.

Pearl looks at me through gold-rimmed glasses that grip the tip of her nose and clarify the indistinctness of a world once clear to her. "People from Main Street wear shoes in December, Lizzie." Then she goes back to picking my heel with the tweezers.

"It's eighty-five degrees outside. I didn't think about shoes."

"Well, this is what happens when you don't think." She holds up a greenish chip of glass trapped in the tweezers. "Dangerous debris." Then she says what she always says when I disappoint her. "If you don't want to go to Cincinnati, then don't get on the bus." It's a favorite adage she picked up from her second cousin, the only Judge in Highlow.

By now, I know how to respond. "Cincinnati is a dangerous place, not half as nice as Highlow. I don't ever want to go there." Pearl gives my foot a congratulatory pat.

And Peck gives a defiant slap to the fuzzy red and white Santa Claus pinned to the screen. The bells on its feet jingle. "Well, I'm going there. Our daddy's in Cincinnati and I want him to paint my portrait."

Pearl stands, holding a cane with the ebony head of a lamb, that belonged to her father, and to his father before him. "It's your mother who's the artist, not your father. If he was an artist, he'd have cared about what he created. He'd have painted you both in his mind and he wouldn't have forgotten you!"

Peck winces at her words. The mystery of our father's identity feeds on his heart like an unhurried dragon. But it doesn't bother me so much. After all, we have Pearl and Izear. And even though our mother often borders on crazy, at least she's right upstairs.

Pearl cools quickly, compassion in her bright blue eyes. Then Peck says, "I'm going next door to Hobart's." The bells jingle again as the tight door spring slams the screen behind him.

"Oh, my. He's such a sensitive boy." Pearl says. "And so mistaken about his father."

But when Peck says our father is an artist from Cincinnati, I believe him. I don't know how he came to that conclusion; I only remember that one day he did. And now, my brother's greatest desire is to go there and find that man he doesn't know. I want what he wants, so when I told Pearl I wouldn't go to Cincinnati, it wasn't true. I'd follow Peck anywhere.

Earlier today, I followed him next door to the McSwain house. We often go there on Saturdays, if Hobart's not working at the used car lot in Dixie. Hobart opened his door with a smile (he has perfect white teeth) then stopped whatever he was doing to hand us each a bottled Coke and some silver tops from a candy jar shaped like a snowman. Then we sat on the sofa in his living room and Hobart took out Mrs. McSwain's leather album to show us black and white pictures of beautiful Mama who seemed a happy, sensible girl, and him, a clumsy-looking, little boy, tagging behind her like a sad afterthought. He told us about growing up next door to Mama and how Mama used to treat him so sweet. Then oddly, he stroked her photographed face and lovingly mumbled her name, "Lila, Lila." Without even saying good bye, Peck got up and left the house, with the bottle of Coke still in his hand.

 I went after him, as always. But today, he was mad enough to holler, "Stop following me, Lizzie!" That was when he threw the bottle against the concrete. It burst like a new star in formation, exploding around both of us. Except, it was me who stepped into the pieces.

 Pearl is wrapping the chip of glass in a napkin, shaking her little chins over Peck's slamming of the screened door. "What do you and Peck see in that Yankee boy next door?" she asks me.

 I shrug. "He gives us candy." It's the only thing I can think of.

 "Hobart's way too old to be playing with thirteen year-olds. Maybe if he was actually from Highlow it might be different, but he's never belonged here." Then she reprimands herself, "Oh Pearl, be kind. Hobart can't help where he came from."

 Actually, I think Pearl likes Hobart. She often discusses him with her cousin, The Judge. Pearl says while they're talking about Hobart, The Judge takes notes. He takes notes on most everyone in Highlow, because The Judge is responsible for conclusions so he needs to keep track of the circumstances leading up to them.

 Sometimes I like Hobart, too, now that I'm old enough to notice him. He's twenty-something and very good-looking. I'd like to follow Peck to his house again, but Pearl needs me here. It's the Saturday before her Christmas open-house, a party that Mama never wants to come to, but always does, because Pearl insists.

I watch my grandmother slowly climb the stairs and go into Mama's room where their voices sputter from high to low like a broken radio. After a while, Pearl comes out. She is just beyond the threshold when the door closes and the lock clicks from inside. She stops right there, against her own wall of black and white photographs, leaning on her lamb's head cane. She does not look back when she says, "Lila, you are expected tomorrow night." Then her tone softens. "Please darling, the party only comes once a year."

Pearl doesn't wait for an answer. She taps forward to the holly-wrapped landing above me; a small, old woman, curved like a question mark.

"Do you think Mama will come?" I ask.

Pearl stops to straighten a crooked red bow tied onto the holly. "She was painting a girl's face with a party ribbon in her hair. That's a good sign."

Mama paints faces on china plates, but not the fine porcelain ones from Pearl's cabinet. Pearl scans the garage sale classifieds then sends Izear to look for all the unwanted plates he can find. Pearl and Izear are proud that Mama renews discarded things. Years ago, when he was a little boy, Izear was discarded, too, until Pearl rescued him from his mean Cherokee Indian daddy and gave him a happy home in her Highlow house.

Mama paints a fresh face on each worn plate and when she's done, she carefully prints a name, hidden in the raw umber shadows of a temple, or under the pale cadmium highlight of a chiseled chin, or in the black pupil of a familiar eye-. She prints it real tiny so you have to look hard to find it. She prints dates, too, for when that fine face was born and died. There's a little boy up there now, born in 210 and died in 223. She said she painted him because he once carried the Bread of Life to men in prison, and then was killed for it by his so-called friends. His face looks a lot like our faces, Peck's and mine. Imagine us looking like somebody almost two thousand years old! But Pearl said no matter the years, people have always looked pretty much the same way, which is mostly the wrong way, but no surprise to her. Two thousand years from now, if the world's still here, it'll be the same thing. Pearl said looking the wrong way is the hand-me-down thing that's messed up the world.

Mama calls the little boy on her plate, Tarsicius, and Pearl thinks Mama painted him with real sweet-looking face. Pearl's partial to little boys with sweet looks, even the ones who look the wrong way.

"If Mama's painting a girl dressed for a party," I say, "that means she's coming to the open-house." I try to keep Pearl's spirits high.

"I don't know about that. Sometimes you might as well be talking to a pile of pine straw as talk to your mama." She disappears around the corner wall of the landing, tapping ebony.

Last week, on our side of Main Street, Miss Billie Nana Spratling's yard man was hauling off pine straw and accidentally stepped off her curb when the wheel barrow tipped over because it was too heavy for him. A dark-skinned, white man, driving a yellow pick-up truck, looked the wrong way and ran into him. It broke her yard man's leg, but Miss Billie Nana had him in a cast that very day. He's fine, now. I saw him at her house just this morning, finishing up the raking.

Pearl thinks there're too many accidents on both sides of the street. She said it's getting about as dangerous to step off on Main Street in Highlow, Alabama as it was for Mama to step off the bus in Cincinnati when she ran off to art school against Pearl's better judgment. Mama was too young and too fragile to go anywhere on her own; and when she came back nine months later, big as two watermelons, Pearl said Mama was so spent-out she couldn't even carry her own pocketbook. Izear had to carry that heavy thing for her. And from the looks of her eyes, Pearl said, she was pretty sure Mama'd cried all the way home.

Two days after she got back, my brother and I were born and Mama nearly died. Pearl said she shuddered to think of what might have happened if Mama had tried to have twins up there in that cold and distant place without a trace of family. Even now, all those bright lights Mama used to have in her eyes?--they're gone. Pearl said it was Cincinnati that snuffed them out. It's the one thing in this world she's positive about.

Peck has been at Hobart's all day while I've been helping Pearl chop pecans and raisins and shred coconut for her Lane Cake. I wanted to help Izear put up Christmas lights in the front yard instead, but Pearl said no, just leave him alone because Izear has his own way of doing things. By the time night comes on, Izear has bright lights strung up everywhere; winding up the porch rail, all around the front door. He's even got lights on the two leafless Japanese magnolias that stand next to the street, way down below the fat live oaks and tall pines in Pearl's long front yard. Izear had to run seventeen, eight-foot extension cords up the yard for that and you'd think he'd never done anything better in his whole life the way he stands out there now, small as my thumb in the middle of Main Street, so proud of the beautiful lights he's strung.

Watching Izear through Pearl's parlor window, seeing him stuck in the center of all those lights, reminds me of a gingerbread boy set on a plate with colored candies all around him. Remember that gingerbread boy that got it in his head to run away and all those hungry people and animals that ran, ran, ran after him? Ran fast as they could, but none of them could catch him because he had a right to leave if he wanted to. Then he met the wolf, and you know what happened. I think that was kind of like what happened to Mama in Cincinnati. And lately, I worry it might happen to Peck, too.

Highlow's Nice
But It's Not the World

When the upstairs window creaks open, I'm out on the front porch watching the moths attack the gas coach light and Izear is standing in the street looking up at his handiwork. Pearl's concerned voice crackles from above. "Izear, get out of the street before you get run over!" But Izear won't budge an inch unless he's got a mind to. "Then do not expect me to pay for your burial, Izear!" Pearl warns.

"Ain't go'n be dead enough to get buried, Miss Pearl. Ain't no trucks coming." He looks both ways, up and down the street. "Nome, ain't a truck in sight." He crosses his arms over his chest and stands very still for several seconds to make his point, then comes on up the yard, stopping to rearrange one of the light strings on a Japanese magnolia.

Pearl gives a sigh of exasperation and the upstairs window creaks back down.

Izear crosses the grass beyond the porch then rounds the side of Pearl's ancient house without seeing me, or knowing I'm thinking up something to say to him. If you're from Highlow, you have been taught to say polite stuff. It lets people know you appreciate them. "Hey Izear," I call. "Those lights you put up sure are pretty."

He does a little jerk; voices coming out of nowhere scare him sometimes. He tilts his head and squints up at me. "Ain't it time for you to be in bed?"

Izear likes to act gruff, but he's really nice. Pearl says he got his good disposition from his pretty black mama who was much sweeter than his mean old Cherokee daddy. I don't tell him how nice he is though, even if I do love him. You can take polite too far, especially when Pearl says I'm supposed to mind him like I would my own daddy, if he was here.

"It's too early for bed, Izear. You want to play Pin the Tail on the Donkey?"

"I certainly do not. I don't play no assy games."

His words trail the shadow that curls in front of him, around the camellia, between the gardenias, and Izear follows it like he's sneaking up on a black cat's tail. The tail stretches out, long and pointed, on the other side of the loaded bushes, leading him back to the one hundred and twenty year-old carriage house. Thirty years ago, when Izear turned sixteen, Pearl decided he was a man, not a boy anymore, so she turned the carriage house into a garage apartment and moved him in. He's stayed there ever since.

I stay on the porch, thinking of the gingerbread boy and wondering why in the world he'd want to run away when he had a happy home on a plate. Then Peck calls to me from inside the house. He's finally back from Hobart's where he stayed all afternoon.

"I'm out here!" I holler, but wish I hadn't when Little Benedict Spratling follows him onto the porch like a three-quarter midget. I can't help but say, "I hope you're not spending the night with us, again!" When he does, Little Benedict starts out in Peck's room, but ends up in my bed, crying to go home and I don't get any sleep at all.

"Pearl said he could," my brother answers. He defends even the most obnoxious people. Besides being polite, he's what people from Highlow call 'a real nice boy.' Pearl says Peck might be sullen sometimes, but that's because he's very intelligent and thinks beyond his years. I don't know about that, but he does have some big words written in the diary he hides in his closet.

"My mama and daddy's gone to a par-tee," Little Benedict squeals like it was something to be proud of and like Peck and I ought to wish we had a daddy and mama with a party to go to. But

I don't need to wish for a party. Pearl's is coming up. And crazy or not, I do have a mama. I'll bet a silver dollar she's having a party right now, talking to the faces on her plates. As far as my daddy, Peck and I wouldn't know his face if we saw it, but I'll bet another dollar that man has been to a lot of parties in his lifetime. Maybe more than Mr. Benedict, Sr. and Mrs. Billie Nana Spratling ever heard of.

"How come Hobart won't baby sit you anymore, Little Benedict?" I ask the skinny pip-squeak. "You got too wild for your other next-door neighbor?"

Of course, Little Benedict is anything but wild. He's just a pansy and always will be. Peck thinks he's lonely inside; but outside, Little Benedict is as sickly pale as the yellow-ochre sketch Mama draws on the china before she puts the color on. And he always has a cold. Miss Billie Nana will tell you Little Benedict has inherited allergies from Mr. Benedict, Sr.'s side of the family. In fact, she'll tell you anything she can plug in a conversation to let you know that she married a man who did not come from the same kind of good stock she did. But whatever Little Benedict's got, and wherever he got it from, it drools and snuffs just like a cold. Put that in with the nighttime crying and there's enough pitiful little boy to grate on your nerves 'til it snows a blizzard in Highlow, Alabama.

"Hobart can't baby sit me tonight 'cause he's got him a date," Little Benedict sniffs. He wipes his drippy nose on the sleeve of his plaid flannel shirt, then grabs at a fly-by moth.

Peck gives a loud hee-haw laugh, so I laugh, too. "It's not a date," Peck says. "It's Mrs. McSwain's sister's child, come to visit from Crisscross, Georgia." Peck pats Little Benedict on the top of his pale orange crew cut like a daddy might do. "That makes her his cousin, Little Benedict."

"Yes, it is a date. They're going to the picture show!" Another trickle, another swipe with his shirt sleeve.

"Who cares about a date?" I say to them. Except I care. I'm

thirteen, now, and I have dreams.

"You're just jealous because nobody ever asked you to the picture show and prob'ly never will," Peck says, but I can see he's sorry he said it. His eyes get soft-looking real quick when he thinks he's hurt your feelings.

So I ask him, "You want to play Monopoly?"

"He don't wanna play nothin'." Little Benedict chirps. "We saw the Osprey up there on the McSwain's roof." and we're fixin' to go catch it, ain't we, Peck?"

I yank at a wisp of Little Benedict's fruit-colored hair. "That's a plain lie. Osprey's hunt for fish and there're no fish on the McSwain's roof. Anyway, it's just an old bird."

Little Benedict twists away from me. "It ain't a lie and it ain't an old bird. It's a big ole Osprey; big as a dog."

"A dog with wings? Shoot boy, does it bark, too?"

"Hush up, Lizzie," Peck says.

"Oh, what do you want with it, anyway?" Since we first saw it circling the river in Dixie, Peck's wanted that hawk. Izear told him then it was an evil thing. 'You better not be wanting no evil thing. Claw out yo' eyes, you ever caught it.' But Izear hasn't changed Peck's mind about the hawk any more than Pearl changed his mind when she said our father was not an artist from Cincinnati.

"Even if the Osprey was here'," I say, "ya'll couldn't see it out here in the dark."

"It ain't dark. Look at all the lights!" Little Benedict snatches at another moth and starts down the steps.

Peck snatches him back by the collar of his flannel shirt. "Stay on the porch, Little Benedict."

"Yeah, there's some awful mean folks ride up and down that street." I take absolute delight when I hear Little Benedict's fearful, sucked-in breath.

"You're the one being mean," Peck says to me.

I give Little Benedict another yank to his hair and he punches me in the stomach. It doesn't hurt. Little Benedict couldn't hurt a fly if he tried to.

Peck is studying the McSwain's roof, so I try to distract him. "Pearl said we could ask Hobart to come over early tomorrow night to help her get ready for the party."

"Okay," Peck says, but he's still scanning the treetop.

"I'm coming to the par-tee!" Little Benedict squawks. "I came last year and the year before that, remember Lizzie?"

"I remember who had to watch you so you wouldn't get into trouble. I'm not watching you again. I plan to enjoy myself on the twenty-third of December."

"Me too!" he says and tries to grab my hand. I snap it away from him. Nobody in their right mind would want to hold Little Benedict's snotty hand after all he's wiped up with it.

"Come then, but you'll have to find somebody else to carry your cake."

"I'm big enough to carry my own cake, dummy. Watch this." Little Benedict steps up on the base of the porch railing which puts him chin-level to me. "See? I'm strong." He flexes his piddly muscles, loses his balance and stumbles back onto the porch, then we all laugh like hyenas because it feels good, until Peck returns his eyes to the tree tops and Little Benedict whines that he's sleepy. He grabs my arm. "C'mon, Lizzie. I wanna go to bed."

"Listen, little worm," I say, prying off his fingers. "I am not seven years old like you. Teenagers don't go to bed the same time babies do"

The front door opens. Pearl says to Peck, "Time to unplug the Christmas lights, honey, and lock up." Then pointing to me with a teeny finger, her tone of voice flips to firm. "Take Little Benedict upstairs and help him into his pajamas."

"Why do I have to do it?"

"Because I said so, and I don't want to hear one more peep about it, Lizzie."

I can't stand the smirk on Little Benedict's face when he gets a grown-up to agree with him. I grab the back of his scrawny, doll-like neck and I don't even move my lips when I whisper so Pearl won't hear. "You can put on your own pajamas!" I push him up the stairs and the thought occurs to me that I am in control of his puny life, except that Pearl is watching. "Good night, Pearl," I say sweetly, squeezing Little Benedict's neck like Edgar Bergen squeezes the neck of his dummy, Charlie McCarthy, and makes Charlie say whatever Edgar wants him to. "Say goodnight to Pearl, Little Benedict."

"Night Miss Pearl," he says. A dummy if there ever was one!

Of course, I do help Little Benedict with his pajamas, and he does cry and sniff and snuff, then ends up in my bed with his arm flung over my ventriloquist mouth. And the tiny wisp of warmth he gives lying beside me almost makes me forget that Little Benedict's mama and daddy are known for staying at their 'par-tees' for two or three days. I even think how we might make a good ventriloquist team--me and my dummy, Little Benedict--him on my knee and saying whatever I make him say, like: "Oh Lizzie, you're the most beautiful princess in the whole entire world and someday your prince will come to take you away from Highlow. Would you like that, Lizzie?"

And I would answer in my own royal voice, because every princess must widen her viewpoint. "You'd better believe it, dummy! Highlow's nice, but it's not the world."

Call me Knucklehead

The Spratling House

"Little Benedict! What are you doing under the bed?"

"Hiding from Mama."

"Why are you hiding from your mother? Come out from under there, now."

"I can't, Daddy. My shirt's got hung on a spring."

"Dammit, move this way. There. Now, get out!"

"Is Mama asleep?"

"No, just lying down. She's a little tired and nervous. Look Benny, you know she doesn't mean those things she says to you."

"Then why does she say them?"

"Because she's angry with me, not you."

"But I'm the one she yells at, and she calls me stupid, too. She's not like my grandmother, Pearl."

"Pearl is not your grandmother!"

"I wish she was. I wish I lived with Peck and Lizzie."

"The grass is always greener, Benny."

"Huh?"

"Pearl's is not a perfect house."

"Pearl doesn't yell at me."

"Because you don't belong to her."

"She doesn't yell at Peck and Lizzie."

"You don't know that."

"Pearl doesn't drink whiskey like Mama, and Peck and Lizzie don't have to run from her."

"My God, Benny, they have other problems."

"No, they don't. Lizzie and Peck have everything."

"You have two parents."

"They have Pearl and Miss Lila, and they have Izear."

"But do they have a real father like you do?"

"No, not like I do; but they have one. He's from Cincinnati. Lizzie and Peck are going to take the bus to Cincinnati and find him. Lizzie said so."

"Well, see? You don't have to take a bus anywhere to find your father. I'm right here."

"Not always. You take mama's side and then I don't have anybody on mine. And you buy her whiskey. You shouldn't buy her whiskey."

"Dammit Benny! Don't tell me what I should do."

"Knucklehead, Daddy."

"What?"

"You forgot to say, *Don't tell me what I should do, knucklehead.*"

"I've got to go; your mama's calling me. You stay out from under that bed, Benny."

"Say 'knucklehead.'"

"Alright, knucklehead. You know I love you, Benny."

"I know. Don't let mama come back here while she's tired and nervous, okay?"

The Osprey

Peck

Pearl said I'd have to let go of stuff I couldn't have, no matter how much I wanted it, or got used to chasing it. "Don't hold to such things, Peck," Pearl warned--things like my daddy, who made his bed then refused to lie in it, or like the Osprey, hovering just low enough to tempt, then flying too high to touch. But Pearl was wrong. I couldn't let go. Those needs lived inside me like the words in my diary. Closing the book never made them disappear. Some things just *are*, whether or not you can see them, or touch them, or hold them.

    I never held my father. But once, I held the hawk. Lizzie and I had ridden our bikes down River Road to Dixie, where Pearl told us not to go. It was early morning and the sun was just beginning to rise over the river, making peach-colored ripples on the gray-blue water. We stopped to watch a great Osprey circling overhead, its wing-span enormous as it sailed on currents of air; a black-masked bird with a piercing golden eye. We saw it scan the water, inches from the surface, searching for prey, then rise, roll, and swoop downward again, skimming the river's mirror, then up, down, around once more. For almost half an hour we waited for the hawk to dive. Then, all at once, it plunged feet first, talons spread, its wings held up and back for the powerful stroke it would take to raise its prey.

    Except it couldn't rise; the fish was too large. And it couldn't let go, its talons were embedded in the fish's flesh. All it could do was thrash about, defeated. "Oh Peck, do something," Lizzie cried. Already I was wading into the river.

    Strange how it seemed to will itself into my hands when I

reached for it, like a father to his son. Its breast beat steady and warm. Its golden eye dared me to keep hold, challenged me to loosen it from the fish. But as I did, the hawk immediately punctured my palm with its claws. Blood ran into the water. Lizzie gave a cry of alarm, but I kept hold.

My thought was to ignore the pain, to bind its wings so it couldn't fly away, then tie it to the limb of a backyard tree with a piece of old twine and keep it close forever. But nothing's forever. Almost as a painful goodbye, it sank its talons deeper into my hand then abruptly soared away; shrieking the sound of my name, "peeeeeck--peeeeeck." It taunted me from the distant treetops. It kept me captive. It had drawn blood, it had left scars, but that didn't matter. And it didn't matter that I was left afraid of the Osprey. I still wanted it, as much as I wanted my father.

That December afternoon, after Lizzie stepped into the broken glass and Pearl insisted our father cared nothing for us, I return to Hobart's because I hadn't liked the way he stroked Mama's picture, like he loved her. I want to tell him he isn't good enough to love her. But when the door opens and Hobart stands in the threshold -- so tall, so commanding--my intention dissolves and I can't make the words come.

He seems glad to see me back, and says he'll pay me a dollar to help him pack up stuff from Mrs. McSwain's room, things he says his adopted mother doesn't need any more--layers of wrinkled white handkerchiefs with lace around the edges, threads and needles and crochet hooks, a woman's waistcoat spotted with what looked like blood, a broken rosary, the wood-framed picture of an old man in a string bow tie who squinted with one eye as if he had something on me. I put all those dusty things into a cardboard box that Hobart marked, 'Junk,' while old Mrs. McSwain rocks on the porch, unaware of what we are doing, because her mind is too far away, now. She's not curious like Pearl.

Pearl said Hobart wasn't born in Highlow, or even in

Alabama. Hobart was born in Detroit, Michigan. When he was a boy, he was adopted by the McSwains who attempted to raise him within the boundaries of Main Street; but it wasn't long until Hobart felt boxed in and began walking the River Road to Dixie, the part of Highlow people didn't like to remember. Dixie's river had started to rise again, and that concerned them. Pearl said she knew, then, he'd never belong, though she admitted she feels empathy for Hobart because she could see he wanted to go somewhere in life, even if his destinations were wrong ones.

When he was still too young to drive a car, Hobart tried to get back to where he came from. He stole some money from his adopted daddy's cash box and paid two old black men from Dixie's car lot to drive him up there. But don't blame Hobart, Pearl said, he didn't know any better. He didn't know those men were way too old for a new trip like that. Plus, they couldn't read a map. The one driving the truck they borrowed from the car lot, ran it off the road into a ditch somewhere in north Georgia. Just a little bump of his head on the steering wheel killed him. The other one, stupid from birth, ran out on the highway when he saw his friend bleeding, and got hit by a car that never stopped. At the first squeal of a siren, Hobart took off into the woods and ran ten miles to the nearest gas station to telephone Mama and Daddy McSwain and tell them he'd decided to stay, and that he intended to make Highlow love him, no matter what.

From that time on Pearl said Hobart acted lots nicer, nice as he could be to everybody. She said Hobart took a big gamble starting all over. Pearl is always partial to people who gamble. They remind her of her dead husband, William Crawford Todd, a man who could smell a poker game from fifty miles away. Pearl loved that old man. She thought she knew everything about him, then found out she didn't. She doesn't know everything about Hobart either. Hobart likes to talk. He's going on and on while I pack up the boxes, but I'm the one he talks to about secret things.

Secret Things

Hobart

I talk to the boy, Peck. But I don't tell him everything. I tell him about Detroit, that it was a dingy place as I recall. It's only light came from the swooping white-winged women who fed us, forty unwanted boys under the care of hooded bird-women. Sister Perpetua--she smelled like lilies--took me to the car when Mama and Daddy McSwain came to save me from a sad life as an orphan. Mama McSwain and Sister Perpetua cried, the only two people ever cried over me, but Daddy McSwain had a tight-lipped look on his wide-eyed face that said he couldn't believe he was taking a pale-looking, eleven year old Yankee boy home to Highlow, Alabama. He kept that look 'til the day he died, then Mama McSwain resurrected it to keep his memory alive.

I was in the care of the bird-women from the time I was four so I don't remember much of my real parents. I heard they were both of no account. I heard it in passing, but I knew it already. They never took account of me, though my mama gave me a box to sleep in; a tall, cardboard box with a scratchy blanket folded in the bottom and a stone in the corner too heavy to lift so I couldn't turn the box over and get out of it. She left me for long lengths of time, maybe days, in the box. Then I'd hear the door open and she'd come in with a man that could have been my father and they'd stand over me, looking down. Finally, she'd lift me out, smelling like something burnt, and she'd laugh and call me "little doggy.' That's all I remember, except for how cold it got in the box. But Sister Perpetua said Detroit was a cold place anywhere you were.

Still, I tried to get back there once, when Sister Perpetua was dying. I chose an old man to drive me. A mistake, but I hadn't met D.C. Carter then--he has plenty of other used cars in his Dixie car lot that'll get you where you want to go. So the white-hooded, bird-woman died without me. I regret that. And when I think about her, I still smell lilies.

Peck's piling stuff in the cardboard box and asking me about cars in the Dixie lot. I tell him that D.C. said he'd give me a deal on a convertible. I do not tell him what else D.C. said; that I ought to have plenty of money to buy it with, after my next powder sale. I say nothing about that, or that D.C. calls the powder 'Fine china.' "Sell 'em that pure white stuff and nobody in Highlow will ever say nothing about where you come from anymore," D.C. says.

D.C.'s got heart, but he's a fool. Day's gonna come when I'll own his car lot, own my mama's house, and even be rich enough to buy acres and acres of land. Maybe I'll turn them into a town like Pearl's wealthy grandfather did with Highlow after the Civil War. I won't give the land away like he did, though--just offered it free to any homeless, damn Confederate left maimed and penniless! I heard the story from Daddy McSwain. He said Pearl's grandfather was crazy.

Hell, Pearl's whole family's crazy--bunch of rich fools that ought to lose, but they end up winning! But I plan to win, too. So what will Peck's mama say then? How will Lila paint me?

"Hobart," she used to say, with her brush in her hand, "turn this way, turn that way," like I'd do what she said because she was Highlow blood and above me. So I showed her where I fit in. I showed her who was under who. And I felt no guilt in making love to her. Yes, it was love. Maybe I took it, but I paid for it, too; I gave her Fine China in return.

Not so long ago, before Cincinnati, I followed her everywhere; watching her back, her swinging, dark hair shining in the sun like a blackbird's wing. "Go away!" she said, glaring at me with her crazy cobalt eyes. Hell, she was lucky I was there the morning of her sixteenth birthday when she attempted to fly from Pearl's attic window. Fly! Her arms raised above her head, pushing down in a powerful stroke as she stepped off the sill as if even the laws of physics were under her spell.

"It was some hereditary thing made her do it," Mama McSwain said later, pouring witch hazel over the long, wide bruises on my arms that came about when I broke her fall. "That family's always been deluded. Nice, but nevertheless, deluded."

Deluded? Or had somebody Lila wanted to get away from sprinkled her with dust and told her she was an angel?

Now, there are times when Lila doesn't want to get away from me. She wants to be where only I can put her, in an unfailing world with no consequences where only the present matters. And sometimes after the powder takes effect, she slips away from Pearl, slips inside my kitchen door while Mama McSwain sleeps upstairs. She slides her hand around my neck and kisses the lobe of my ear. Then she's the one who wants love, while the Fine China lasts. When it's gone, she pays me in insults. "Go back to hell." But always, another craving comes and she opens her palms for more. Lila wants me. Rich or not, deluded or not; she *wants me* in Highlow. Lila knows I belong here. But those are secret things I'd never tell Peck. He wouldn't like me then, and I might need him someday.

The Unfortunate Poker Game

Peck

From the McSwain porch, I hear the squeak of Hobart's mama's rocker. The sound of it is right in tune with the song she's singing about power in the blood of the dead savior. "Why do you reckon they killed him?" I ask Hobart.

"Who?"

"Jesus. I don't see why they had to kill him."

"Because he didn't fit in! And if you want to earn your dollar, quit running your mouth." He rummages through a drawer inside a large chiffarobe as if looking for something particular. Finally, he takes out a small, round jar of what looks like ladies' face powder and starts to put it into a long, green metal box that has a lock and key, but it accidentally opens and some of the moon-colored powder spills on the floor.

"Damn!" he shouts, hurrying to sweep up what he can with his hands to put it back into the jar. He wipes off what's left on his fingers with a piece of creased, yellowed paper he's found in the drawer, then throws the crumpled paper into the box marked, 'Junk.'

"You ought to read that paper first," I tell him. "Pearl says you should never throw away anything until you're sure what it is.'"

"You read it," he says. "I'm busy."

I un-crumple the paper. It's an Alabama real estate deed, dated 1865, entitling Pearl's grandfather to the house on Main Street. At the top of the page there is a written note: *Transferred to A.W. McSwain after a game of poker, August 5, 1924.* And then there's an angry-looking signature: William Crawford Todd.

Was it possible that Pearl's husband had gambled away her house all those years ago? Surely it isn't real, but why is it here at the McSwain's? I stuff the paper into my pocket to hide it from Hobart, meaning to show it to Pearl. But Hobart eyes are hawk-keen.

"So what does it say?" he asks, interested now.

"Nothing. It's just an old piece of paper."

"How come you want it, then? Give it here. It's mine; it was in my house."

"But you were going to throw it away."

"Well now, I ain't. So give it here!" He holds out a hand and there's meanness in his eyes when I hand it over, but as he reads the meanness turns to surprise, and then to joy. He touches the paper lovingly to his chin as if all at once, he has everything he yearns for. Then old Mrs. McSwain pipes up louder from the porch, "Power in the blood, power in the blood of the lamb."

Hobart clinches his nice, white teeth, and talks through them like he sometimes does. "You coulda' told me about this paper, old lady. You coulda saved me a lot of grief all these years." He takes a breath and grins. "Now, it's me that's got the power."

I can't let him have it. "She didn't tell you about the paper because it isn't legal."

"What do you know about *legal*? It's legal, alright. I've learned a lot about real estate law." He seemed confident, carefully folding the paper, locking it in the long, green box. "Don't tell Pearl about this; not yet."

"Why don't you want Pearl to know--if it's really yours?"

"You think it's not mine? You saw it in writing. Old William Crawford lost Pearl's house to my adopted, dead daddy, and I'm his rightful heir." Hobart's entire body vibrates as if he's stuck a finger in a light socket. "Christ, just think of the years it's been hidden. My birthright!"

"If Pearl finds out about the deed, she won't like it. Nobody in Highlow will like it."

Hobart gives a spiteful smile. "Well, they'll just have to live with it, won't they?"

"But where will we live if you own Pearl's house? We'll have to move."

"You won't have to move. Pearl will pay me rent."

Rent? He doesn't know Pearl! "When are you going to tell her?"

"When it suits me, not you. So shut up about it!" But Hobart has sense enough to know he'll have to bargain with a true Highlow son. He puts a hand on my shoulder. "If you don't tell her, I'll help you catch that damn Osprey. We'll hunt the hawk together. I'm the best hunter around you know. Only one that's ever caught one."

"I'll think about it." I like the bit of control I have, but I can't be sure of Hobart. Like the Osprey, he sometimes frightens me. I've seen the carcasses of deer he's killed, and once I watched him skin a doe. Its blood ran all the concrete floor in his garage, made such a mess that not even a stinging spray of water and sand could take away the stain. He left the meat hanging for a week in the garage, a porthole air-conditioner running, door locked, windowpanes covered, so no one who came to visit could see inside, especially not Pearl.

Pearl doesn't know that Hobart is a hunter, that he owns three rifles. She hates guns, even though she has one, a revolver from the Civil War, her grandfather's gun; and she makes sure everyone in Highlow knows about her "just-in-case" gun--just in case somebody breaks into her house on Main Street looking for what isn't theirs. At her Open House, Pearl used to call aside visitors caught stalking her ancient rooms, to remind them of their status as guests. Now, her vision has weakened, and she relies on younger, easily distracted eyes, like mine, to keep disguised hunters at bay.

Hobart hunts in green fatigues with dark splotches so he can hide from his unsuspecting prey. If I don't tell Pearl about the deed, he says he'll buy me some fatigues, too, at the new Army Navy Surplus store. And he says again, he'll make sure I catch the Osprey.

I tell him, "All right."

So, we close the boxes marked, "Junk," with masking tape and take them down to the corner of the driveway for the garbage man to haul them off. Mrs. McSwain sees us pass the porch. She stops singing and says, "Ya'll better be careful standing so close to the street. Accidents happen."

"Yes Mama," Hobart says politely.

In the Army Navy Surplus store, I stand in front of the cracked mirror while Hobart rolls up the green-splotched pant legs. "You can stick that excess in your boots."

"I don't have any boots."

"We'll get you some then." Hobart checks his wallet. "How much?" he asks the big man with bulging muscles who stands watching from behind a counter cluttered with pieces of metal, rusted guns, and old hand grenades.

"For the outfit or the boots?" the muscle man asks, and spits some tobacco in a beer can.

"Both."

"Fifteen bucks." The muscle man moves a hand over a line of army boots on a shelf behind him and picks up a pair. "These oughta fit him."

"Try 'em on," Hobart says, snatching the boots, dropping them on the floor beside me.

The muscle man eyes Hobart. "You look familiar. You serve in Korea?"

"Wasn't in the war. I was an only son," Hobart replies, looking down to take the money out of his wallet while I shove my foot into the new boot.

"How do you know, Hobart?" I ask.

"Know what?"

"That you're an only child."

"Last time I looked, I was the only one there."

"You could've had a brother, before you were adopted and came to Highlow."

The muscle man immediately raises an eyebrow. "You ain't from here?"

"I am from here!" Hobart says. "Got me some old money and I own some prime Highlow property, too!" Hobart gives me a look that says I'd better agree.

"He does own property," I say. "I found that out about him."

"Yeah?" The muscle man looks doubtful. "I wouldn't take you for Highlow blood."

"Gimme my stuff," Hobart orders, shoving the fifteen dollars across the counter. The muscle man keeps an eye on Hobart as he sticks the hunting outfit and boots in a bag.

In the truck, Hobart glances at his face in the rear-view mirror like he's wondering what the muscle man saw in it that made him doubt. It is a handsome face that Hobart has, but it's not a Highlow face and never will be. Like Pearl says, you can't buy a birthright. It's freely given. And you can't steal it either. Pearl says you are what you are, so you might as well be satisfied or else expect a life of misery hunting for things that don't belong to you.

Hobart turns the truck onto Rebel Road and then to Dixie, run-down with bankrupt rednecks trying to escape the river that is rising too fast. They hang around the new Stop-Crime sign on the corner of Rebel and Cat Alley looking for tricks and money from drugs--that's what Pearl says-- but Hobart says it's a short-cut to owning Main Street.

In silence we pass several black men and two young white boys under the Stop-Crime sign. They see us coming and nod to Hobart in recognition. He pays them no regard. He does not want to be reminded that these are the people who acknowledge him. He does not want to admit that he hasn't been washed in the blood of Main Street. When we pass D.C. Jackson's used car lot, Hobart slows down and cranes his neck to look over the seven or eight cars, as if he has money to buy one. Finally, he takes the turn home.

Mrs. McSwain is no longer on the porch when we pull into the driveway, passing the stacked, cardboard boxes. One of them has already fallen into the street. "Hell!" Hobart says, getting out and kicking it to the curb. I wait in the truck until he gets back in and drives into the garage, over the old stains of deer blood. Grabbing the bag from the Army Surplus store, he shoves open the truck door, then slams it behind him and heads for the house as if he's forgotten I'm here.

"You have something that belongs to me," I remind him. "The hunting outfit."

He won't let me take it. He's worried I might try it on for Pearl and cause a stir. "You put on an obvious uniform, it lets people know what you're up to."

"We'd better catch the Osprey soon, or I'll tell."

"Yeah soon," he says in a tired breath, walking up the steps, opening the door. For a minute, his mama's singing escapes, again: "Would you be whiter, much whiter than snow? There's power in the blood, power in the blood." Then the door to Mrs. McSwain's house bangs shut and all is quiet.

Three o'clock in the morning there's a tapping on my window; pebbles thrown by Hobart from below. I follow him to Mrs. McSwain's. He tosses me the bag and tells me to go to his room and change into my hunting outfit. I can hear his mama's snores rising and falling from a bedroom down the hall; then I notice the key, on Hobart's dresser, beside the long, green metal box. So, I use it.

The deed is still inside the box, folded so the signature of William Crawford Todd is the first thing I see. I ought to take the paper and destroy it. I ought to save saved Pearl's house. Instead, I close the metal lid and lock it back, because I want the Osprey so bad, that hawk Hobart can help me catch. Then out of shame, and maybe the thought of some future reconsideration, I put the key in my pocket.

Hobart and I take our place on the edge of the woods, next to the river. The high, wild pampas grass blows gently in the wind and a piece of it sticks to my cheek as if pasted there with glue. In the dampness of the December dawn, the green-splotched jacket and the heavy pants stuck into my boots smell musty and ancient, something like Pearl when she speaks to me of patience, when she tells me that time changes perspective and that imagined desires often fade. But Pearl is old and she is wrong. Many a man has sacrificed his home, even his life, for a passion. Isn't that what William Crawford did? And don't I have his blood?

Hobart spots the Osprey in the tip top of a tall pine with the crescent moon behind it. Its wings are folded, its beak bowed into its breast like a humble angel on a Christmas tree. Everything inside me craves it.

Quietly, Hobart unzips the canvas bag he's brought with him, takes out one of his rifles, and lifts it.

I whisper loudly, "No, I don't want him dead!"

"Hell, I thought you were a hunter! It's the only way you'll have him." He aims, but misses when I push down on his arm.

"Dammit," he says as the Osprey flies off. "I'm not bringing you out here again!"

The key in my pocket gives me courage "Yes, you will. I'll tell Pearl, if you don't."

The Osprey circles above us. "Fine," Hobart says. "Tell her, and do without what you want most in the world. I'm the only one who can give you that."

But Hobart can't give me what I want most in the world because he's never understood that it's my father I want; to know him, to love him, and have him love me. I want to hunt with my father, not Hobart. I want to smile like Little Benedict does when his own father tousles his hair and calls him knucklehead. I want to watch my father paint my face on a real canvas, not a china plate. He would be someone to talk to besides Lizzie, to play games with instead of Izear. My father is somewhere in Cincinnati, and one day, I'll find him, and bring him home to Highlow where he belongs.

Above us, the Osprey calls-- peeeeeeck, peeeeeck, peeeeeeck-- and the scars on my hands begin to throb, and inside my chest is a pressure, like furious wings unfolding. It doesn't matter. I'll catch him one day, even if he kills me. All at once, Pearl's ancient house and the yellowed piece of paper seem of no consequence whatever.

Each Bird is Different

Lizzie

In our grandmother's ancient house on Main Street, there is a tall, mahogany cabinet, its pediment scrolled with flowers in perpetual bloom. Behind the beveled glass doors, Pearl secures her collection of Fine China, rimmed in gold, and colorfully painted with birds of prey. Each bird is different, and each so finely fired that when a plate is held before the lamp, the hand behind it is clearly seen.

On these plates, she serves her family, the only collection she treasures more than her porcelain. In advance of any special occasion, she takes out each piece and studies it to determine fitness for her table, then assesses her family for the same sort of wear: chips of neglect, willfulness, or simple time. Pearl says any plate, or person, can become imperfect because everything exists in the distance between perfection and imperfection. That's why she's always ready with a new invention she recently found at The Jitney Jungle grocery store: Super Glue.

Today, is the twenty-third of December, the day of Pearl's party. Peck is sweeping up the parlor. I'm dusting the music room. Pearl, with a tube of Super Glue sticking out of her pocket, is taking pieces of fine china from her glass-doored cabinet, and putting it on the mahogany table for inspection.

Pearl's china was originally a gift from her grandfather to her grandmother. She has a picture of them on the piano. I wipe a rag over the photograph, and Pearl notices. "Lizzie," she says. "Your great, great grandmother was a generous woman in height and heart, just like you; and oh, how she loved to dance!"

I look at the woman in the picture. She's dressed in a light-colored dress with lace sleeves, and she's laughing, her palms open as if she's inviting me to dance with her.

"Her name was Grace," Pearl says. "She had copper-colored hair, like you and Peck, though you can't tell it in the black and white photograph."

I smile at that. When I was younger, I wondered if Peck and I might have been adopted like Hobart, because no one else in the family had reddish hair.

Standing straight-faced beside Grace is Pearl's grandfather, Joseph, the founder of Highlow. He is leaning on the lambs head cane and is shorter than his wife, the top of his head level with her pearl-drop earring. He has a tidy beard and bow-tie and a worried expression like he's unsure of what his wife will do next. I've seen the same expression on Peck's face.

"How did my great grandfather make enough money to build all of Highlow?"

"He didn't build all of Highlow. He bought land after the Civil War and then gave it away, and others built the town. And however he made his money," Pearl says, with a wrinkle between her silver brows, "he put it all to good use." Then she sweeps her palms apart as her grandmother might have done in a dance, looking up at the white wood-worked ceiling, and around the room with its elaborate furniture. "He built this house. He built it for Grace. Now it's ours, and isn't it a wonderful house?"

"Yes. I wouldn't leave it in a million years," I say, because it's what Pearl wants to hear.

A loud noise comes from the parlor. Peck has tripped over a small, embroidered foot rest. His elbow is bleeding, so Pearl goes for the Witch Hazel. After the Super Glue, it's her second choice for making things better, but my brother goes back to sweeping the floor and won't let her dab it on him, so Pearl returns to checking the china.

"Besides being the season of the Good Lord's birthday," Pearl says, "the twenty-third of December is when your granddaddy--

my husband, William Crawford Todd-- was born on the other side of the tracks, in Dixie. If he was alive today, William Crawford would be eighty-eight years old."

"Imagine that!" I say to humor Pearl, while I dust around the last of the fine china plates on the dining room table.

Peck is studying a hawk painted on one of the plates. He gives me a sideways glance. "That's nothing," he says pragmatically. "Just think how old George Washington would be if he was alive, but he's not either."

I almost mention the age of little Tarcisius, up there on a plate in Mama's room, and how she talks to him like he was alive, but that might upset Pearl. Anyway, Peck likes to have the last word. He's a real nice boy. I love him, and don't want an argument to spoil the party.

Tonight, Pearl will whip up her special eggnog and open her house like she has ever since 1934, when William Crawford Todd, who was sixty-eight at the time and thirty years older than Pearl, got drunk and fell over the railroad tracks trying to get back to where he was born. Pearl says she cried and cried when they told her William Crawford had been cut slap in half when the caboose on a Coastline train backed over him. She says she loved both parts of that spunky old man from Dixie, body and soul. Pearl says it's true William Crawford wasn't bred well, and he certainly wasn't good-looking, but that was because he took after his mother.

William Crawford's daddy was a handsome colonel in the Civil War who met an ugly nurse in a Yankee prison hospital, where he was recuperating from a lost leg in a battle for the Confederacy. The ugly nurse didn't care if he had one leg. She was taken in by his looks and his southern charm, and William Crawford's daddy was so lonely they started William Crawford. Naturally, William Crawford's daddy felt obliged to marry her and brought her south to Dixie. But the nurse didn't stay long after William Crawford was born. Being ugly, and a Yankee, she had two strikes against her, because Dixie had her standards then. So the nurse went back north, leaving her handsome, one-legged husband to raise a baby as ugly as she was. But Pearl says good looks and good breeding aren't the biggest things, if a person has a good heart.

Pearl's party is one big thing, especially when the twenty-third falls on Sunday, like today. Highlow's what they call a Baptist town; liquor on Sunday does not set well with most of the people born here. I know because somebody stuck a note on Pearl's front door about how she would go to hell if she threw a liquor party on the Lord's Day. It was the same day Miss Billie Nana Spratling's yardman got his leg stuck under that truck's wheel. The note was signed, *'Somebody that loves the Lord, from Highlow.'* But Pearl's not scared. She says the Lord from Highlow can't hold a candle to Our Father in Heaven.

Hungry Party Guests in a Baptist Town

Lizzie

    Pearl and Mama and Peck and me, we are all from Highlow and we all love the Lord. That makes us like most of the people, but we do have one strike against us. We're the only Catholics ever lived here, except for the family of Miss Rose Sabertini Jackson, the wife of our redneck garbage collector. Miss Rose was born in Highlow, down in Salt Alley, but her parents came over from Italy just after the war. They grew the best strawberries in the world out on Highway 101. Miss Rose was real poor until she married Mr. Jackson and came up a little. That didn't keep the Klan from going after her Catholic family though. One night, when Mr. Jackson was gone, they showed up at her house with their capes and hoods on to cover their real selves. But Miss Rose knew who one of them was. She'd helped her mamma sell strawberries downtown, and her mama, who'd lived through the Depression without any pretty shoes, had a habit of noticing the shoes of people who bought her berries. Always, she pointed out the best shoes to Rose. Mr. Edwin Ard, who ran the hardware store, had the finest ones. So, when the Klan came, Miss Rose only had to look down at his shoes to recognize Mr. Ard standing in her doorway with a torch and telling her that she and her Catholic family better get on outta this Baptist town.

    "I don't intend on going anywhere, Mr. Ard," she told him.

    He was stunned and took a few steps back. "I'm not Mr. Ard!"

    "Well, your shoes say you are," Miss Rose told him. "Now you get outta here yourself, or I'll call Miss Pearl's cousin, The Judge. Miss Pearl's a Catholic, too, you know."

"The Judge" was all the threat Mr. Ard needed to hear. He corralled the others and left because everyone, including Mr. Ard, knew The Judge always came to Pearl's rescue. Once, he'd sentenced an unruly guest at Pearl's Christmas Open House to six months of cleaning up all the slop on the floor of a Highlow chicken breeding business--without gloves. Besides keeping a notebook, The Judge is fond of unique and uncomfortable sentences.

Most everybody, Baptist or not, comes to Pearl's Christmas open house. The hoity-toity and the poor white trash; they all come. Pearl doesn't even send invitations anymore. It's plain 'word of mouth.' She sets out her china and opens her door to all of them, stuffs them full of her bourbon-soaked lane cake and pours out the eggnog and Izear's homemade scuppernong wine 'til they can't see anything except the bright lights. Oh what a party! But the best part is this: whoever finds Pearl's little porcelain Baby Jesus, hidden in their slice of her lane cake, gets a hundred dollar bill from Pearl's tin box with the rose Mama painted on it. The tin box is where Pearl keeps all her money from William Crawford's life insurance. Pearl says she might have been a lot younger than William Crawford, but she was also a lot smarter. She took out that policy two months after she married William Crawford, just after he lost seven of Pearl's mama's cut-glass crystal goblets in a gin-rummy game. Pearl's always known how to prepare.

It's a real hundred dollar bill Pearl gives away. Always, a hundred dollar bill you can keep. Nobody seems to keep the porcelain Baby Jesus though. He's always left on the table. Not to worry. Pearl expects that, too. After the party, she'll wrap Him back in brand new tissue paper and put Him in her top bureau drawer where she keeps her undies smelling good with yellowed gardenias, and save Him for the next year.

All in all, Highlow, Alabama's a good town to live in if you're born here. Even if you're not, you can get over it by thinking up extra nice things to do for Highlow's true blood. They'll like you, then. That's what Hobart McSwain does. Hobart's always doing extra nice things for Pearl. He would for Mama too, if she'd let him. But Mama can't stand the man.

Hobart, Mrs. McSwain, and Leona--Hobart's pretty cousin from Crisscross--are the first party guests to arrive. When she puckers up her lips, Leona looks a lot like one of those goofy, blonde movie stars, and right now, Hobart's in Pearl's living room acting exactly like her big-headed leading man.

Pearl notices and jabs Izear in the ribs with an elbow and a grin. "Hobart thinks God sent him down from heaven as a gift to the ladies."

"Well, I reckon he was sent from somewhere," Izear says, "but it looks to me like he's used to sweating." Like Mama, Izear can't stand the man.

"C'mere, Peck," Hobart calls to my twin brother who hops on command. "This is Leona, my cousin from Crisscross. Talk to her while I go help Pearl."

Leona re-puckers her lips then takes a deep breath so her chest sticks out. Just in the V- neck of her white blouse, the corner of a blue Kleenex peeps up. Peck looks at Leona like she's the prettiest thing he's ever seen. He does not notice that Leona's stuffed. He sees only what he wants to see. Boys get like that, even nice ones.

Leona tugs at a piece of her yellow blonde hair, probably bleached with a bottle of peroxide while she was at Panama City Beach, Florida. South Georgia people are famous for bleaching their hair then lying about it. Last time Izear drove us to the beach, Peck and I saw a bunch of those bleached-white heads on sun-browned bodies stuffed in little bitty bikinis and smelling like vats of Hawaiian Tropic. I asked one of them how she got her hair so white. "Why Shugah," she purred, "it's natural." Like I was born yesterday!

Hobart's hair is blonde, too, but when he says it's real, I tend to believe him.

He comes in my direction with his hobbling mama, aiming her for the empty chair right next to me, just below Pearl's big painting of the Sacred Heart of Jesus. Peck calls it Pearl's Mercy picture because whenever she passes it, she says, "Sacred Heart of Jesus, have mercy on us." Mama painted it for Pearl when she was a teenager, before she got interested in fine china plates. It's hung where it is for so long that if you move it a little you can see that the painted wall underneath looks brand new.

"Is Lila coming down?" Hobart asks me, showing his perfect white teeth. Hobart always wants to know how Mama is doing. I shrug my shoulders and draw an intentional frown on my face. I tell him she won't come down for anybody tonight, not even me. I tell him this, hoping he'll feel bad for me, hoping he'll put his arm around me like he did Leona from Crisscross. But he doesn't. And even though Hobart looks his best in a brand new suit that's dark gray-blue and so shimmery you want to touch a finger to his sleeve, and even though he looks spotless, his shiny chin brushing over a starched white collar, white as that sliver of December moon I saw from my mama's window not an hour ago, and even though Hobart looks so fine in his pretty red tie with a green Christmas tree painted on it; even with all that, I make myself remember how he's usually dirty and sweaty, fixing the plumbing up underneath Mrs. McSwain's house,. Then I don't care one little bit that he didn't give me a hug. Smelly old Hobart.

"Oh, I think she'll come down," Hobart says like he knows everything. He sits his mama in the chair by me then pushes through the swinging door to the kitchen.

Peck says Hobart has a crush on our mama because he's always sending her things like wrapped-up face powder that used to be Mrs. McSwain's. Peck brings the powder into Pearl's house because Izear won't let Hobart in the door except during Pearl's open house at Christmas.

I say that's stupid. Hobart can't have a crush on Mama; he's much too young for her. Peck says Hobart's only a year or two younger than she is. I say, well maybe he does have a crush on her, but there is certainly no turn-about on Mama's part. She sees clean through Hobart.

Mrs. McSwain smiles at me like she wants to talk, but I pretend I've got an itch on my foot and bend down to scratch my leg. From the corner of my eye, I see her stare up at the picture of the Sacred Heart. Pearl says Mrs. McSwain's one of those 'don't-want-to-own-up-to-it-in-a-Baptist-town-but-feeling-guilty-closet-Catholics.' And I think Pearl's right, because there's a tear running down Mrs. McSwain's cheek. I set my hand on her old shoulder and give it a squeeze. Then both of us watch Hobart.

Pearl has given him the key to her scrolled mahogany china cabinet, so Hobart takes out Pearl's seven cut-glass goblets, one by one. After Pearl's husband, William Crawford Todd, got himself cut half-in-two on the railroad tracks, Pearl bought back the crystal goblets he lost in the poker game. Said she paid the old codger that won them twice what they'd be worth to anybody else, but she had to do it for posterity. Now, Hobart's got his finger curled around a crystal stem, pouring wine into it like it was him that bought the bottle.

Soon as Little Benedict's daddy and mama enter Pearl's front door for the open house, Mr. Spratling says, "Where's old Izear's sour cream pound cake?" Except for the hundred dollars and the bourbon soaking, Izear's sour cream pound cake rivals Pearl's lane cake any time of the year. Pearl is quick to say that she's the one who taught Izear to cook. She says she's glad that his sour cream pound cake is first of the two things he's famous for. The second thing is, Izear had to go to jail in another town for poking out the eyes of some white man; but nobody talks out loud about that famous thing anymore. Pearl went to her cousin The Judge and got him out in less than a week. Now, it's just history, tucked away.

Before Little Benedict's clean-cut daddy can take off his fine leather overcoat, Izear's brought him a piece of the sour cream pound cake, set just over the engraved 'T' for Todd on one of Pearl's best sterling dessert plates. Izear's grinning, waiting for his usual pat.

"Um Umm! When I go to heaven--" Mr. Spratling hands Izear his coat with one hand and takes the silver plate with the other--"I ain't going 'less I can take me a piece of your cake with me."

"Don't worry," Mrs. Spratling says, real mean-like, "you're not going to heaven." Her mouth's all twisted to one side, and her eyes look kind of glazed like she's had enough partying already, but she lets Izear take her mink. It's not cold enough for her mink or his leather, but the Spratlings have appearances to keep up.

"Some Lane cake for you, too, Mrs. Spratling?" Izear asks. I can see his nose twitching from the fur. Still, Izear knows to do extra nice things for people.

"Thank you, Izear," Mrs. Spratling says with that hum-drum look people that got rich, but weren't born that way, learn to put on. She'd never admit it, but Mr. Spratling is the one who came from money; she just married into it. There used to be talk that her mama was a mulatto, though Miss Billie Nana is as light-skinned as Little Benedict. Naturally, she'd made an appointment with The Judge, swearing up and down it wasn't true. She said her mama and daddy were both aristocrats from New Orleans. She'd asked The Judge to write that down, just in case he was questioned about her. No one knows if he did.

All at once, Little Benedict who's standing in between his parents; hair all slicked down and pale-faced, like what's left of a dreamsicle at recess after you've licked most of the orange sherbet off the vanilla part. He tugs on Miss Billie Nana's dress and says, much too loudly, "Mama, I'm gonna get you that hun'erd dollars!"

Miss Bille Nana shrugs away, looks around to see who's heard. She seems so unnerved I almost feel sorry for her. "Make him be quiet!" she says to her husband.

Mr. Benedict, Senior pops Little Benedict on the head with the knuckle of his index finger. "Knucklehead!" Senior says without moving his lips. I guess Little Benedict brings out the ventriloquist in his daddy, too.

"Ow!" Little Benedict squats quick, then spies Hobart at the dining room table pouring the wine for Pearl. "Hobart, lemme help," he squeaks, and runs toward him.

I've heard some silly girls at school say Hobart really ought to be a movie star. They gurgle and giggle and stomp their feet when they see him like they've stepped on hot coals at a Girl Scout camp out. Hobart is handsome, but as I've said, I hardly notice it. I do notice he's hanging over the neck of Leona from Crisscross who must have re-stuffed herself since there's no sign of the blue Kleenex, anymore. And I see how he's still got his old mama parked in the chair with nobody talking to her but me and merciful Jesus. Hobart hasn't even bothered to bring her any eggnog or even a glass of the wine he acts like belongs to him. He knows he doesn't have to do extra nice things for his mama; she'll love him no matter what he does.

I go over to Hobart who's draped over Leona. "Your mama needs some wine." I say this to let him know he has other duties besides pretending he belongs in our house.

"Take her some then, lady girl." Hobart winks at Leona, pours a cut-glass stem full and hands it to me like his mama's my responsibility, not his. I give him a look to let him know where I was born and where he wasn't. And even though it's not me that has to watch about being extra nice, I take the stem to Mrs. McSwain and hand her that pretty glass goblet filled with velvet red wine reflecting all those green and white lights from the Christmas tree.

Mrs. McSwain' coughs to find her voice. "Thank you, Lila," she says, reaching for the wine. She's always mistaking me for mama.

"It's Lizzie, Mrs. McSwain," I say to the old thing.

"Oh yes, yes. Alizarin Crimson Todd," she says. "I remember the day ya'll were born."

Lord God! I am hoping she didn't say my full name loud enough for anyone else to hear. It's bad enough to know that your mama named you after a tube of paint without having it broadcast to the world. Peck got off easy; I think Mama named him after our daddy, but nobody's squeezed the truth out of that tube yet.

"Lizard!" Little Benedict pokes his boney finger into my ribs and sings, "Lizzie's named Lizard!"

You just don't know when that boy's around until you step right on him, like a piece of somebody's chewed-up gum, spit-out on the floor of a dark picture show. I grab him by the throat. "Don't you call me that again or the next time you sleep in my bed, I'll smother you!"

"I won't say it again, Liiii--zard!"

I ball my fist between the folds of the poinsettias printed on my pretty Christmas skirt so he can see it. Of course, he will say it again; he's an absolutely disloyal bedfellow and always will be.

Hobart is taking a break from pouring wine. He re-situates his arm around the shoulders of his kissin' cousin from Crisscross. Peck stands beside Hobart, staring at Leona like she's vanilla malt from Colcutt's drug store with whipped cream and a cherry on top. Little Benedict yanks on the sleeve of Hobart's suit jacket and Hobart bends down to hear what the brat will surely tell him about my name. The silly Pendleton girl is trying to get Hobart to notice her from across the table. She looks entirely disappointed when Hobart gives me a wink. Ha! The trick's on Little Benedict, too. Hobart's known for some time about my silly name, and he's never told anybody. I think that's real nice of him, but I'd never admit it out loud.

Pearl taps around from group to noisy group. Izear follows, cutting through the voices, holding a silver tray loaded with liver pate and rum balls rolled in coconut flakes. You can smell all that rum when Izear passes with the tray, the one Pearl took out from under the sterling tea set that sits on the buffet because she said it was the biggest one and Izear had made too many rum balls for anything smaller. "Izear overdid the rum balls this year," Pearl is telling the mother of the Pendleton girl. "Maybe you'd like to take some home with you."

"Oh, honey, would I!" the Pendleton girl's mother says, a ball stuffed half-way in her mouth while she picks up another one. She stomps her feet just like her daughter. It's like Pearl says; hungry means different things to different people. Both Miss Pendleton and her Girl-Scout-fire-stomping-daughter look just starved.

The Tall Man in the Eagle Jacket

More and more people come in. Izear puts the tray back on the white lace-covered table with the angel hair and the figures of the Nativity on it, so he can take some more coats. The later it gets, the stranger the people who sometimes do, and sometimes do not, give their coats to Izear. The tall man who just came in doesn't hand over his coat. He keeps it on; a jacket zipped up to his chin. He walks past Izear with half-shut eyes as if Izear is not even there. But Izear keeps looking at the tall man like he thinks he might have seen him before, until Pearl says to go get another tray of bourbon balls and to pack some of them up in wax paper for Mrs. Pendleton to take home with her while he's at it.

On the back of the tall man's jacket is a painted eagle with a golden eye and wings that spread out onto the sleeves. The tall man touches the furniture as he passes it; the backs of chairs, the sofa. He dodges the hum-drum voices of the people, and heads to the dining room table like he knows just where the cake is. Within the commas of conversation, from the corners of their eyes, everybody watches the tall man in the eagle jacket as he moves his hands over the table, as he takes the next to the last piece of cake. Then quiet falls on Pearl's living room because people know the tall man's got a real fighting chance for the hundred dollars. Nobody's gotten lucky, yet. Pearl never allows seconds on her lane cake. You take what you get the first time.

I don't think the tall man in the jacket knows what he's bitten into. He looks surprised when his teeth come down on the little-bitty-porcelain baby. He spits it into one of Pearl's white, tatted napkins and blinks his half-shut eyes as if he's looking to see what it is. But I can tell you right now, he doesn't see it. The tall man in the eagle jacket doesn't see anything. I believe he is absolutely blind.

I look for Peck, to let him know that a blind man has bitten into the baby Jesus, but already my brother is staring at him, staring at his painted jacket with its eagle wings like he wants it for his own.

The blind man wraps Baby Jesus with Pearl's white cloth then puts him into his pocket as if everyone else is blind, too. Maybe he doesn't know to ask Pearl for the hundred dollars. Maybe I should politely tell him. I take a step forward, just as Mama floats down the stairs.

Whispers. Whispers.

"Ooh...What a pretty dress."

"Doesn't Lila look beautiful?"

People don't know who to pay attention to--the tall, blind man who's won the prize, or Mama--all except for Hobart; he doesn't take his eyes off Mama.

She's dressed in white; a dark-haired angel with a purple ribbon tied around her waist, and a soft pink blush on her cheeks and lips. The whispers continue, but Mama doesn't hear them. She doesn't see the faces. She does not talk to these people; they don't know her language. No one except the tall man with the Baby Jesus in the pocket of his eagle jacket, the blind man who is holding out his hand toward Mama as if he feels her coming toward him; no one, except this man who everybody watches but nobody knows, receives the favor of my mama's glance.

Mama holds Pearl's tin box with the rose painted on it, her fingers cupped around it. She sits the box on the white lace table in front of the tall man in the eagle jacket. Then she opens it, and offers him the hundred dollar bill. Whispers. Whispers.

The tall man bows his head into the neck of the eagle jacket like he's trying to disappear inside the collar. He pushes out a long-fingered hand as if to keep Mama away. The tips of his fingers are stained pale pink like the blush on Mama's cheek. Mama smiles, takes his hand, and places the hundred dollar bill inside it. Then she kisses the tall man in the eagle jacket on the cheek, like he was her cousin. And he kisses her back, on her lips! Whispers. Whispers.

Izear swoops around Mama, encircling her shoulders. He draws her away to the corner where Pearl stands, leaning on her lamb's head cane, but Mama's still smiling at the tall man.

Hobart yells abruptly, "The party's over!" His words slice through the soft rumblings of voices, as if it was his house and up to him to decide endings. He rushes to open the heavy front door, and a cold rush of air slaps the faces of the guests.

The blind man doesn't seem to know what to do. He shivers a little from the cold and walks toward it. Hobart holds the brass door handle tightly, watches as the tall man in the eagle jacket comes closer. The man looks as if he feels Hobart's presence, as if he would speak to Hobart, if Hobart made the first move. But Hobart does not have to be polite; the tall man is not from here.

Hobart opens the door even wider. The tall man passes over the threshold and outside. Mama gives a slight whimper. Whispers tumble over whispers; about Mama, about Hobart and the real nice thing he just did, getting rid of that foreigner, that un-welcomed stranger who dared to kiss an angel.

Pearl sent us to bed early after the party was over, and Izear took Mama to her room. Now, he and Pearl are cleaning up. I hear the china clinking downstairs. I hear Pearl asking Izear to tell her again about the second thing he's famous for. I think she mentions Cincinnati. I call across our Jack and Jill bathroom to Peck's room, "When are we going to Cincinnati?"

"You told Pearl you didn't want to go there."

"I didn't mean it. If you want to go, you know I'll go, too."

"Well, it's not a good place, Lizzie." His voice is almost too soft to be heard.

"But our daddy might be there and we could find him."

"I don't care about Cincinnati anymore. I don't want to go. I don't want to go anywhere."

"I'll bet you'd be dumb enough go to Crisscross if Hobart's cousin, Leona, asked you."

I hear the bed springs squeak as Peck turns over. Oh, let him sleep. He's not dumb. He's a real nice boy and I love him. But no matter what he says, he wants to go to Cincinnati. I know that for sure; I've read his diary. Peck writes everything down, just like Pearl's cousin, The Judge.

Something of Value

From The Official Notes of Pearl's cousin,
The Judge
In the section tabbed: History of Highlow

Pearl comes from a family of survivors, people of strong blood with a rainbow of ways to endure. Her grandfather, Joseph--my own Great Uncle--was thirteen when his brother was killed in a Yankee raid and his parents died from grief and yellow fever. He was left all alone so he ran away from Boligee in Greene County, Alabama where he was born and came further south to live with his aunt, my grandmother, who'd also lost a son. But after a few months in her care, he joined the Alabama Cavalry, vowing to kill the damn Yankees who'd killed his brother and his aunt's boy. He was quickly captured in the woods of North Georgia and taken to a Federal prison camp in Ohio, eight months before the War ended.

It was rumored a bitter, young Yankee sergeant from the camp who'd lost his own sibling to the Confederates, immediately took Joseph as his personal whipping boy, literally beating him day and night for the remaining months of the War, until his ribs were broken and his back bleeding and rotting from infection—because even when the chips were down, Pearl's grandfather, Joseph, never failed to fight back.

Physically, he was no more than a bent skeleton when he returned, and most believed he was quite mad. At first he would not eat, fearing maggots in his food. He would not sleep on his back unless holding a sharp, kitchen knife across his chest. He washed himself in the river at least three times a day, believing his skin was rotting away and frequently forgot to re-dress afterwards. He was often seen naked in the woods hunting with no weapon except his bare hands. Everyone expected he would fall to the wrath of a wild animal, but twice he came home with a bear carcass slung about his shoulders.

    If it had not been our strong-armed grandmother, Pearl's and mine, Joseph would have eventually come to harm. She sent him to Montgomery to be under the care of one of its most prominent citizens, Joseph's former Confederate colonel, Isaac Jameson, who'd also been imprisoned in the Ohio camp and singled out for starvation. Colonel Jameson was from a very wealthy family who owned hundreds of acres of undeveloped land that stretched into South Alabama. By letter, he made it known to my grandmother that Joseph had saved him from certain death in the prison camp, stealing bits of food and water from the Yankee tents, until he was caught for doing so and put into a dark, wood-covered hole where he was kept like a wild dog for the last month of The War. For this, Colonel Jameson wrote that he wanted to repay Joseph in any way that he could. My grandmother had written back with a request, and the Colonel came to get him and took him to Montgomery. For nearly a year, Joseph lived in Colonel Jameson's home, tended to by Colonel Jameson's personal doctor, and fed by the Colonel's mild-mannered wife. But it was the Colonel's copper-haired daughter, Grace, who soothed his night terrors by sharing her emerald absinthe.

    When Joseph finally came back to my grandmother's farm, docile as a lamb, he brought with him gifts from Colonel Jameson: a deed to two hundred acres of the land in South Alabama, and copper-haired Grace who loved to dance. But Joseph was generous. He kept only the land on which Pearl's house stands, giving away the rest to those afflicted southerners who promised to build something of value on it. And Highlow was born.

Trip to Crisscross

Peck

Pearl's always said, "Peck, if you know something for a fact, but try to hide it, the truth will still make itself known. You can push it way back, or disguise it, or cover it up with any lie you want to, but it's stronger than you are. Nobody has ever beaten the truth."

Well, I'm going to try. But about Pearl's house and what I know, I have to be careful. Anything I say to Lizzie, or Pearl, or Izear, might hasten the discovery that our house is not our own, that all our desires are rented ones, that Highlow is not always as it seems.

In Pearl's front yard, there are many camellia bushes, each a parent of identical flowers; but the oldest and tallest bush, the one closest to the street, is different. One side of it produces large, pink-petaled flowers centered with yellow stamen while the flowers on its other side are tight and small, an ugly red color with no centering crowns. I was there some years ago, when Pearl discovered the deviation.

"Why is this?" Pearl asked Izear, as if he and the bush had betrayed her.

"Some flowers are blessed with a crown you can see, and some of 'em just hide it inside," Izear said. "You know, like an ugly person that's got a good heart?"

"Pearl's not ugly!" I remember saying, thinking Izear was talking about her.

"No, she's not," he was quick to say. "Miss Pearl's a pretty little thing, inside and out; but some ain't. You remember Miss

Eileen I almost married? She was some kinda ugly! But Lord God, on a cold night that woman could love ya like--"

"Izear!" Pearl snapped. "Hush that talk."

Izear gave her a teasing grin. "Now, you ain't forgot William Crawford, have you Miss Pearl? He weren't too pretty, either; but you and him use to--."

"If you don't hush up, Izear, I'll put you on the bus to Cincinnati."

"Put me on the bus, Pearl," I said, because all I dreamed of then was finding my daddy

"See what you've done?" Pearl said, scolding Izear. "If that ever happens, I will hold you responsible!" Then she grabbed my hand and yanked me up the yard.

"He's got to go off one day," Izear called out. "If he don't, he ain't ever gonna know Highlow's home."

The night of Pearl's party, I recalled Izear's words, and a few days later, I went off to Crisscross. I took the bus to see Leona. Hobart bought me a round trip ticket when I asked him to, after I reminded him what I knew.

Pearl thought Hobart was taking me fishing—it's what I told her so she wouldn't worry, that we'd leave at dawn, but I'd be back before dark. "Fishing is good for a boy," she'd said.

But Lizzie argued. "You don't know how to fish!"

"That's why I'm going. To learn."

The next morning, Lizzie followed me out into the yard in her pink, seersucker pajamas with her hair stuck straight out on both sides like wings on her head, and the coming sun turning her gold. Next door, Hobart's truck engine was running, waiting for me in his driveway. "Maybe I'd better go with you," Lizzie said.

"No!" I think it hurt her feelings when I ran quickly for the truck.

"Well, I wouldn't want to try fishing anywhere in South Georgia!" she hollered across the yard. "Ya'll don't know those people like I do. They don't fool me. There's probably not one real fish in a Georgia river!"

Hobart and I took off down Main to the bus station. When I got off in Crisscross, Leona was there, just as Hobart said she would be. She was so pretty, her hair piled on top of her head, shining like a yellow crown. She had on a tight, red dress that Pearl would have said "was cut down to heaven knows where." It showed the rising of her bosom when she breathed.

We went to the picture show where she held my hand, like I was her little brother. We went to the drugstore where she bought me a malt like I was her son. We went to her house where she sat beside me on a sofa and hugged me like I was something else altogether, and I'm ashamed to say it scared me; but more ashamed to say it was what I wanted when she kissed me on the lips. And she would have again, except that the telephone rang. For a good thirty minutes Leona talked with her hairdresser who'd set her up for a date with a cowboy from Texas. While she talked, I watched the fish in her aquarium across the room, lots of little guppies and their mama who was eating them, one by one. By the time the phone call was over, there were only two fish left, and it was time to go.

Leona took me to the bus station. I told her, "I'll be back," and she kissed me on the cheek and said, "Okay, Shugah. Anytime you want, you just come on." And as the bus moved out, I turned to see Leona waving to me in her red dress, her bare arms spread wide as wings.

Back in Pearl's kitchen, I slapped the counter with the fish that Hobart had bought from Larry's Fish Market, strung on a line to fool her. "My goodness," Pearl said, putting an arm around my shoulder. "Would you just look at this fisherman?" Lizzie didn't say anything. She just followed me with her eyes as I passed her to go up to Mama's room.

Mama was painting my face on a fine china plate. She looked at my empty hands, disappointed because I held no bag of the face powder Hobart sends her. Even after I hugged her and said I loved her, her eyes told me to go back over to Hobart's and get her some. So, I went.

Hobart sat me down at his kitchen table and wanted me to tell him, again, what happened with Leona. He had the same half-grin as when I told him the first time. She was nice, I said, and it was good to get out of Highlow for a while. Then I thanked him for buying me the ticket. That was what he wanted to hear—"Thank you." Hobart liked for a person to owe him. He got up in my face. "Well, since you ain't got a daddy," he said, "I reckon somebody's got to show you the world."

But I was getting tired of being his errand boy, of keeping his secrets. "I have a daddy, you know I do!" I snatched up the powder Hobart had set on the table and got up to leave. Outside, the hot air of night slid over my face like a mother's soft hand.

"Next time you tell your mama to come over here herself, to get that stuff," Hobart called through the screen; the same thing he says every time he gives me the powder. "And don't expect to visit Leona again. She's my cousin. I was just letting you get some practice."

"Go to hell, Hobart," I said when I was too far away for him to hear.

"You tell your mama now!" His words trailed me through the tall thin pines that used to be the border between his property and Pearl's.

But I'd never tell Mama to go to Hobart's, again. I saw what happened the last time.

Lies

Lizzie

The morning after Peck's fishing trip, I half-wake, keeping my eyes closed in my dark, rosy room, thinking about the tall man in the eagle jacket and putting myself in his skin. I wonder what it's like to be blind. I imagine my fingers as the only vision I have, moving them across my eyes, down my nose and mouth, around my face. It's the same face as Peck's when there's nothing but touch to judge with. When you're blind, you see only the picture you draw in your head and that is sad, but there's one thing good about blindness. You can make things up as you go along, you don't even have to notice what some people do. You don't have to acknowledge some people at all. If you're blind, it's easy to see things just the way you want to, even if you're what Pearl calls a 'cock-eyed optimist.'

In a doze, I hear a soft, muffled tapping on the window pane and imagine that I am the one who is tapping. I am standing outside Mama's window, between the tall man and Hobart, and we are trying to get Mama's attention, but she won't hear us. Then I wake up enough to know I am in my own bed and the tapping sound is a tall bush scraping against the lower pane. Cotton Tree, it's called by some of the ladies in Pearl's Highlow Horticulture Society, because of its abundant white flowers. But Pearl calls it Confederate Rose, because its spotless white blooms last only through the morning, turn pink by noon, and bleed to a shriveled crimson before the day is over. "Just like the Confederacy, all those years ago, when it had its day in the sun," Pearl says. When she looks at one of those roses it reminds her of three things. The first thing is Dixie. The second and third are Mama—before, and after Cincinnati.

One week after the open house, Mama's painting. "Whose face is this, Lila?" Pearl asks, holding up the plate. "It looks familiar."

"It's the man from the open house," I say. I talk for Mama a lot. Nobody understands her like I do. "The one that got the hundred dollars and took the Baby Jesus, remember?"

"Oh, yes." Pearl sets the plate down on Mama's table, but she keeps looking at it. "Somebody should have taken the porcelain Baby Jesus away from him. I don't know where I'll find another one."

"I know where there's some, Pearl. I saw bunches of them at Woolworth's, in a basket over there with the plastic baby-doll stuff."

Pearl does not like my suggestion. "A plastic Baby Jesus?" she says. "I would never give away a plastic Jesus." She gives me a glare of disappointment and taps from Mama's room.

Mama's eyes follow Pearl as she leaves, then she stirs her brush in turpentine. "He brought it back," she says.

"Who?"

"The Baby Jesus that he put in his pocket. He brought it back."

"The man in the hawk jacket?"

"Yes," Mama says quietly. "He was here yesterday. He gave the Baby Jesus to Izear." She holds her plate up to the light of the window with her hand behind it. Her fingers shine clearly through the china as if they were painted on. "I don't know what Izear did with Him, but He's somewhere in this house."

Immediately, I go downstairs to ask Izear about the incident. He slaps the heavy, lemon-smelling dust rag down on the dining room table so hard it shakes a pink rose petal off the centerpiece. "I don't know nothing about that man bringing Jesus to this house."

"Mama said he did."

Izear picks up the petal, puts it in his pocket and starts dusting, again. "Well, he mighta' brung Him back. I don't remember."

"Who was he, Izear?" I have on my best 'boss' voice. "I believe you know him, don't you?"

"Too many fingerprints on this table. Ya'll quit touching it when you go whizzin' by." He is scrubbing a dark shiny place on the edge of the table, but I don't see one fingerprint.

"Izear, if you don't tell me who that man was, I'll tell Pearl about Miss Eileen up there in your place last summer." I may have used this up on Izear, and it is old news. Miss Eileen, who used to be his girlfriend, is long gone. She ran off with the head caddy at the Highlow Country Club. They say two hundred dollars from the Pro Shop was missing after the caddy left, along with six dozen boxes of my favorite candy from the caddy shop freezer.

"Go on and tell her then, little Miss Tattle-Tale," Izear says.

But he knows I won't. Izear knows I love him. In the wood of the table, I can see our faces, Izear's and mine, side by side; creamy and caramel, like the inside of a Milky Way.

I visit Mama again. She's finishing up the blind man's face. "All done," she says, then kisses the edge of his plate and hands it to me. "I want you to have this, Lizzie. I've painted your father, for you and Peck."

Just like that, our father. But what my mama says is not always what she means. She comes from a place that's different from Peck's and mine. Our father couldn't be the man in the eagle jacket.

"Where's he from?" I ask her, looking at the face on her plate.

"Cincinnati." She answers plain as day. It was Pearl who told us our father came from Cincinnati. Until now, Mama never gave us a clue.

"But he came to Pearl's open house," I say. "How did a blind man get so far down south?"

"He came on a bus, of course. He doesn't like flying." Mama

looks at me with her angel eyes like there is no surprise in what she said. Her revelation is definitely something I will have to think about before I tell Peck.

I'm thinking about it, looking down from the window of Mama's room, when I see Leona come up Mrs. McSwain's driveway and take the back steps to her house. Hobart opens the door and kisses her on the mouth, not like she was his cousin, at all. "What a liar!" I say.

Mama hears. She mistakes my words as commentary on the face of my so-called father. "Not always," Mama says, looking at her plate; "and he might have been a good daddy." But Mama hasn't seen what I see--ever. She is still in Cincinnati, so to speak. And since it doesn't do to get her riled up about Hobart—she can't stand the man--I let her think I'm in Cincinnati, too.

I take the plate and study the painted, half-shut eyes. "Why don't we know our father?"

"Why?" she repeats, as if I have asked a question with such a simple answer, like why does Little Benedict sniff and snuff, or why does Pearl walk with a cane? "You don't know him, Lizzie, because you haven't been to Cincinnati."

That settles it. I will have to go there.

A Necessary Bargain

Peck

My diary is spiral-bound. It's a notebook with *PECK'S DIARY* printed in big letters, right on the front. I plan to give it to my father, so he'll know something about me. In it, I write about the things I want: him, the Osprey, and maybe Leona. I write about the people I love: Lizzie, Mama, Pearl, and Izear. I even write about Little Benedict because someone needs to take account of him and it seems no one does. But there are some things I don't write about. Those things, I keep inside my head so nobody will be hurt by seeing them on paper.

Hobart has lots of girlfriends who come to his house, Leona and others. But sometimes Mama goes, too. I didn't tell her to go, as Hobart had ordered on the night I got back from Crisscross. She goes on her own. Once, I followed her; saw Hobart fold her into his arms and kiss her on the mouth. I saw him lead her down the hall to a room where the window was low to the ground and the curtains didn't fit. I saw pieces of Hobart, pieces of Mama. I saw things twisting: legs and arms, a bare back, an uncovered breast, things that are supposed to go with love. Except there was sadness in Mama's eyes, so I knew it wasn't love I'd seen.

Pearl told us about sex and love. On our thirteenth birthday, she said we needed to know. Pearl told us how bodies are given as a gift from Almighty God, and that Matrimony was a sacrament upon which a dream is built. But sometimes, Pearl warned us, the sacrament is forgotten and the dream becomes costly.

The day after I saw Mama with Hobart, he showed me the

blueprint of his dream; a real-estate agency he planned to build with plenty of his adopted mama's money, after she left it to him. I didn't want to see his blueprint. I wanted to ask about Mama and why he'd made her so sad. But all I could get out of my mouth was the weather report. "Izear says we're ripe for a flood."

Hobart looked up from his plans, irritated. "How does he know?"

"He heard it on the six o'clock news on his rabbit-eared TV. It's going to rain for days and the river's going to rise up out of its banks on Dixie. It won't get up to Main Street, though. We're on high ground."

"You ain't as high as you think you are," Hobart said, folding up his dream with his smooth, quick hands. Then his handsome face became so transparent I could almost see his thoughts, ready to erupt. I didn't want to be anywhere near Hobart then.

"I don't need you to catch the Osprey," I said in a burst of courage. "I'll do it myself."

Hobart laughed. "Dreamer! Ya won't get him without me."

"I've held him. I've touched his wings."

"And look at your hands, like mincemeat after it got through with you. I'd have killed the damn thing; killed it, stuffed it, and had a damn trophy. You got nothing to show, but scars."

I looked down at my palms and remembered the pain.

Hobart came closer, an odd softness in the air around him. He thumped a playful fist against my shoulder. "Look here, Peck, if you want it alive, we'll get it alive; but there just ain't no hope of your getting that hawk without my help."

It seemed the time to ask him, "Did you hurt Mama last night?"

He paled a little. "Of course not; I only gave her the powder she came for."

"But why does she need it?"

Hobart shrugged. "Why not? It makes her feel good."

"I don't think it's good for her to want it so bad."

"Is it good for you to want the Osprey so bad? We all got stuff we can't do without."

"What is it you can't do without, Hobart?"

He laughed. "Not much."

"It's Pearl's house you can't do without, isn't it?"

"You haven't said anything about the deed, have you?"

"No."

"I wanna be the first to tell Pearl who owns her house."

"I wish William Crawford hadn't been a gambler."

"But you wish you had the Osprey, too; don't you? Keep your mouth shut and you will."

"I'm not taking Mama any more powder, Hobart."

"Fine!" he said, all softness gone. "She knows where it is."

An Empty Plate

Hobart

A hunter can find new things before anybody else does. I found the waterfall first, years ago when I was hunting in the woods near Dixie with Daddy McSwain--a monstrous waterfall with a black and silver-mouthed cave opening behind it. Even Daddy McSwain was impressed after I drug him through the trees; him in the middle of spotting a squirrel in his rifle sight, and just about to squeeze the trigger.

"Well lookathere, Hobart!" he declared. "I started hunting these woods over fifty years ago with my own daddy and in all that time I never once caught a glimpse of that."

"Maybe you didn't go deep enough, Daddy McSwain."

"Maybe not." He sat down on a flat, algae-covered rock and starred at the silvery water splashing on the river. "That thing is something!"

"Let's go behind it; see what's in the cave."

"No, boy. Even if we found a way to get behind that powerful water, we could get boxed inside and never get out."

"I been boxed before and I got out. Come on."

"I don't need to go inside to know what's in there," Daddy McSwain said. "There's rotting carcasses, old bones, darkness and danger. I've been in other caves, in the Pacific in World War II. Too many old memories."

"But this is a new cave, and I found it."

"Then we'll call it yours," Daddy McSwain said. "It belongs to you now. You don't even have to tell a soul about the cave, or the waterfall."

Of course, I couldn't keep something as impressive as that to myself, especially if it was mine. I had to show Lila.

Back then she often went in the woods by herself, even though I'd heard Miss Pearl warn her about being alone in such a wild place. "You could have an accident!" But Lila was obstinate, always had her own mind. She'd cover her ears and walk right through those pines, with Pearl wringing her hands and calling for Izear to bring her back.

One day, soon after I discovered the cave, Lila headed for the woods, again. Pearl called for Izear, forgetting she'd sent him for milk.

"I'll go after her, Miss Pearl," I said.

"Oh, please bring her back, Hobart."

So I followed Lila. She was used to me following her; but that day, I kept out of her sight. That day in the woods, I hid when she stopped to admire a purple thistle, when she picked a goldenrod then bent to touch a tiny mushroom growing between the roots of a tree. She went deeper and deeper into the woods, while the thoughts in my head urged me, "Call out to her; say something to the prettiest girl in Highlow." But it was nearly an hour before I did, and that was because she tripped on the edge of the bank and fell into the river. Then I shouted, "Lila!"

She broke the surface of the water quickly and looked up at me, stunned for a minute, her hair clinging to her face. Then she laughed and started swimming away, fast. I dove in and swam after her, the bell-ringing echo of her laugh expanding my head like some drug. Oh, I followed her-- beat my arms, my legs, my body, against the river for her—until she slowed, panting and tired, just below the waterfall. Then she reached out for a glistening, blue-algaed rock protruding over the water like a shelf, and pulled herself onto it. "Look at this! Have you ever seen anything so beautiful?" she asked me, passing the palms of her hands over its surface.

"It's mine. I found it." I climbed up beside her.

"You did not; I did."

"I found it with Daddy McSwain, over a week ago."

"Then why didn't you tell me?" she asked, just like that, as if we were best friends and ought to have no secrets between us.

"Look what else I found." I pointed toward the waterfall. "There's a cave behind the falls."

There was no hesitation, no talk of fear or danger; she simply slid off the rock. "Come on," she said, and we swam toward the waterfall. Closer, closer to that beautiful thing meant to be mine.

It's hard getting through a power like water. It pushes you back; it stings your face and takes your breath. It fills your lungs, even tries to take your life. But if you want to pass through badly enough, it can be done. Five minutes, and we were scrambling over a slippery bolder and inside the cave on another shelf-like ridge with the river a few feet below. Daddy McSwain was right. It smelled of rotting carcasses, it was dark, and maybe dangerous. On the ridge were several small bones, like the bones of a child, and there were spiders, mice-- and immediately, mosquito bites on our arms and legs. A disturbed bat flew in our faces, then into the blackness behind us. But Lila didn't appear frightened. Without sight, with her hands walking the walls, she edged further into the nothingness. "Are you coming?"

Of course, I went without seeing, only hearing a very peculiar whisper that must have been Lila's. "I adore this place. It's like nothing exists in here, except *now*. An empty plate, waiting to be filled with whatever I choose."

I remember thinking: choose me! I extended a hand in the direction of her words. It brushed her lips. She kissed it with a loud smack then laughed; the chime-like ring of it echoing through the cave. Then there was silence, only the sound of her breathing and the gurgling of the water below us. It seemed over an hour we were on the ridge, both blind in the middle of emptiness, a gift to Lila from me. Finally, she said, "Let's go."

Pearl was frantic by the time we got back. "Lila, you're soaking wet!"

"I would have drowned, if Hobart hadn't saved me," she said, giving me a wink that Pearl didn't appear to notice.

"Well Hobart!" Pearl chimed. "You might not be from here, but you sure come in handy." It was the first time I saw a social possibility for myself on Main Street.

Not a week afterwards, I watched Izear carrying a crate of old china plates into Pearl's house and asked him, "Where'd you get those?"

"From a yard sale down the street," he said, not looking at me.

"I thought Miss Pearl had plenty of plates."

"Ain't for Miss Pearl. Now, go on home."

I suspect it was the day Lila began painting faces; the first of her passions I had a hand in.

Highlow Blood

Lizzie

In the light of a full Spring moon, my twin brother's breath hits my cheek as we sit side by side, cross-legged in the grass of Pearl's back yard watching Little Benedict do somersaults. Peck looks gray and cold in the moonlight and there's a familiar boy smell rising from the back of his neck, the tang of trouble. I'm sure it's due to one of the three things he's had on his mind: our father, the Osprey, or over-stuffed Leona. I give his hand a pat, but he moves it away without a word.

Then Hobart's kitchen lights up, giving a clear view of him through the window.

"Look, there's Hobart!" Little Benedict squeals, scrambling up from the grass after a flopped somersault.

Hobart is holding a long, green metal box that he slaps angrily on the kitchen counter. He rummages through a drawer, finds a hammer and then beats it against the lock on the metal box. Little Benedict yanks my arm. "C'mon, let's go see what he's doing!"

We run to the fence and start to climb it, but Peck stands back, biting his lower lip, as if hesitant to climb the fence, so I motion for him. Finally, he comes, and then we all crouch under the window.

Hobart has gotten into the box and is taking papers from it. One at a time, he reads them and throws them aside as if he hasn't found what he's looking for. Then he gives a happy-sounding grunt and smiles, holding up an old, yellowed piece of paper. "Highlow blood," he says.

"Ooooh, he said 'blood!'" Little Benedict whispers.

"Damned old Highlow blood," Hobart repeats, grinning like the Cheshire cat in Alice in Wonderland. And there's something about the way he says it--Highlow blood-- that makes mine boil. It's like he's kicked a helpless baby, or dropped the host at Mass, and it brings out what Pearl says is my worst quality-- spite. If I had Pearl's just-in-case gun, I'd aim it at Hobart and put the fear of Main Street in him for the way he put us down.

The light goes off in the kitchen then back on in the bathroom. Hobart is looking into the bathroom mirror. Now there's a conflicting flutter in my stomach, just seeing his handsome reflection.

"Look, he's still got that box!" Little Benedict says.

Hobart squeaks open a cabinet door and lays the box inside.

"I wonder what that paper is for," I say to my brother whose face shows a thousand thoughts fighting with one another.

"Let's sneak in and find out." Little Benedict starts for the McSwain's back door.

"No!" Peck says too loudly and grabs him by the collar.

Hobart glances our way and we all duck as he peers through the window, but he must not see us because he turns around again.

"Did you hear what he said about Highlow blood?" I whisper to Peck. "He acts like he's better than we are. And what if there's something awful in that box?"

Hobart's bathroom light goes out just as Peck whispers. "It's just an old piece of paper."

Little Benedict sides with me, "I'll bet it *is* something awful."

"Ya'll better keep this to yourselves," Peck warns, heading for the house. "Or Pearl will find out we've been looking in windows."

Peck is our leader, so we follow him home. I forget about Hobart's handsomeness and recall the hateful tone he used when he mentioned Highlow. I think Pearl ought to know how Hobart really feels about us. I think Pearl will be so appalled that she'll call her cousin The Judge to take notes.

    Pearl isn't appalled. She takes me by the shoulders instead. "Looking in other people's windows is unacceptable behavior for those of Highlow blood. Quit being so spiteful or one day it will backfire on you."

A Favor

Peck

With the hot summer rain, steam rises from Main Street, but when the street gets used to the heat, the steam disappears and only sheets of water run down the pavement, washing away the edges of Pearl's yard. She calls on the men of her house to save it. Izear and I put on our plastic raincoats and stack concrete blocks along the slope to keep in the new grass he planted last spring. Izear works hard because Pearl's house is his home, too. I work alongside him with the key to Hobart's secret in my pocket. The key is no longer needed after Hobart destroyed the lock. I keep it to remind me of what I should have done, but did not do.

After Izear and I finish, we head for the house, an open faucet of rain pouring down our plastic coats. "Gonna need us an ark if this keeps up," Izear says.

Little Benedict waits for us on the covered porch. "What's a ark?" he asks.

"Ain't they never sent you to Sunday School, boy?" Izear takes off his raincoat and shakes it until Little Benedict starts sneezing again.

"Sure I been to Sunday School. Aaahchoo! I been to Monday School, too," Little Benedict giggles, wiping his ever-running nose with the back of his hand. "Even been to Tuesday and Wednesday and Thursday school."

"Hush up, boy; if you'd been to Sunday School you'd know what a ark is." Then Izear tickles Little Benedict underneath his scrawny arm and Little Benedict doubles over in laughter. "Sweet Jesus!" Izear says. "Ain't no Sunday School could stand the likes of you, no way."

Little Benedict gives Izear's waist a bear hug. "Well, you can stand me any day of the week, can't you, Izear?"

"Aw, I reckon," he says, unwrapping Little Benedict's arms, "Long as you brings along a Kleenex."

I knew then I wanted my father, when I found him, to be like Izear, somebody who would love you even when your nose ran all over your face.

By the sixth day of rain we are still dry in Pearl's house on Main Street, but Dixie is underwater. Izear says, "That rabbit-eared TV reporter was sent down south to stir up a show, and now, he's standing on the corner of Rebel and Cat Alley under the Crime Stop sign, sticking his microphone under the noses of all the druggies and whores and asking 'em about the Federal Government's suspicion of Dixie's drug problem and what's gonna happen to their civil rights when the FBI put guards in all the red-neck bus stations, so nobody can send anything out to the people up north drooling to make money off it?"

"What is gonna happen to their silver rights, Izear?" Little Benedict asks.

Lizzie howls with laughter. "Silver rights? It's civil rights, dummy!"

"Hush, girl" Izear gives Little Benedict's head a pat. "That TV reporter don't know what he's talking about anyway. He's stuck ankle-deep in an ongoing redemption by the Lord, a real Southern Baptism and he's too blind to see it, even with Dixie's river soaking into his sole."

"Yeah, he's just a Yankee carpetbagger from Chicago," Lizzie says.

"Chicken in the car and the car won't go," Little Benedict sings. "That's how you spell Chi-ca-go." Izear laughs, then we all laugh.

"Let's play *Pin the Tail on the Donkey!*" Lizzie says, pulling out the tattered box containing the poster of a grinning donkey and ten different colored tails. Lizzie likes being our social director.

"I ain't touching that thing," Izear says. "My daddy told me don't never hang around with no jackass."

"Oh alright, Izear; I suppose we'll have to play canasta, just for you." Lizzie takes a deck of cards from a kitchen drawer and deals four hands on the table. She is winning, as usual, by the time Hobart knocks on Pearl's kitchen door.

"Whatcha want?" Izear asks him from the other side of the locked screen.

Hobart stands on the steps, water rolling down his green plastic raincoat and the bill of his hunting cap. "I want Peck," he says.

Lizzie shoves away from the table. "We're playing canasta. I've already dealt Peck's hand and he doesn't want to quit."

"I don't mind quitting." I step in front of Izear and go out onto the stoop to see what Hobart wants.

"Hey Hobart, you want me, too?" Little Benedict asks hopefully.

"Don't want anybody but Peck." Hobart unfastens his green plastic coat and holds it open for me.

"Get out of that rain!" Lizzie hollers as we crossed the yard to his house. "You might get struck by lightning!"

When we get inside, Hobart opens his pantry and pulls out a small, brown paper bag. "I got a favor to ask," he says, reaching into it for a saran-wrapped bundle of white powder.

I back away.

"This ain't for your mama. It's more powerful stuff; worth a lotta money."

"What is it?"

"Dixie's special sugar for a man in Detroit. I need you to put it on the bus. Pack it up with one of Izear's sour cream pound cakes."

"It's not Christmas. Izear doesn't make sour cream pound cakes if it's not Christmas. He makes chocolate."

"Hell, chocolate then!"

"How come I have to put it on the bus, and not you?"

"Because you're innocent and I'm not, that's why. An innocent child nobody will suspect."

"Why aren't you innocent, Hobart?"

"Dammit boy, I grew up a long time ago."

Izear makes me a chocolate cake when I tell him it's to take over to Mrs. Spratling because she's been sick and already had to forego three parties. Nobody stops me at the bus station, although two men in dark glasses and wet hair, sitting behind the baggage counter drinking beer with the clerk, ask me about my sick aunt in Detroit, the aunt I said I was sending the chocolate cake to. I tell them that my aunt is next to death's door and that she wants to come back to Dixie, but nobody has the money to send her a bus ticket. One of the men says I'm a real nice little redneck to be so concerned about the elderly.

Later, when I tell Hobart about it, he laughs and says I oughta win an Academy Award. He says he can see that lying will pay off for me.

After the rain is over, the TV weatherman says he won't be back for a while and the TV reporter from Chicago says he wouldn't be back either, because the FBI hasn't been able to hang a thing on Dixie. So Hobart and I go hunting again.

Hobart sticks his rifle in the rack on the back of his truck and motions for me to get in. He stretches his arm along the seat behind my head, grips the leather-wrapped wheel and looks back through the cab's rear window to steer us out of the driveway. He is quiet as we drive toward the river; maybe he's thinking about Leona, or Mama. But I'm thinking about the lies I've told, the secrets I've kept--all those things I never write about in my diary.

In the woods, Hobart is drinking a bottled beer and offers me some. "Your mama likes beer, too." An odd softness creeps into his eyes again as I take the bottle from him. The glass slips in my palm from the sweat of Hobart's hand.

"I don't like it," I say, taking a swallow, then one more.

"Yeah? Why're you drinking it then?" I give him back the bottle and he grins. "You don't know what you like; don't even know what you really want."

"I know what I want."

"Hell, 'less we kill it, you ain't never gonna have that hawk." He raises his rifle and aims as if he sees the Osprey, then lowers it. We share a stubborn look at each other.

"How do you know Mama likes beer?"

"I've seen her drink it. There's lots goes on you don't know about." Hobart laughs. "I got a lotta stuff on you Todds, boy."

"I know you've got our house, what else is there?"

"Never you mind. Now, let's hunt."

We wait for hours, guns in hand, but the Osprey doesn't come so we drive home by way of the muddy river road. I go inside the McSwain house to take off my hunting outfit and leave it with Hobart until the next time. Hobart puts it in the top of a closet. On my way out, he gives me a sack of powder. "Take this to your mama."

"No. I told you I wasn't going to do that anymore." I turn to go down the steps.

"You take it, or I'll take your house, tomorrow," Hobart says.

I can't ignore the meanness in his voice.

Mama is starting a new plate; only the yellow-ochre outlines had been drawn. I can see the almond shape of an eye, the shadow beside a nose, the hint of a lip, but it's nobody I know yet. I want to kiss her, and do. She touches my face with her stained fingers. "What was that for, angel?"

I shrug. "You're my mama, aren't you?"

"Always."

From my pocket, I pull Hobart's plastic-wrapped gift. She takes it from my hands then looks at me, as if wondering how much I know. "I don't want this," she says. "Why would I want this old powder?" But she doesn't give it back. Instead, her fingers close around the bag. I touch her shoulder, and she looks up, tears in her eyes. "This is the last time. You tell him that."

"I'll tell him."

I watch Mama's trembling fingers place the plastic in a bureau drawer, then she turns to wrap me in her arms. "This *is* the last time. I mean it."

"You won't go to Hobart's anymore?"

Her face drains of color. "Why would I go there? I can't stand the man."

At once, I'm tired of the lie, tired of keeping secrets. "Hobart owns Pearl's house. He has the deed. I've seen it. I've seen other things, too, like you and Hobart."

She puts her hands over her ears. "No! I won't hear another word!" then she calls for Izear who comes running.

"I just wanted her to know the truth," I try to explain to Izear, but crying overtakes me because I've upset Mama, because I'd betrayed Hobart and Pearl could lose her house, and because I will never capture what I want most in the world.

Izear pulls me close, wipes my tears with his hand. "She knows the truth. It's you that don't."

That night Lizzie and I sit cross-legged in Pearl's back yard again, without Little Benedict. Mrs. Spratling has learned she's going to have another baby, plus she's caught the flu bug and has given it to Little Benedict and his daddy, so they all stay home for a change. Lizzie is making tuneless, harmonica music with a blade of grass between her lips. She keeps looking at me as if she's afraid I might get up and leave. I have no intention of leaving; I see the shadow of a woman in Hobart's window, and it is not Leona's.

I remind myself that Hobart has lots of girlfriends. Then angry, muffled words pass through the window and Lizzie comes to attention. "I can't stand Leona," she says, assuming one of the voices is hers. "I don't know what you and Hobart see in her!"

"It's not Leona." I get up and go into the house.

Lizzie follows me down the hall, into the music room to William Crawford's desk. I pull open the bottom drawer and take out Pearl's just-in-case-gun.

"What in the world are you doing?" she shouts. "You're not going to shoot Hobart over that stupid Leona, are you?"

"It's not Leona!"

"Put that gun back, or I'll call Pearl!"

I drop the gun into the drawer and slam it closed. Lizzie pursues me up the steps to my room. I lock the door behind me.

"What's wrong?" she asks through the door." I thought you'd be glad it's not Leona."

I can't tell her what I know-- that our Mama is hooked on some drug and maybe on Hobart, too, that our house is not ours, but his, or that I never wanted the osprey, only our father who doesn't want us. I love Lizzie too much to hurt her like that. And I can't let her into my room because no one, except Izear, has ever seen me cry.

Just in Case

Lizzie

Hot August is here. Hobart will turn thirty years old before it's over, but Mrs. McSwain will not be at his party if he has one. Last month, he put her in the first nursing home in Highlow. Hobart told Pearl she'd lost her mind.

It got away with Pearl when Hobart took his mama off. "She's no crazier than you are," Pearl said to him. "You bring her back, right now. Bring her to my house!" So Hobart did.

Pearl sat her in the chair below the picture of the Sacred Heart and gave her a glass of scuppernong wine, then Izear fed her some pound cake he'd made especially for her. I took the chair next to hers, like I'd done at Pearl's open house. Then I patted her little hand.

"Where's the Christmas tree?" Mrs. McSwain asked. The wine and cake dribbled out of the side of her mouth when she opened it.

"Good Lord, Bessie McSwain," Pearl said. "Christmas is a long ways off."

"It is not," Mrs. McSwain insisted as Pearl wiped her mouth with a tatted white napkin. "Where have you hidden the presents? I want my presents!" she insisted, pounding a knee with her little clinched fist. "Can't I have at least one present?"

Pearl whispered to Izear, something that sent him upstairs toward Mama's room. I rose to keep my distance, conveniently disappearing behind the swinging door to the kitchen where I could look through the crack and not be asked by Pearl to do anything special. But what Mama did was more than special. With Izear smiling behind her, she came toward the old woman holding a present, a fine china plate wrapped in white lace, tied with a purple ribbon.

"Ooooh!" Mrs. McSwain cooed when she unfolded the lace and saw the face of little Tarsicius, b. 210 d. 223. "Saint Tarsicius," she said, as if she'd known that sweet-faced, thousand-year-old boy all her life. And that afternoon, while Mrs. McSwain held the painted porcelain face of a little boy saint in her lap, she fell from Pearl's chair into a lump on the floor, dead.

On the day of her funeral, Pearl insisted that Hobart put the sweet face of little Saint Tarsicius in the casket along with his mama. I suppose that ancient child is lying there to this day on Mrs. McSwain's old chest.

Now, Hobart's busy turning his mama's house into a real estate business. He's said it will be a first for Highlow. Pearl said she might have known he'd do something like that. She said Hobart's always got to be first. So today, Izear is driving her downtown in the blue and white Buick Roadmaster she bought in 1953 to discuss the situation with her cousin, The Judge. She wants an impartial opinion about Hobart's tacky reconstruction of Main Street.

"Miss Pearl, you know The Judge ain't gonna do nothing except side with you," Izear is saying on their way out the door. "So why're we going to tell him about it?"

"I'm not going to tell The Judge anything. First, I'm going to let him talk."

"And then?"

"Then I'm going to agree with The Judge when he says everybody knows Hobart doesn't belong in Highlow, but we have to accept that he's here and try to find a little bit of good in him."

"You think The Judge sees a little bit of good in that scoundrel?"

"Probably not, but that's what he'll say because that's what a good judge is supposed to say."

"So if we ain't going to hear the truth, then why make the trip?"

"Because Izear, The Judge writes down everything. He always keeps notes, just-in-case."

"Just-in-case we forget?"

"Just-in-case the day comes when it's all we have to go by."

"Lord, Lord, Miss Pearl. You sure are a puzzle." He ushers her through the door and it slams shut behind them.

Peck and I giggle at their conversation, then go to his room---he promised never to lock me out of it again—to look through his National Geographic magazines.

Peck turns a page and finds a naked Pygmy woman with long sagging breasts. "Look at this, Lizzie." He hands me the magazine.

"I bet she gets cold in the winter," I say.

Peck eyes my chest. "Reckon you'll ever get like that?"

"Give it here!" I snatch back the magazine. "Or maybe you want to hang it up in the bathroom like Hobart's naked woman calendar?"

"How did you know about Hobart's calendar?"

I try very hard not to let my eyes stray to his diary, beneath the magazines where he has hidden it. "Little Benedict told me,' I say quickly. "I bet she wasn't any little Pygmy woman, was she?"

"Some movie star, I think."

"Was her name in the picture with her?"

Peck gives his famous hee-haw laugh. "There wasn't anything in the picture with her!"

I shove him. "Stupid boy." He makes like he's hurt and falls down on the rug, then we both laugh. But I'm certain he knows something I don't, and I hate it when we're not--one thing, I guess you'd say. I worry about the tearing sounds I hear in his voice, the splitting away from me I sometimes see in his expressions. For a minute, I close my eyes to get rid of all that, thinking how I love him, how I couldn't do without him. Then I put the magazines back into the bottom drawer of the cabinet in Peck's closet, just above the diary he doesn't know I've read.

The next morning, we have to hurry. We're going to Crisscross for Mass. I think Peck's hoping he'll get lucky and see Leona walking the street; but as usual, I don't want to go.

"Why can't we just be Baptist, Pearl, like everybody else in Highlow? Why do we have to drive sixty miles when there're plenty of churches here?" I say this every Sunday and every Holy Day that Izear drives us twenty miles across the state line to Crisscross in the Buick Roadmaster. I don't really want to go to the Baptist church, but I ask anyway so Pearl will know it's a sacrifice. She likes sacrifices. She says they make a person, a person.

"Catholic is as Catholic does," Pearl answers as always. "If we're going to say we're Catholic, then we must go to Mass, no matter how far we have to go."

"Well, Mama doesn't go," I whine to Pearl. "And Izear just sits in the car."

"Your mama is ill," Pearl answers. "And Izear has made his own unfortunate choice to sit in the car."

Izear shifts a little behind the wheel. "Nome," he says, "I came in one time."

"When Izear?" Peck asks.

"When ya'll was two weeks old and baptized in the Spirit. I came in then."

"Oh yes," Pearl says. "I had forgotten that, Izear."

"Yes'um. I helped Miss Lila when she couldn't hardly make it up the steps holding the babies."

Pearl laughs. "And Monsignor Cullen asked where the father was, and you said, "I guess I'm it!" Then Izear laughs, too.

"I don't think that's funny," Peck says abruptly. "We have a father."

I follow the leader. "Yes, we do have a father. And he is an artist."

Pearl looks sorry she laughed, Izear tightens his fingers around the wheel, and Peck sulks in the backseat until we get to the church. I think Peck might not get out, but he does. During Mass, it seems as if every other word is 'Father.' I watch Peck to see how he is reacting to all those reminders, but I can't always tell about my brother. Sometimes he's too deep a well to see the bottom. If it wasn't for his diary, I'd never know what he's thinking or doing. I wouldn't know he went to see slutty Leona, even though knowing puts a strain on me.

As we are driving down the main street in Crisscross on our way back to Highlow, Peck looks through the back window of the Roadmaster to the sidewalk by the bus station.

"If you want to talk to that silly girl, why don't you just call her up long distance. Or better still," I whisper, just to see his reaction; "why don't you just take the bus to see her?"

He glares at me. "I've never in my life wanted to talk to Leona!" His lie angers me, but I feel guilty, too. Sometimes I wish he'd hide his diary in a better place.

Harsh Things

The Spratling House

"Aaaaachoo!"

"Good lord, Little Benny, you scared me to death! No, don't use your sleeve! Go get him a handkerchief, Benedict Senior. Oh, if only I'd married a man without inherited allergies."

"Now Billy Nana, you got the best when you got me."

"The best of what? You came from nothing. Anything we have is because of my good blood.

"Honeybuns, you ought not to be talking like that, especially in your condition."

"I wouldn't be in this condition, if it wasn't for you."

"We don't want our surprise baby to be hearing harsh things."

"Harsh things? With you, my whole life is harsh things. All I ever wanted was just one, teeny-weeny good time, just one good party."

"You're getting your nerves all frayed. Settle down now. We've got a nice life, you and me and Benny. And soon we'll have little--."

"Don't you dare give it a name!"

"But it will soon be here. We ought to pick out a name; one for a girl and one for a boy."

"Aaaaachoo! Can I name it?"

"No you can't, Benny! And neither can your father. Nobody will name it until I see what it looks like--I mean, if it's alright."

"But Billie Nana, Dr. Sharbel says there won't be anything wrong with it."

"Dr Sharbel! I wanted to go to Montgomery, didn't I? Go to a doctor who'd tell me the truth, just-in-case. But no! My own husband wouldn't take me and now it's too late."

"Don't cry Billie Nana. It won't matter what it looks like."

"Don't cry, Mommy. Aaaaachoo! Maybe it'll look like me."

"Oh I'm so tired of breathing his germs. Just take him out, Benedict Senior!"

"Let's go outside, Benny, and let Mommy rest."

"Daddy, why can't I name the baby?"

"What do you want to name it, Benny?"

"Well, if it's a boy, I want to name it Peck. And if it's a girl, then Lizzie, I guess."

"That could get very confusing, don't you think?"

"No. I'll know who it is."

"Well, we'll think about it, okay?"

"Okay. Aaaaachoo!"

A Little Repair

Lizzie

    Living in Highlow causes nice people to trust. Take Pearl, for example. She trusts the three of us have given up on looking in Hobart's windows. Tonight, we're on our side of the fence, but only about ten feet from his bathroom, where the moving shadows inside entwine to become black knots like those on the trunks of old trees. Peck tried to discourage it. Of course, he did not succeed. Now, he keeps saying, "Sh—sh."
    "Quit breathing so loud, Little Benedict!" I say to please Peck, and jab the dummy with my elbow.
    "I've got to sneeze--aaaachoo!" Then up comes his wiping sleeve.
    "Well, I'm sure Hobart's heard us by now!" Peck snaps.
    "No, he's still kissing her." Even though it's too dark to tell who he's kissing, I can see Hobart's blonde head has not been put off course by Little Benedict's sneeze. Hobart doesn't hear a thing. Maybe when you kiss somebody for that long your ears get stopped up.
    "Oh my gosh!" Little Benedict's nose is running wild. "Where'd they go?"
    "They must be on the floor."
    Peck's voice cracks, "Is it--Leona?"
    "Of course not." I can't see who it is, but why should he get his feelings hurt by a slut from Crisscross who owns a vicious mama guppy and takes up with cowboys from Texas. I almost tore

up those pages when I read them, they made me so mad!

"Let's climb the fence and see," Little Benedict puts his foot on the cross wood to go over.

"I don't want to see!" I snatch him down by the collar of that handkerchief he wears for a shirt.

"Well I do!" Little Benedict contorts himself until I lose my hold and he steps up on the cross wood, again. "Come on, Peck," he says. Amazingly, my brother starts toward him.

I have to do something quick. "Hey, look over there! I think it's the Osprey!"

Peck is detoured immediately. "Where?"

"Over there." I swing around to point at the dark. "On Little Benedict's roof."

Oh, the short attention span of men. How they run toward any false distraction. I am wondering how to keep up the lie when the surprising scream comes from the trees behind us. Peeeecek. Peeeeeck.

"There it is!" Little Benedict stops in his tracks.

Between two light grey swipes across the black sky, the Osprey flies, swooping low behind the pines. "It's back that way!" Peck shouts.

We are off--down Pearl's front yard, onto the pavement of Main Street and across to the other side where the primroses grow thick and high and smell like the perfume Mama dabs behind her ears. The Osprey perches on the top of the street light, shadows the ground, threatens and scatters the moths away from the glow, then folds itself into a place of rest. My brother looks up at it, his face caught in the light of the cold moon, captured like a painting on a fine china plate. If I held my hand behind his head, I am sure I could see my fingers on the other side.

At once, the wings of the Osprey stretch out again and it soars into the thick night, followed by those stupid boys I love. What can I do, except pursue the dream with them?

Two blocks down, the pavement turns to dirt and sharp

rocks press pain against the thin soles of my tennis shoes. There are no primroses here and nothing to smell except the dust sucked into your nostrils whenever you breathe.

"Ouch!" Little Benedict stumbles over a rock and falls. "Peck, wait!" he calls, but my brother doesn't stop. So Little Benedict squats and snuffs and wipes his nose. "Lizzie, I can't go no further. My foot's hurt."

"Just sit then. We'll stay here."

But Peck runs on. At the dead end of Main Street, he disappears into the shadows of great live oaks. Surely, he will look up to see that he cannot win.

In the light from the porch of a nearby house, Little Benedict plops in the road and unlaces his smelly tennis shoe. He yanks off his red sock and eyes his foot. "Oh my gosh, I'm bleeding! Lookathere at the blood, Lizzie."

"It's where your sock's faded on your toes, dummy."

"It ain't. It's real blood and I'm going home!"

"By yourself?"

Little Benedict reconsiders. He puts his chin in his hands and we wait, until we hear Peck's footsteps and see him step from the shadows.

"I almost had him, Lizzie," Peck says on our way home. "Really, I almost had him."

I keep wondering about the different things people run after and why they chase those things in the first place. It's like we're all born with a little eaten-out place inside us that we ignore, so it keeps getting bigger; ripping and splitting until it ruins the whole of us. Except for Pearl. She doesn't let any hole go long without fixing it. Once, a hole appeared in her grey coat with the mink collar because she forgot to put the mothballs in her chiffarobe, but she sewed it up and it looked like a new coat again. She said she had to fix it. That fine coat had already been bought and paid for and she meant to wear it. She wouldn't even let Izear help her sew it up and he's much better at sewing than she is. I said all that sewing was a silly waste of time. Just throw out the old thing, I told Pearl; you've got enough money in your tin box with the rose on it, so just go buy another one. She turned her catching eyes on me, snapped me up inside her head like she had to teach me quick, before something awful happened. "It's never a waste of time to take care of something that's served you, Lizzie. Repair it and it will serve you, again. Why turn something fine into garbage because of one little flaw?"

    That's the way Pearl is about her Highlow house and the people in it. You can trust Pearl to keep fixing things up because she's got a merciful heart. She knows all about our holes and loves us anyway.

What Mommy Doesn't Want Her Baby?

Pearl's Attic

"I don't wanna play in the attic, Lizzie," Little Benedict whines. "I wanna go to the hospital and see the baby."

"Quit kicking me, Little Benedict! The baby's not even born yet, and Pearl said to play up here 'til it is; didn't she Peck?"

"Lizzie's right. Pearl will call us when it comes. Let's look out the window. Maybe we'll see the Osprey fly by."

"Ya'll boys are so stupid. Let's play 'old clothes,' instead. There're plenty of clothes up here."

"I don't wanna play 'old clothes.' I don't wanna look for the Osprey neither. I wanna go to the hospital and wait for the baby."

"Not now, Little Benedict. Here's a big old army hat; even has a feather in it. Put it on, let's see how you look."

"Hey, I'm a general. See Lizzie?"

"Yeah, like Robert E. Lee."

"And Dwight D. Eisenhower," Peck says.

"He was a president."

"Well, he was a general, too, Miss Know-it-all."

"Little Benedict you want some fudge? Peck and I will go down and get you some."

"No, I don't wanna stay up here by myself."

"Then I'll stay with you while Peck gets the fudge."

"You get the fudge, Lizzie. I wanna ask Peck something."

"Oh alright. I'll bring up some cards for Canasta, too. Be back in a minute."

"What is it you want to ask me, Little Benedict?"

"About babies."

"Why me? Girls know more about babies.

"You'll tell me the truth. Lizzie won't."

"Okay, what do you want to ask?"

"Well--if the Mommy doesn't want her baby, what will happen to it?"

"What Mommy doesn't want a baby?"

"Mine doesn't."

"Miss Billie Nana? Sure she does, Little Benedict."

"No, she says she's not bringing home an idiot baby that ought not to be here anyway. What do they do with an idiot baby, Peck, if it ain't s'posed to be here and its mama doesn't want it?"

"They'll probably take it to a place where it will have lots of other idiot babies to play with."

"But I don't mind playing with it."

"Don't cry, Little Benedict. Wow, you do look just like Robert E. Lee in that hat!"

To Live and Die in Dixie

Lizzie

Peck and I are watching Izear pick a chicken he got from Miss Eileen's relatives. Izear is carrying on about how Miss Eileen's relatives wish she'd taken him over the caddy she ran off with. "But that's the way them balls roll," Izear says, holding the chicken by its feet and snatching out another feather. The chicken's head wobbles like a long wet dumpling every time he yanks one.

"Ouch!" Peck laughs. "You sure that thing's dead?"

"Wrung its neck myself, so I reckon it is," Izear says. Snatch. Snatch.

I can't help but ask--seeing the closed blue lids and how the chicken's neck jiggles and wobbles when Izear pulls out a feather--"Izear, did you really poke out a man's eyes?"

Snatch. Snatch. "You been itching like a chigger bug to get back to that, ain't ya?" Jiggle. Wobble.

"Well, did you?"

"I wouldn't poke out nobody's eyes unless they didn't use 'em to start with. Now, ya'll take this bag of feathers to the garbage out there and stay on out so I can finish up the frying."

"But why did you do it, Izear?"

Peck sees Izear is getting agitated. He bops me with the bag of feathers. Some of them fly out and float around before they land on Pearl's kitchen floor. Izear stoops to pick them up, but I don't let him off my hook. "Why?"

He looks up at me with his deep brown eyes. "It mighta' been a 'just-in-case' thing, little Miss Nosey, and that's all you need to know. Now, ya'll get on outta here."

Izear stuffs back the feathers he's picked up and Peck pats them down in the bag and rolls it closed. Reluctantly, I follow my brother to the garbage can at the edge of Pearl's driveway.

"Well, I still don't know why he did it," I say to Peck. "Izear's too sweet to do something like that, and 'just-in-case' is not a good reason."

"Not to you, maybe," Peck says, opening the lid to the garbage can; "but somebody else might think 'just-in-case' is the clearest reason of all."

Across the yard, Benedict Senior is helping Miss Billie Nana into their backyard swing; she's complaining as usual, says the swing needs painting but she supposes she'll have to call someone besides Benedict Sr. to do it because he's nothing but thumbs. They never brought home a baby.

Pearl told us not to ask why they gave it away, but I caught the tail-end of her telling Izear, "The Judge says he's unsure himself whether Billie Nana's baby is an idiot child, so in his notes, he's just going to put: *different from the rest of us*. Oh, if only Billie Nana had let us have it! You and I would have--." Pearl hushed quick when she saw I was listening.

"I'm sorry for Little Benedict," I say to Peck.

"Yeah." He stuffs the bag of feathers in the can.

"Who do you think they gave the baby to?"

"I don't know, but one day I'm gonna find it and bring it home for Little Benedict to play with." Peck's such a nice boy. Two-timing Leona could never in a million years love him like I do.

A Boy Can't Wait Forever
Peck

In the late afternoon of a summer day, Lizzie and I rode our bikes to Wheaton Springs. We sat side by side on the grass on a hill above the main river and for a while we didn't speak; looking at the tremendous waterfall on the other side, listening to its flowing sound. Hobart once told me there was a cave behind the splashing water and that he'd gone there with Mama. I'd written about it my diary, how Hobart said the cave was dark and dangerous. I wondered if Lizzie had read those words when she turned to me and asked, "Do you want to go see what's behind it?"

"No, I think we've got enough old bones and carcasses to deal with."

"It might be beautiful inside. Why do you always look on the dark side of things?

"Why do you always try to brighten the truth? Some things are dark." A fog from the spring below the falls rose and came across the water, spreading between us like the gauzy screen of a confessional, and I knew I had to tell Lizzie. "Mama left the house last night. I followed her to Hobart's. It wasn't the only time she'd been there."

"But Mama can't stand Hobart!"

"She took Pearl's box with the rose painted on it."

"The tin box with William Crawford's money?"

"Hobart opened his back door and Mama went in. He didn't close the door, just the screen; so I could hear them." The splashing of the waterfall suddenly seemed so loud, I hesitated. Maybe it was a sign. Maybe telling Lizzie was a mistake.

"Go on!" she said, crushing a clump of dirt with the sole of her sneaker.

"Hobart put his arms around Mama and asked her if she remembered the day she painted his picture and how she was his first."

"His first what?"

"I don't know, Lizzie."

"Well, we do know Hobart likes to be first, but what else?"

"She told him she'd brought enough money to buy back Pearl's house."

"Pearl's house is Pearl's!"

"No it's not. William Crawford lost it years ago gambling with Mr. McSwain." I could see she was dumbfounded, trying to take it all in. "Now, Hobart has the deed, that paper we saw him reading."

"The one he put in the metal box?" she asked weakly.

"Yes. Hobart and I found it cleaning out his mama's room."

"But you didn't tell me! And it wasn't in your--."

My diary? I'd expected that, still I continued. "When Hobart wouldn't take the money, Mama asked him what he would take for Pearl's house. He laughed and said she ought to know. Then she slapped him."

"I told you, Mama can't stand the man!" She kicked a rock downhill as if she was kicking Hobart.

"Hobart looked angry that Mama had slapped him and said he wouldn't be sending her anymore of Mrs. McSwain's old face powder."

"Why would she want old Mrs. McSwain's face powder, anyway?"

Her interruptions were making it much harder to go on. "She likes it, I guess."

"That does not sound like Mama, at all."

"Hobart said Pearl's house would be his first sale soon as he got his real estate office finished, then he asked Mama, 'What will you do then?'"

"What will we do?"

"Mama said just-in-case he tried something like that, he ought to know she'd be prepared."

"Just-in-case?"

I nodded, yes.

Lizzie grabbed my arm. "We've got to get the deed back. Let's go!"

But I didn't move. "I should have used the key."

"You had the key and didn't use it?"

"Hobart said if I didn't tell, he'd get me the Osprey."

Her eyes flashed infuriation. "The least you could have done was to write about this in your diary. It will be your fault if we end up homeless!" Then she scrambled across the hill to her bicycle as if she was going to leave.

"I'm sorry, Lizzie," I called out, then my voice choked. "I don't seem to do anything right."

She dropped the bike at once and came back across the hill, putting an arm around my shoulders. And the sense of what she said surprised me. She sounded just like Pearl. "You do a lot of things right, Peck. It's just sometimes you look the wrong way. You'll never catch the Osprey, and we'll probably never find our father. But even if we don't, we'll be okay. Don't you know that?"

Knowing a circumstance, and accepting it, are two distant things; as far from each other as high is from low. Still, I shouldn't have worried about telling Lizzie. She pulls the two together. I never have. People chase things when they have an empty place that needs to be filled. And when they can't find the truest thing to fill it, they often hunt something else, even dangerous things like birds of prey. I wanted our father, chased him in my mind until I thought I knew him, except what I wanted most was for him to care enough to know me. A boy can't wait forever for a man to be a man.

I Never Missed You!

Lizzie

For all his life, Peck has run after what he thinks he needs, but doesn't have. I keep hoping that he'll give up trying to catch the Osprey, that maybe he'll change his mind, like he did with the butterflies. Once, for a week, he collected them in jar after jar of lovely, flickering colors. "The people I know who chase butterflies just pin them in a scrapbook," I told him.

"I'd have to kill them to do that," Peck said, holding up one of Pearl's fruit jars to admire the Swordtail fluttering frantically inside.

"Well, you can't keep a butterfly alive in a jar. It will beat itself to death on the glass trying to get out."

At once—because he's too nice to cause harm--Peck opened up all the lids and let his colorful treasures loose. Soon afterwards, he began the other pursuit: chasing the Osprey as if it were our father. Frankly, I don't miss our father that much, but I'd never let Peck know it. If my brother said, "Let's take the bus to Cincinnati tomorrow,' I'd go in a heartbeat, just for him.

Across the breakfast table in Pearl's kitchen, Peck takes a piece of the toast Izear has put on a plate in front of us. "Did you know your father?" he asks Izear.

"Knowed he was a full-blooded Cherokee, ugly as sin, and the meanest man I ever met. People saw him walking down the street, they crossed to the other side 'cause he always carried a plank of wood in case somebody made him mad."

"At least you knew him." Peck rolls his napkin into a snake

shape.

"Most fathers ain't all they're cracked up to be," Izear says. "Eat your toast. I made that blackberry jelly myself."

"But you did know him."

Izear turned from the stove where he was frying bacon. "Lookahere; you got all you need. No reason at all for another man in this house, so quit whining."

"I want just want to meet him."

"I wanna meet the King of Egypt, too, but it ain't gonna happen. You take what you get then thank the sweet Lord Jesus for it."

I hear Pearl's cane clicking on the hall floor, coming toward the kitchen. I know she can hear us, so I say, "I thank the Lord Jesus for you, Izear." Izear smiles, and Peck throws me a haughty glare.

Tapping in, Pearl says, "Have a little patience, Izear. Dissatisfaction is part of the human condition. It's desire that moves the world forward." Then she turns to Peck and me, "But remember to keep a steady eye behind you. Aspiration is often a delusion. Only history is real. It lasts forever."

She knows Peck and I love history--family history, or the history of famous people like Abraham Lincoln, or Dwight D. Eisenhower. I like to know what they looked like, how they dressed, what sort of wife, husband, or wedding celebration they had. Mostly, Peck wants to know who their fathers were.

Pearl goes on. "You might bury a person in a cemetery, but you'll never bury what his life meant to the people who loved him, or didn't."

That gives me the idea. "Let's ride our bikes to the cemetery, Peck." I'm not big on cemeteries, but Peck likes them so we often ride there. He gets up from the table without comment and I follow him to the garage where our bicycles are.

Highlow's cemetery, Memory Hill, is on River Road, just

before you get to Dixie. Peck rides like crazy and I have a hard time keeping up. Our shirts are wringing wet with perspiration by the time we get off our bikes and push them down a pine-lined path to the most elite section. Beneath an enormous granite star is Pearl's grandfather, Highlow's founder, its first mayor, and longest serving sheriff; Joseph Shelley. Beside him is his wife, Grace Jameson Shelley.

"Joseph Shelley was the forefather of Highlow, and one hundred and two when he died. For nearly eighty years he wore the badge, trying to keep his Highlow safe from intruders." It's Pearl's script, but we know it by heart. We've heard it every Cemetery Day since we could walk, brought by Pearl and Izear to wash the graves.

In the shadow of the big star is the grave of Pearl's father, Harper Shelley, Highlow's second sheriff and then mayor. Next to him is his wife, Ruby, Pearl's mother.

Peck takes his turn. "Harper Shelley was wounded in France by a German during World War I and was sent home with a Purple Heart and a permanent limp. He was leaning on his lambs head cane, ordering a German beer from the bar at the Highlow Hotel, when he was shot dead by a shell-shocked soldier who'd fought there, too; an old friend of his who mistook him for an armed Kraut. The whole town came out for Harper's funeral and the very next day, the friend who'd shot him jumped off the third floor of the hotel to kill himself, as well, but he only broke both his legs and one arm. He was in a wheelchair and sent to the mental hospital in Tuscaloosa for a while. Eventually, he came home and was able to be a father to his son, while Harper's wife, Ruby, and his daughter, Pearl, were left devastated and alone." Pearl's words, reproduced by my brother, carry his own resentment.

Not far from Ruby's grave is a small stone with carved flowers, a lot like the ones on Pearl's china cabinet. There is one word engraved within the flowers: *Sister*. Oddly, Pearl never explained it, so Peck and I pass it by, as she always does, to stand before the resting place of William Crawford Todd, Pearl's much-loved husband. His is one of the more recent family graves, left of the granite star, and is overseen by a tall angel standing on a pedestal engraved with "Todd." The stole upon the angel's shoulders is provided by the oldest pine in the cemetery, an enormous tree that began long before the sheriff or the mayor, even before Highlow was founded by Joseph Shelley.

"William Crawford Todd was run over by a Coastline train, exactly five years to the day that Pearl got Izear out of jail--the first time," Peck says, continuing our tour.

"And he was split in half." Usually I feel compassion at this point, except now, I add my resentment, too. "But not before he gambled Pearl's house away! How could Pearl's husband do that to her?"

"I don't know, Lizzie. If only he hadn't."

"I hate Hobart."

"I don't suppose it's his fault."

"Well, he's taking advantage of it. Do you think he'll put us out soon?"

"First, he'll have to tell Pearl," Peck says. "He hasn't done that. I don't know why he's waiting. Maybe he'll forget about it."

"Hobart? I don't think so!"

"He's really not that bad, Lizzie. He's sort of scary, but I really think he likes us."

"Likes us enough to tear up the deed? Of course, you could've done that last night if not for your silly Osprey hunt."

Peck turns his face away. "Maybe I'm crazy like Mama."

"Mama's not crazy; she just doesn't see things as they are."

He looks at me, puzzled. "I don't think you see things as they are, Lizzie. It's like you're too happy to miss not having a father."

"I told you I'd go with you to Cincinnati. You're the one who changed your mind. And what's wrong with being happy?"

"How do you do it?"

"Why should I think about him at all? He hasn't thought about me, or you either. I hope he's paid back for that. I might even pay him back myself, if I ever see him. The first thing I'll do is call him worthless; then I'll say, *I never missed you!*"

Peck turns his face away. I think he's crying, and it breaks my heart.

The Ride

Peck

 Lizzie, Little Benedict, and I are playing canasta on Pearl's back steps because Izear has hidden the Donkey Kong game. This afternoon, there's a lot of hammering and banging going on next door. It's Hobart's thirtieth birthday, and construction of his new business has begun; the first real estate agency in Highlow. I notice Hobart in his driveway, re-cranking Mrs. McSwain's old car that has been dead in her garage since 1959. Nobody knew it still ran. Little Benedict jumps up, dismantling Lizzie's neat discard pile, and calls across the yard, "Hey Hobart, can we go with you?"
 "Nobody wants to go anywhere with Hobart!" Lizzie says, yanking at his trouser leg.
 "I do, and Peck does, too," Little Benedict retorts.
 "He does not!" She gives him a knuckle on his knucklehead like his daddy does. "And look what you did to my pile, dummy."
 "We don't even know where he's going," I say to Little Benedict.
 "Well, I'm gonna find out." He runs for Hobart who is cranking the car for a third time since it has died on him again. "Where're you going, Hobart?"
 Hobart rolls down the window and grins. "Dixie!"
 Because of the hammering noises and the continuing gunning of the car engine, I can't hear what else is said. Hobart finally drives off and Little Benedict comes running back. "Hobart's fixin' to go buy himself a new car for his birthday. He said he'd take us to ride when he gets back. Anywhere we want to go!"

From The Official Notes of Pearl's cousin, The Judge,
Who happened to be driving down Main Street

On the day Hobart McSwain turned thirty years old, he bought a car from the used-car lot over by the railroad tracks where people from Main Street try not to go. He bought it from D.C. Carter, Dixie's most infamous entrepreneur. And he bought it for himself because he's got no adopted mama anymore, and who else would have thought enough of him to give him such a present?

It was a dark-colored car; a long convertible with a dysfunctional top, always down. And like Hobart, the car didn't come from Highlow. It used to belong to one of D.C's uncles who wasn't really a blood uncle, just D.C's mother's boyfriend from Chicago. The car had Illinois plates, so until he could get the plates changed, Hobart had D.C. stick a loud horn in the car that played a tune to fit Highlow.

It was around dusk, according to Pearl. Lizzie, Peck, and Little Benedict were in the music room waiting for Hobart's return. They ran onto the porch when they heard the horn blowing on the street in front of her house--an automatic tune about good times not forgotten.

"I'll take ya'll for a ride now. Come on!" Hobart yelled. The twin white headlights, like embracing orbits, played on the pavement, while the horn in that gift to himself impersonated glory: *To live and die in Dixie. Away. Away.*

Little Benedict was first to run for the car and get in beside Hobart. Hobart stretched across him, calling to Peck and Lizzie.

"Hurry up! We'll drive to the river."

Lizzie wrapped her fingers around Peck's arm to hold him back. "We're not going."

Hobart hollered again. "I found the Osprey's nest on the big bank in the top of a pine. I'll show you!"

Little Benedict pushed up with both his hands, craning his scrawny, yellow-ochre neck, dirt beads circling beneath his pale, little boy chin. "We'll catch the Osprey this time, Peck. Let's catch him!" He pressed a hand over the heart in his little bird chest, whipping the other high into the air and then down in a crisp salute; his homage to an unseen general.

The first flash of yellow moonlight hit Peck's shoulders. He yanked away from his twin and ran for the car.

"Just go then!" Lizzie hollered. "Let it claw out your eyes!"

"I won't be long," he called back.

"Long enough for it to kill you. And I don't care if it does!"

He was just shy of the car when he turned to look at her. A sudden moment of doubt? But all he'd inherited made him destined to hunt. The boy just couldn't help it. He got in.

"Yeee—haw!" Hobart shoved his palm into the horn, and the car sped away. *Away. Away.*

Only half an hour passed. And the horn re-blew in front of Pearl's. Only half an hour, and Peck lay across the back seat of Hobart's gift to himself, bleeding over the knees of Little Benedict who held Peck in his arms, defeated in a lost cause. Hobart got out and lifted Peck's body to his chest, staining his cotton shirt with the life of Lizzie's twin. He walked away with him. *Away. Away.* Between the purple border grass. Past the branches of bottle brush rustling against the bannister of the steps. And up to Pearl, with Peck in his arms.

Only Little Benedict could say how it happened; how Peck's eyes had glistened with wanting in the cool, wet air, and how his breath nearly stopped, seeing the Osprey swoop low enough to touch. "The hawk was close, so close," Little Benedict said. And Peck was so enticed by its white breast and masked face, its golden eye, and painted wings shimmering against the moonlit screen of night, that he stood on the back seat and reached for him. "Just like a child reaches for his daddy," Little Benedict said. "And Peck almost had him!" But Hobart was driving fast, so fast, up the narrow, river road; the Osprey passed just beyond Peck's grasp. He turned to look back at what he had missed, and it must have happened then--the whipping of the sharp tree limb against the skin of his neck, the lashing just under his chin, the scourging rip that opened his vein and released his blood. "Peck was dead in an instant!" Little Benedict cried.

From within Pearl's house came the wailing of two women, then the cracking sound of a just-in-case-gun. And from Lizzie? Recollection of her last words to the person she loved most in the world: *Long enough for it to kill you. And I don't care if it does!*

Hobart stumbled back onto the porch bleeding from his chest, his own blood mixing with the young blood of a Highlow son. He shouted back to the women in Pearl's ancient house, "I'm gonna kill that goddamn bird, once and for all!" And his new car skidded off. *Away, away* from Main Street.

I Belong Here!

Hobart

"So, Hobart; you don't want to file charges against Lila Todd?" the redneck, pock-faced policeman asks me as if I have a choice. He stands in superiority beside my hospital bed, cleaning gun oil from his left thumbnail with the index finger of his right hand; no intention of filing anything.

"The gun backfired. Lila's not responsible."

"The Judge wants to know if you're responsible for the boy's death."

"No."

"So nobody's responsible for nothin', eh?"

"Yeah. Some damn bird that flew by."

The policeman nonchalantly closes the door, then grabs the front of my hospital gown and wraps it around his fist. He yanks me forward, "Yankee punk! You ain't got an old Southern mama to hide behind, now. I believe De-troit's callin' you, son. Why doncha take the next bus out and go back where you belong?" Then he cracks my head on the metal frame of the hospital bed.

I close my eyes from the pain. "I belong here! I own property!"

"Like hell!" the policeman shouts.

When I open my eyes, he's gone.

Do You Know My Little Brother?

Little Benedict

"Where's your daddy, little boy? Quit crying and let me see your wrist. Okay--no hospital bracelet. You don't belong here, do you? Where's your mama, little boy? Where's your family? What're you doing here all by yourself?"

"I'm looking for my baby brother."

"What's his name?"

"I don't think he has one."

"Well, what's your name?"

"Benny. What's yours?"

"Miss Candy. Now, what's your last name, Honey?"

"Spratling. Do you know my little brother? He prob'ly looks a lot like me."

"Then he must be a handsome boy. C'mon and we'll see if we can find him, Sweetie."

"It smells funny in here."

"It's a hospital smell. Piney Woods is sort of a hospital. How long's your little brother been here?"

"I think he was born here."

"No honey, I don't think so. We only get them after they're born. Sit down in this chair and let Miss Candy find out what we need to know. Now, tell me where you live, Peanut."

"On Main Street."

"Here in Headland?"

"In Highlow."

"How'd you get to Headland, Sugar?"

"On the handicapped bus. I got on at school."

"Just sit there, Angel. I need to make a phone call."

"I'm looking for my baby brother."

"Yes, darlin'. Be just a minute more."

"I want to name him Peck, if he doesn't have a name."

"Now don't start crying, again, Sweetheart. Miss Candy will find out where you belong and be right back."

. . .

"Alrighty now. We've called your daddy, Sugar-pie. He's on his way. Wanna see your little sister?"

"You mean my little brother?"

"No, you have a pretty little sister, Lollipop. She has lovely, caramel-colored skin and lots of curly, black hair. Come on, you can play with her until your daddy comes to get you.

Mama's Shadow

Lizzie

  I know 'dead,' but I will not see 'dead'. I will not look at my twin brother in the casket, though they say he is in there. I hear Mama's soft cry. I hear Little Benedict's sniffs. I hear Pearl's cane tap down the aisle beside me as we leave the church in Crisscross. I do not hear or see Hobart. He knows not to come.

  Izear drives the Roadmaster. His eyes fill with so many tears that he runs over the curb backing out of the church parking lot. We follow the black limousine to the cemetery, to the family plot, to the tent between the sheriff's star and William Crawford's angel marker. Mama sits beside me in the backseat. Her long fingers are stained with paint. She will not get out of the car, so I stay with her; our lovely mama, our sad and crazy mama. From a distance, I watch the red veil of silt cover the box they bury. He is so *far away* from me now. If I could go back to the night of his death, I'd cut out my tongue before I could say what I said to him. I did not mean those words. I loved Peck. Always. And I always will.

  Mama cries quietly, "Our Father, who art in heaven, take care of my angel boy." I stroke her hand, thinking that I hope He will, because our father on earth never did.

  Seven days after Peck's death, Mama tries, again, to kill Hobart with the just-in-case gun. She shoots through her opened window as he walks toward his new car, still bandaged from the first time, but all she hits is the rear-view mirror.

  Izear hears the shot. Before Mama can fire off another one, he grabs the gun from her and hides it in the top drawer inside Peck's closet. He hides Mama, too, in the attic; after Hobart yells that he's going to call the police. This time, he's going to file charges. But when The Judge, notebook in hand, comes to interview him, Hobart recants his story. He says he can't imagine why he's called the authorities; Lila Todd is sweet and gentle as they come. That's because—just before the Judge arrived-- Izear pushed Hobart down, slammed his head into the grass between the twin concrete paths of the McSwain driveway, and threatened to poke out his Detroit eyes.

That day, Izear lets Mama out of the attic and back into her room of china plates, after he's boarded up the side window so she'll never have to look at Hobart or his new car again. Mama cries for days though, because her room is so dark.

Pearl doesn't like her to cry. She has Izear rip off the boards.

Tonight, I hear Mama in Peck's room. I see her shadow as she opens the drawer in his closet where I saw Izear hide the "just-in-case" gun. Should I tell this to Pearl?

Make-Believe Mother

Little Benedict

I'm at Hobart's house because he's my babysitter tonight. He's heard the kitchen door open, but he doesn't want to get out of his lazy-boy chair, or put down the chocolate chip cookie bag we're sharing. So he says to me, between chews, "Go see who it is, Little Benedict." I go into the kitchen, and just about strangle on a chocolate chip cookie when I see Miss Lila standing there, holding the just-in-case gun. "I want Hobart," she says.

"Hobart, *don't* come in here!" I call out to him.

But he comes immediately into the kitchen. He sees the gun, too, and offers her some kind of powder to put it down, but Miss Lila, the gun dangling in her right hand, screams, "No!"

He opens his long metal box and offers her the yellowed piece of paper.

She snatches it from him, stomps it on the floor, and raises the just-in-case gun.

Hobart heads for the pantry, slamming the door behind him. Miss Lila shoots through it.

Hobart yells that she's hit his heart and she needs to call an ambulance, but Miss Lila does not call an ambulance. She turns to me, instead, like she has no idea what she's done. She puts her arms around me, and the sound of her voice in my ear seems to come from far away. "Peck," she calls me, instead of Little Benedict. I start to tell her I'm not her son, but it feels so warm, so wonderful to be held by a mother. Then she takes my face in her hands and says, "I'm going to tell you who your father really is, Peck darling; but you must tell no one. Can I count on you?"

I snuggle against her breast, soft as a bird's. Of course she can count on me not to tell. Would a son betray his mother--make-believe, or not?

She whispers the name of Peck and Lizzie's father, but I don't believe her. Miss Lila's got a great big imagination. Still, I stay in her arms for quite a while, until Hobart's hollering from the pantry is nearly too much to bear, though it doesn't seem to bother Miss Lila at all. When he quiets down, she lets me go. She picks up the official-looking, yellow paper and starts tearing it into little pieces, so I run next door for Miss Pearl and Izear.

"Oh, Lila; no!" Miss Pearl says after she's tapped, fast as she can ahead of Izear and me, into Hobart's house, and sees the gun lying on the kitchen table. "Sweet Jesus!" she cries when she opens the pantry and sees Hobart bleeding and, by now, mostly unconscious.

But Miss Pearl thinks quickly. She tells Izear to undress Hobart who's awake enough to shield his eyes and whine every time Izear touches him. "Dress him in his hunting clothes," Miss Pearl orders. Then she takes the just-in-case gun from the table, wraps Hobart's fingers around it, and tells Izear to take Miss Lila home. "And clean up that paper, Little Benedict."

I pick up the confetti of paper Miss Lila tore up and take it out to the garbage, while Miss Pearl telephones an ambulance, the police, and her cousin The Judge. When they all arrive, she tells them that she'd asked Hobart to clean her just-in-case gun, and while he was doing that, he accidentally shot himself. Then she whispers to me, "Remember Little Benedict, you and I are Highlow blood and in this together. Plus, the Judge will write down whatever you say."

Naturally, I side with Miss Pearl, and keep my mouth shut.

The Judge goes home and the ambulance takes Hobart to the hospital where the police will question him, but before they do, Miss Pearl and I visit him in the Intensive Care room. With an odd smile, she tells him, "Hobart, there is no piece of paper left in the world to say you belong in Highlow." Hobart looks sad. He tries to speak, but no words come out. "Despite that," Miss Pearl says, "I've decided that you might belong here, after all."

Hobart's eyes light up because she's mentioned the one thing he's craved all his life.

"Because where there's good, there's evil," Pearl continues, "And people have to live with the evil until they can fix it." She takes out the super glue from her pocket and holds it in front of his face. "Now, the question is: Can you be fixed, Hobart?"

"Oh yes, Miss Pearl, I'm fixable. Just tell me what I can do to prove it?" So she does.

When he's questioned by the police, Hobart agrees that the shooting was another accident, then Miss Pearl takes my hand and we walk to the house of her cousin, The Judge, to tell him the news so he can put it in his notebook.

The Judge makes us hot chocolate served in a fine china cups with re-glued handles while Miss Pearl tells him what she wants him to know. He nods his head, writing it all down in his notebook as she talks. Then he tells Miss Pearl that she can pick up her gun at the police department. "Do you have anything to add, Little Benedict?" The Judge asks me.

"No Sir."

Miss Pearl pats my thigh, and The Judge says I'm a fine little specimen of Highlow's best. He shuts his notebook and calls the case closed--after he draws up papers to send Miss Lila to an out-of-town hospital for a short respite, at Miss Pearl's suggestion.

A week or two later, my daddy reads aloud from the Highlow Eagle: "A long car with no top exploded on the river road. Nobody can say, after the explosion, whose car it is. The Judge believes the out-of-control burning is just another unsolved Highlow secret, best left untold."

Then my daddy says, "The Judge is right. Some secrets oughta stay secret."

"Like my Little Sister?" I ask him.

My daddy doesn't answer. He doesn't even look at me. He lays down the Highlow Eagle and leaves the room.

Like a Father Might Love His Son

Hobart

I never asked for Alabama; I never asked to be her son. I had no choice over my deliverance. A child has no muscle, at all; he's only a displaced leaf riding on a stale wind, blowing this way and that. But when the wind stops, the leaf descends. I descended into the high side of Highlow and was raked aside, and it hurt that I wasn't good enough to be noticed.

I felt the lack for years, watching those twins swim in the deep river of Highlow's blood while I clung to the dirty roots protruding from its banks. So yeah, I was envious. I wanted Pearl's house, and its transfer was legal; by law it was mine. But in the end, I gave the deed to Lila, and not because she held Pearl's just-in-case gun. I made the concession because of the boy. I never meant him harm. In fact, I believe I loved him, like a father might love his son.

I was sixteen when Lila's twins were born. I rode with Izear to Cincinnati to find their daddy. D.C. gave us a car to drive, one of two or three he had back then. He gave it at no charge except the gas. Pearl didn't know we'd gone. She was too busy tending to Lila, hiding in her room because she was ashamed of herself and wouldn't let anybody near her. She should have been ashamed, shoving me aside to take up with some fool artist. She should've known he'd never take care of her.

I made him pay for what he'd done to Lila. Hell, he should have seen it coming. Instead, he denied it. "I never did a thing to her. She was just some kid artist I took in," he'd said. Greedy bastard wanted more than his share. He should have known to be nice. Now, Peck's dead. Hell, it's all the fault of that damn artist from Cincinnati, that blind bird in the Eagle Jacket who slinked into Pearl's Open House.

If You Don't Want to Go to Cincinnati . . .

Lizzie

    Pearl once told me, "Lizzie, if you don't want to go to Cincinnati then don't get on the bus. But when you have a hole in your heart, you'd go just about anywhere, do just about anything, to fill it. Our Cincinnati father ought to be told about what he could have kept from happening, and I mean to go there and tell him. It isn't fair he's still on this earth while Peck is not.

    Bus stations smell. Something in your stomach gets all scrunched up in a bus station. Your nose burns and there are sounds; screeching brakes, cranking noises in these places of transfer. Anybody will talk to you on a bus. You don't have to be related to them, or even know them. There's a woman beside me and a boy in front of me. Both of them got on in Phenix City and they're carrying on such a conversation you'd think she was his mother. She's not. The boy doesn't have one, he says; he's on his own, has been since he was twelve.

    "All I can say is--." The woman stops talking to open her purse. She has on a black dress with strawberries printed all over it and her purse is big and black, and crammed with little pill bottles. She rummages through it until she finds the bottle she wants, unscrews the cap, and pops a pill through her bubble gum-colored lips. "All I can say is," she continues, "I'd never let one of my sons go off on his own at twelve years old."

    "I ain't twelve, now. I'm seventeen," the boy grunts. He's not a handsome boy like Peck, but pleasant-looking.

"Whatever." The woman in the strawberry dress brushes through the air with her hand.

"How many sons do you have?" I ask the woman, trying to be polite.

"I ain't got none, but I wouldn't let 'em anyway." She cocks her head to look at me. "Are you by yourself, too?"

"I'm going to meet my daddy in Cincinnati." That's what I wrote in the note I left on Pearl's kitchen table this morning. Plus, I put an IOU in the tin box with the rose on it because Pearl didn't have her party in December and said she didn't know if she would ever have one again, so there were plenty of hundred dollar bills available. It's not stealing. The money would have belonged to somebody if Pearl had given another chance to find the baby Jesus, and maybe that somebody would have been me.

"Cincinnati's a long way from here, ain't it?" the boy asks. He cranes his neck a little to see over the seat. He looks short, but I think he'd be a tall boy if he stood up.

"Yes," I say. "A long way."

"Well, you'll have a wait in Atlanta," warns the strawberry woman. "They got me waiting an hour and a half for a North Carolina bus going to Charlotte; I got connections, there--an ex."

"An axe?" I gasp. What kind of woman is this?

She laughs and her bosom shakes the berries. "Ex. You know, ex-husband? Well, maybe you don't. Don't nobody know 'less they been there."

"No, I've never been to North Carolina," I say. I don't tell the woman I've never been to Cincinnati either, but the boy looks at me like he can tell. He gets a tiny little wrinkle between his eyes that gets deeper the longer he looks at me.

"Where're you going?" I ask the boy to joggle his irritating expression.

"Atlanta. That's where I live." He says this proud.

"On your own?" the woman asks.

"Yes ma'm; since I was twelve years old, like I tol' you."

The bus turns into the Atlanta Trailway station and stops. The strawberry woman is the third person to get off. On her way down the steps she drops all her pill bottles "Damn!" she says to nobody in particular, but behind her, a bald-headed man runs after the rolling bottles. One by one, he hands them to her, and one by one the strawberry woman looks at each label and packs them back in her purse. Then she tells the man she has them all. But I don't hear her say thank you to the bald-headed man. Maybe Charlotte's different from Highlow. Maybe people don't have to be nice.

I follow the strawberry woman until she's swallowed up by a crowd of people that don't look particularly friendly, so I stop to open Peck's old duffel bag. I have my own duffel bag back in Highlow, but I brought Peck's bag. I packed it with some old magazines, personal things, and my wallet. I pull out my wallet and check my ticket to be sure I've got the side that says Cincinnati. The other used-up side was to Atlanta and since I'm here now, I figure I can throw away that torn-off piece.

There's a garbage receptacle next to a stone planter with colored plastic flowers stuck in it; a tall planter that comes up to my nose. It's situated in the corner next to the 'his and her' bathrooms. I can hear the toilets flushing all the way out here. I throw the used ticket into the can then feel a breath on my back. It's the boy from the bus.

"Wanna see where I live?" he asks.

"No," I say, although the boy has put on the sweetest expression. "I better not go off anywhere. My bus leaves in an hour."

"You don't have to go off anywhere. I live right here." He points to the stone planter. The sweet-looking boy could be a real nut, but I don't want to hurt his feelings, so I go along.

"Oh, it's a lovely place," I say, "with those flowers and all."

"Yes, but don't worry, there ain't no dirt in there. It's hollow as a chocolate Easter bunny."

"How do you get in?"

"Look." He shoves the tip of his worn-out sneaker on a big square stone until it opens like a door. "You'll see there ain't no dirt in here." The boy's eyes dart from right to left around the station, then he squats and goes in. "Come on," he calls from somewhere underneath the plastic flowers. I follow the voice because it cracks a little and sounds familiar.

At once, a flashlight flicks on and I can see something of where I am, a rectangular space almost high enough to stand in. "Ain't it nice?" the boy says, grinning. "All the comforts of home."

That's not exactly true, but there is a sleeping bag down toward the end and next to it, a stadium chair like you'd use at a football game, and a heavy box, turned on its side, that has all sorts of chip bags and cookie bags in it, even a Milky Way or two.

"I declare!" I say to be polite. Again, he looks proud.

He offers me chips and cookies. I ask for a Milky Way. He un-wraps the candy bar and pokes it toward me then un-wraps one for himself. "You can stay here if you want to 'cause I know you ain't got a daddy in Cincinnati."

"I most certainly do, boy!" I choke a little on my Milky Way, then give him a superior look. "What's your name anyway?"

"J.D. And if you had a daddy in Cincinnati, how come you ain't been there before?" He takes a bite of his candy bar and chews until the chocolate covers his bottom lip

"Who says I haven't?"

"I can tell a lie when I hear one," J.D. says. "I've had experience. You know what they say; takes a sinner to know a sinner."

"I am not a sinner and I'm not lying. I have a daddy and I have a home, a real one. It's got real dirt in the yard and everything." I cram the rest of the Milky Way in my mouth and pick up Peck's duffel bag from the floor beside me with the intention of shoving open the stone to leave.

"Why ain't you home then? They throw you out?"

"No!" In fact, I'm sure they're wondering where I am.

"Then why'd you leave?"

I tighten my arms around Peck's duffel bag and start to tell him that's none of his business then my voice breaks and tears come.

"Cry, girl. Just go on and cry." I think those are the words I hear when J.D. puts an arm around my shoulder, but I don't know for sure. I haven't cried over Peck yet; so I don't know. I only know I'm empty without him.

"It's okay, girl," J.D. says, patting my back like Peck used to. "People got to cry."

J.D. and I have been in and out of this planter for several days now. He is one sweet angel, that Jay--I call him Jay because J.D. sounds so impersonal. I'm still going to Cincinnati, just not now. Jay says my ticket is good for a week, so why not stay a while? He's so much like Peck, such a sweet-looking boy, even if he is from Georgia.

I Loved Peck, too, Ya Know

Little Benedict

"I'll go hunting with you, Hobart, if you want me to."
"You never liked hunting before, Little Benedict. Go hang around with Lizzie.
"I can't. Lizzie's not home."
"Then get in the truck."
"I do like hunting. I always wanted to go hunting with you and Peck."
"Shut up about that!"
"I saw you cry when Peck was hurt."
"I did not! I did not cry!"
"It wasn't your fault, Hobart. It was the Osprey's fault."
"Damn right."
"Did you kill it?"
"I've killed plenty. Stuffed 'em all, too."
"But did you kill the one that killed Peck?"
"It's hard to say unless you kill 'em all."
"Maybe we'll get him today."
"Maybe."
"I got a baby sister."
"Yeah?"
"She's hiding from Mama, so don't tell."
"That idiot baby?"
"Uh huh. She smiles a lot though. Wanna go see her?"
"I don't like babies; they ask for too much. Look, if you want to go hunting, then get in the truck!"

"Okay Hobart."

"I mean you can talk, but not about idiot babies."

"Okay. Can we talk about Leona?"

"She ain't much to talk about. Fasten the seat belt, Little Benedict."

"She's pretty."

"I reckon."

"I saw ya'll kissing."

"Yeah?"

"Are you gonna marry her?"

"You ain't got to marry somebody just 'cause you kiss 'em."

"Oh."

"She's just a bleached whore from Georgia."

"A what?"

"Never mind, Little Benedict. Just be quiet while I'm driving. Take a nap or something."

"Okay Hobart."

. . . .

"You can wake up now, Little Benedict. Get on out; this looks like a good place."

"Uh huh, it's nice."

"You ever shot a gun?"

"I saw how to do it on TV."

"Well, TV ain't real. They use ketchup for blood."

"I've seen real blood. I saw Peck's blood and it was real."

"I told you to shut the hell up about that!"

"Okay, Hobart."

"Look, hold the gun like this and look through that sight. When you see the damn hawk, pull the trigger and kill it."

"Okay . . .but what if we get hungry out here?"

"When you hunt, you got to be patient. And quit that damn sniffing. Here's a handkerchief, wipe your nose."

"What's that fell out of your pocket, Hobart?"

"Somethin' D.C. gave me. Dixie sugar. It's for Leona. I don't use anymore; I'm trying to fix myself up for Miss Pearl."

"My daddy loves sugar. He loves all that sugar in Izear's pound cake. Mama says it's why he's got a spare tire around his waist. Peck loved sugar, too."

"Listen Little Benedict, maybe we oughta go on back if you're hungry."

"We haven't seen the Osprey. If Peck was here, he'd wait."

"I told you not to talk about--. Little Benedict, get back in the truck, we're leaving!"

"I don't want to go."

"Hell, I'll give you a rain check, okay?"

"Okay Hobart, but--"

"But what!"

"I loved Peck, too, ya know."

"Yeah. I know, Little Benedict."

A Bird of Prey

Lizzie

There are lots of distractions in this world and sometimes they blind intentions; that's what Pearl says, and she's right. Take this bus station. I could live in this place forever with Jay and never go home again. We have everything we need because Jay knows how to find it. He brings me all the True Story magazines I can read. He says people leave them behind on the benches when their buses come in. Today, he brought us a transistor radio somebody left and now we have music. Any song at all, we've got it, Jay and me. And sleeping on the bag next to Jay beats sleeping with Little Benedict anytime. Jay has not had one cold and he does not sniff. It's all so good that sometimes, I forget about finding my father, until the whining flush of toilets from the 'his and her' bathrooms sends out a high-pitched sound, like the Osprey calling a name.

"Jay," I ask him, chewing another Milky Way. "Have you ever seen an Osprey?" I point the flashlight on his sweet face as he sits in the stadium chair eating chips.

"What's an Osprey?" he asks squinting, his hand in front of his eyes. I lower the flashlight to the floor and let it lay where the light shines up on him. His face looks two-colored, like a mask.

"It's what you'd call 'a bird of prey.'"

"Well, I don't pray much. Do you?"

I wonder about the sense of this boy, but I answer. "Yes, I do. I prayed for Peck last night." By now, I've told Jay all about my brother. Jay even wishes he'd known him. "I prayed for you, too,

Jay."

"What for?"

"That you'd have a family someday."

"Why do I want one? Must not be so great if you left yours." He crams another handful of chips in his mouth and wipes his lips with the back of his hand.

"I left to find my father."

"You ain't got one. If you had a daddy, you'd have seen him by now."

"I saw him, once."

"I bet he didn't pay you no attention at all."

"He couldn't. He was blind."

"Blind." Jay says like he can see the word in front of him. He crushes the empty bag of chips and tosses it in the box. "Ain't they all?" Then Jay stands, too quick. He bumps his head on the top of the planter and it must have hurt because I think I see a tear in his eye. "I'm going to see if anybody's left some more chips on the bench."

I feel sorry for this boy without a family, "Here, take my wallet," I say, "just-in-case nobody's left any." I still have lots of money in my wallet, plus the other half of my ticket to Cincinnati.

He looks at me funny, but he takes it. While he's gone, I stretch out on the sleeping bag. I dream that Jay is Peck and we're out searching for the Osprey. I want to kill it with Pearl's just-in-case-gun, but Peck won't let me. Then Peck is Jay again, and we're on the bus to Cincinnati. I know we're going there to get married because Jay turns to me and says, "Lizzie, I love you." In my dream, I am just about to kiss him when I see the Osprey outside the window of the bus, and in its beak is a jiggling, wobbling, featherless chicken. Jay makes the driver stop the bus so he can get off and run after it. I wake up then, and can't go back to sleep.

Jay has been gone a long time. I sneak out of the planter,

listening first, then easing out slow like he showed me. But I don't see him. On the other side of the loading door are people waving goodbye to a bus leaving the station. In big letters over the front windshield, I read its destination: Cincinnati. And I think I see Jay's face in a window. At first, my heart sinks, but it couldn't be him. He's probably in the bathroom.

I sit on a bench where I can watch the bathroom door and keep an eye out for some chips or cookies or some more True Story magazines, but there's nothing on the benches near me. Somehow, that makes me very hungry, not finding anything left on the benches. And I can't find Jay—Jay, with my wallet and my ticket to Cincinnati.

Then a hand pinches my shoulder. "What in the world are you doin' here?"

Izear!"

"Least you ain't took the bus, yet." He yanks me up.

"I was going to take the bus. I bought a ticket to Cincinnati, but I met this boy and--." I stop right there because Izear's face is twisting up into a knot. I try to explain about Jay and how much I love him. I tell Izear that someday Jay and I will go to Cincinnati together and get married like Mama did.

Izear's lips are tight over his teeth when he says he wants to meet this fine fellow, Jay.

"Here's the planter, Izear," I put my hand on the concrete, "Where we live, Jay and me. We even have flowers, see? Plastic ones, but flowers, still." I push back the stone.

"Ain't it got no lights?" Izear asks.

"Wait a minute," I fumble around for the flashlight and flick it on. "See?"

"Uh huh. I see. But I don't see no boy. Where is he? And where's your ticket to Cincinnati?"

The rising smell of the buses gives me that scrunched-up feeling in my stomach, again. "Jay has it. It's in my wallet," I say over the sound of three toilets flushing, one after the other, and then the whine.

Izear is angry as I've ever seen him. At once, I understand that he could easily poke out a man's eyes. He snatches up Peck's duffel bag. "Come on. We're going home!"

"I don't want to go home, Izear! I miss Peck too much. And Jay told me he loves me." I didn't say that he told me in my dream; it would only complicate things.

Izear glares at me for minute or two then he touches my shoulder. "Young people love to say they love each other, Lizzie, but it's what they see on the surface they're talking about. And you're a pretty girl." He screws his mouth to one side. "Plus, you're the one that had the ticket."

Jay will be back, you'll see." I've begun to have doubts about that, but I follow Izear through the swinging door of the bus station and down the sidewalk. "What if Jay comes back and I've gone without saying anything to him?"

Izear stops abruptly. "Then I reckon you'll know how that feels." His eyes are piercing.

"But Jay was sooo sweet!"

"Sooo sweet," he mimics. "Don't let no fake, plastic flowers stuck in concrete fool you. That boy stole your ticket! Ain't got a drop a' sweet to him. If you want sweet, then pick you a real flower, one that's grown in Highlow dirt!" Then he ushers me down the sidewalk and back to Highlow where he says I belong.

Except everything in Highlow seems to have changed, even me. And soon, I feel as displaced as a leaf on a stale, old wind, just killing time before it descends.

She'll Strangle that Bird

Little Benedict

It's almost suppertime. Lizzie's sitting beside me on the top step to Pearl's. Izear hasn't gotten around to pruning the Bottle Brush, so it hangs over the banister like a red hand gripping the back of her neck. Except she doesn't seem to notice. She's staring at Hobart's house, prob'ly still angry about him causing Peck's death. "Quit thinking about Hobart," I tell her. "My daddy says there's some stuff we got to forget."

"Hobart doesn't belong here, Little Benedict," she says, suddenly sobbing. "He's a thief and a murderer. He tried to steal Pearl's house, and he took Peck's life!" Her nose is running, so I hold out my arm so she can wipe it on my shirt sleeve, but she shoves it away. "That's three strikes against Hobart. The Judge should run him out of town. Hobart needs another place to live."

"Hobart didn't mean for Peck to die. Anyway, he doesn't need another place. He already has a house."

Her eyes get real green. "You have always been a dummy, Little Benedict, a bonafide knucklehead who can't even put on his own pajamas!"

"I can, too! I do it all the time when you're not around."

"Well get used to it. I'm not going to be around much longer."

"Yes you are; school's about to start. Miss Pearl won't let you leave again. Izear says she's watching you like a hawk."

That's all it takes. Say the word and it's back. Peeeeeck, peeeeeck, peeeeck.

At once, Lizzie turns her eyes to the dead-end street, where the pavement stops and the dirt road leads into the woods. Then she takes off running, through the blooming primroses, beneath the bright red Pyracantha berries that make an archway into the pines. If she finds it, she'll strangle that bird. Like Hobart, she wants it dead. I wait over an hour for her to return, getting hungrier by the minute, because the smell of food cooking is in the air, then I hear my daddy calling me to supper, "Little Benedict!" And I fly home.

Can You Love Somebody You Don't Trust?

Lizzie

Not a year after my brother's death, Pearl and I are in the back garden on a hot day in May. She is filling the hummingbird feeder with sugar water. "You know, Lizzie, I came close to losing my house and everything in it, without even knowing it."

I'm surprised! I didn't think Pearl knew that Hobart once had the deed to the house we live in. Of course, it doesn't matter now. Little Benedict told me Hobart tore up the paper. "Hobart is disgusting," I say.

"No, this was long before Hobart came to Highlow,' Pearl says. "It was around 1910, when I was just a little girl. The Spratling's house was where I lived then, with my parents."

Another surprise. "Little Benedict's house was once yours?"

"Yes. My grandparents, Joseph and Grace Shelley, built that house for my father Harper Shelley and my mother, Ruby, so they'd be right next door to them. It was only after all their deaths and my marriage to William Crawford that we moved over here." Balancing on her lambs head cane, she hands me the pitcher, empty of sugar water, then starts pinching yellow leaves off the rose bushes.

"You mean you owned two houses?"

"Actually, we owned three."

"I'll bet William Crawford gambled them away, too."

She taps her cane on the ground. "He did not! Be patient and listen, Lizzie. The elder McSwains, A.W. and his wife Agnes, built the house on the other side of my grandparents, where Hobart lives. My grandfather, Joseph, gave them the land, the last piece of property he kept after founding Highlow. My grandmother, Grace, encouraged her husband to give it to them. She said A.W. might not have been a Confederate veteran, but he came from good southern stock, so he was probably hard-working. And Agnes was from Montgomery, the capital of the Confederacy, the same place Grace was from. You know where a person comes from says an awful lot about him. It *does* make a difference."

I think of Hobart. "Yes, it does."

"Anyway," she goes on, "A.W. and Agnes McSwain were good neighbors to my grandparents and parents. They had a son, Junior; he was about fifteen then. He became Hobart's adopted father. Our families held parties at each other's houses, and danced, danced, danced--all except Grandfather Joseph who couldn't dance because of a bad leg, but he never refused his Grace a good time. My parents, Harper and Ruby, were fun-loving, too-- for a while."

Pearl sits on a wooden bench in the garden, takes out a lacey handkerchief to wipe a few beads of perspiration forming above her lips. "Did you know I had an older sister?"

I remember the gravestone she always overlooked during our visits to the cemetery. "Why didn't you tell us about her?"

"I'm telling you now." She crumples the lace hanky in her hand and indicates across the yard to the dense woods behind us. "My sister died in those woods. She was six years old, and I barely knew her."

I sit beside her on the bench. "How did she die, Pearl?"

"She was shot." Pearl takes my hand in hers. "A sad story indeed, one you're too young to hear. I only mention it so you'll know that bad things happen to an awful lot of people, not just to you. But time does heal, if you'll let it."

I don't want to listen to her good sense; I want the story. "I'm not too young to hear about it, Pearl!"

She looks steadily at me for several seconds, as if trying to decide what to reveal, then she says, "You and Peck were very different, you know. Of course, you were twins, but poles apart in some ways."

A lump rises in my throat. "He was nice. He'd give the shirt off his back if somebody needed it. I'm not nice as that."

"No, you're not. Truth be known, you're quite spiteful."

Sometimes Pearl is brutally honest, but I guess it's a fact I have to admit. Still, what does that have to do with the story she started to tell me? Lately, it's harder and harder to keep Pearl on point.

"Yes, Peck was generous, like Grandfather Joseph," Pearl is saying, "but being charitable, or not, isn't what I mean about being different."

"What *do* you mean, Pearl?"

"Both Grandfather Joseph and Peck were quite compulsive. Your mother is, too. Certain traits run in families. After the tragic losses of civil war, Grandfather wanted a manageable world for himself, so he founded Highlow. Your mother wants to manage her world, too, so she withdraws from most people, painting her china with only the faces she wants to see, faces that can't disrupt her life. Then there's Peck and that bird he was so consumed with. He never captured it, but he always chased it. Isn't that the way he felt about his father, too?"

I don't want to hear any more about Peck, it hurts too much. "Just tell me the story, Pearl. Please? I'm old enough. What happened to your sister?"

"It didn't just happen to her, it happened to all of us. A family's a unit, like a set of fine china. You know that, don't you?"

I do know that. Peck's death happened to all of us, too, even caused Mama to be sent away. "If only Peck hadn't chased after that hawk."

She pats my hand. "At least you're not blaming Hobart now."

"But I do! I hate Hobart, and I always will. I don't see how you can be nice to him. I'm sure you weren't nice to the person who killed your sister."

"No one knew who that person was for many years, so I *was* nice to him. And then I forgave him. Finally, my parents forgave him, too."

"But why? I could never do that!"

"We learned it had been an accident. A poor man from Dixie, hunting for his supper, fired a shotgun at a squirrel just as my sister stepped from behind a nearby tree. The woods were so thick, so dark, that she didn't see him and he didn't see her. The spray from the gun hit her temple, but she made no sound when she fell. So he just picked up his squirrel, went home and ate it for supper."

"That's awful!"

"Yes, awful for the young man, too--years later, after he realized what he'd done."

"Who was the man?"

"Don't jump ahead, Lizzie!" Pearl gives the ground another tap with her lambs head cane. "Now. When my sister didn't come home, the family searched for her, searched the woods, too, but there were hidden places in there nobody could find. It was nearly two weeks before my father, Harper, discovered her body; so shriveled by then he wouldn't allow it to be laid out in an open casket. I remember how dark the parlor was; drapes pulled, mirrors covered, and all the clocks stopped. The single light was from a candle in a tall stand at the head of her casket. My mother, Ruby, went into the parlor only once. After that, she took to her room and wouldn't come out, not even for the funeral. For many months, she remained in that room; rocking in her chair, overcome with grief and despair that she hadn't kept her little girl safe. Oh, it was sad!"

"What about you, Pearl? Didn't your mother think about you?"

At first, she didn't seem to notice me, though each night I'd climb into her lap. Then one night she looked down at me and spoke my name, as if she'd suddenly remembered that she loved me, too."

There is a tear in Pearl's eye and a few moments of silence until she goes on. "My grandfather Joseph was the sheriff at the time. Of course, he called my sister's death a murder, the murder of his granddaughter; so everyone in the town went looking for whoever did it. They found an old Cherokee Indian and his young son and blamed it on them--somebody said they once saw them on the edge of the woods. But my grandfather couldn't prove it, and the Cherokee didn't own a shotgun; so for nearly a year, my grandfather hemmed and hawed, while Grace, Harper, and Ruby, cried for justice, day after day. Finally, my grandfather gave up and put the two Cherokees in jail with a ten year sentence. The old Cherokee died before the time was up, so they let the son go. Everybody said the son was mean as a snake after those years in prison. Later, he married a black woman from South Carolina, had another a son, and--."

"But Pearl," I interrupt to keep her on course, "who was the man from Dixie, the one with the shotgun?"

Pearl presses her lips together, looks steadily at me, again. At first, I think she's irritated because I interrupted her, then I see she's not sure she ought to tell me. A few more minutes of silence when she picks at a button on her pink-flowered housedress, and I tie the lace on my tennis shoe that's come undone, and then she says, "It was your own grandfather, William Crawford Todd, the man I married thirty years later."

"Good grief, Pearl! You knew he shot your sister and married him anyway?"

"No, I forgave him and married him, anyway. I declare, Lizzie, I don't think you listen. I told you it was an accident. An accident calls for a little mercy."

I start to ask how she knows for sure it was an accident, William Crawford being the only one present at the time. Then I remember William Crawford is my blood, too. It's sort of like betrayal to suspect your own blood, so I go back to the beginning of our conversation. "You said you almost lost your house and everything in it, once before."

"Oh yes. That did have a bearing on things as they are now. You know William Crawford was a good deal older than I was, but by the time we married--well, I wasn't so young either, for a new bride. I'd spent most of my twenties taking care of one or the other of my grandparents until they died, and then I took care of my very distraught mother after my father was shot in the Highlow Hotel. I didn't know what it was like being around young people. William Crawford was what I was used to. He was a good man with only one big fault; gambling. But I can honestly say I loved him to death. Of course, I never trusted him."

"Can you love somebody you don't trust?"

"I'd have to say you can, because I did it."

"So he *did* gamble your house away another time?"

"Oh, for heaven sake, Lizzie, I've already told you he did not," she snaps. "A.W. McSwain's the only man he lost the house to. By the way, if you're talking about that old deed, I've known about it for years. Do you think sweet old Bessie McSwain would have ever called the note? Absolutely not! Now, there was someone you could trust." She un-crumples her hanky and wipes her face, again. "Don't you think it's too hot out here? Either we'll go inside, or you'll have to go tell Izear to bring out some iced tea."

I stand up and holler, "Izear!"

Pearl puts her hands over her ears. "I mean go *inside* to get him, and tell him to bring three glasses."

So, I go in and Izear makes me squeeze the lemons and measure the sugar. By the time we bring the glasses out on a tray to Pearl, she's put the hanky over her face and dozed off, with the afternoon sun and the delicate shadows of a Mimosa playing on the lace.

"Go on, wake her up," Izear says, hovering over her.

"You wake her up."

"You scared she gonna bite ya?"

"Are you?"

He gives a grunt and snatches a powder puff off the Mimosa and tickles the thin stretch of her forehead above the hanky. "Miss Pearl, somebody ticklin' you?"

She pulls off the white lace and starts laughing before she opens her eyes. "William Crawford, you quit that now. Oh, uh Izear." She clears her throat and takes her glass of tea from the tray. "Now, Lizzie, where were we? Izear, you might as well sit, too."

"I was fixin' to put on the chicken noodle soup."

"It's too hot for soup. Just sit." She pats the bench for Izear, so I take my tea and sit on the grass. "Okay. We were talking about how I almost lost my house--the first time."

Izear jolts up. "I ain't sittin' out here in this heat for that!"

"But you're in the story, Izear."

"You don't tell it right."

"Then you tell it, if you think you can do it better," Pearl sniffs.

"Naw, you go on. I reckon I don't like the story no matter who tells it. Just make it short," he says.

Pearl looks pointedly at him and then at me. "The reason I almost lost my house, the first time, is because of Izear's daddy."

"He was a full-blooded Cherokee, and ugly as sin," Izear interjects, with a description I've heard him give before. "Meanest man I ever met. Anybody saw him coming down the street, they'd cross to the other side 'cause he was always carrying a plank of wood."

Pearl says, "I thought you wanted the story short."

He gives her a nod. "Go on then."

Pearl gives a sigh, takes a sip of her tea. "That Cherokee Indian boy Grandfather Joseph let out of jail became Izear's daddy, and he *was* mean. But jail did it to him; he might have been sweet as Izear without jail. Anyway, after he got out, he went up to South Carolina because there was a Cherokee reservation there and he couldn't find anybody else down here that looked like him. That's where he met Izear's mother, a teacher on the reservation." She turns to pat Izear's arm. "See? That's why you're so smart." And then back to me. "But she died soon after Izear was born."

Izear gives her an eager smile. "Talk about my mama, Miss Pearl."

I think even Izear knows Pearl is making it up when she goes on. "Oh, she was a sweet, sweet woman, and pretty, too, with shiny, dark skin the color of a mink coat."

"And she loved me," Izear says.

"Of course, she did."

"But how'd my daddy get back down here, Miss Pearl? I forgot," he said, but I could tell he only wanted to hear the story again.

"Your daddy decided to leave the reservation because he was tired of stringing beads for the tourists, so he packed you up and hitched a ride back to Highlow with A.W. McSwain's son, who was sent up to that state by A.W., on the business of buying some of those beads to hang in the hardware store he and Agnes had opened in Highlow. Then A.W.'s son, Junior—the one that later became Hobart's adopted daddy—took a liking to him, enough to get him hired at the hardware store, sawing lumber and all. Of course, that was a big mistake!" She takes a breath. "I declare, Izear, you ought not to forget your family history, tainted or not."

"Well I do know what happened next, if you think I don't," Izear pouts. "My daddy—Razor's what he came to be called—well, nobody liked him, but he got to be real good at making a clean cut on a board; so, lots of people, even the ones who was scared of him, asked him to make them stuff, like cabinets and such. William Crawford wanted a new poker table so he called for

Razor. By then, I was 'bout ten years old and my daddy always brought me with him on his jobs to hold things steady, and because most people wouldn't run from a little chile."

"Is that when you met Pearl?" I ask from my cross-legged position on the grass.

"It is."

Pearl smiles. "You were the cutest little thing, Izear, and sweet as candy, but even you couldn't stop your daddy from making an enemy of William Crawford, right on the spot."

"Don't it look like they'd a' gotten along, Miss Pearl, both of 'em ugly as they was?"

Pearl sighs again. "It does seem as if they should have. I'm not really sure what went on while Razor was making the poker table, but when it was done, your daddy was mad enough with William Crawford to light a fire in four places around the foundation of my house before he ran off down Main Street. I still remember seeing you, Izear, from my upstairs window, running like the wind to catch up with him." She puts a hand to her bosom and breathes deep. "Then I smelled the smoke. If it hadn't been for the Highlow Volunteer Fire Department, none of us would have a home. Naturally, William Crawford had your daddy arrested, and of course, they took you, too, Izear. You had no other relatives."

"But when my daddy died, you came," Izear says, lovingly.

"Yes, and that was the first time I got you out of jail. It took a little doing since my own father was dead by then and the sheriff who took his place wasn't worth a lick, though he did pay me a little homage. Actually, I think he was as afraid of me as most people were of Razor. Of course, I never carried a plank of lumber, just my Highlow blood."

"Ain't it strange, Miss Pearl, how both my old granddaddy and my daddy, Razor, died in prison? And if it hadn't been for you, I mighta died there, too."

"Yes, it is odd how history repeats itself, but I can't say I'm sorry for it. If things had been different, I wouldn't have had you either. The Lord has everything and everybody in the palm of his hand."

They smile at each other. I smile, too; sadly though. Peck ought to be here. He'd have hung on their every word, and in the end, he'd have agreed with Pearl about forgiving William Crawford. Of course, I don't agree. I think people ought to be paid back for every bad thing they do.

Every Brother Should be with his Sister

Little Benedict

Two years after Peck died, on August 15, the handicapped school bus that will take me back to Highlow pulls up in front of Piney Woods. I'm waiting for it at the entrance door, holding Little Sister, wishing I didn't have to get on the bus and leave her. Miss Candy comes up behind me, kisses me on the top of my head, and says, "Benny, you're the nicest boy in the whole world." I say, "Thank you, Miss Candy, but you didn't know Peck." Then I kiss Little Sister and give her back to Miss Candy 'til the next time I come. Miss Candy walks away, with Little Sister peering over her shoulder. Little Sister's got puddly look in her big, black eyes because she wants to go with me.

For the third time, Lizzie is waiting for me when the bus gets back to Highlow Elementary. She'll walk with me, four blocks to Pearl's where I'll stay until I'm called to supper. Mama and Daddy won't know I've been to see Little Sister, they'll think I've been at Pearl's all afternoon. Lizzie figured all that out. She doesn't grab me by the neck anymore; she puts a hand on my shoulder, like Peck used to do.

"Did you hold your little sister?" she asks.

"Uh huh. She's gettin' heavy."

"Every brother should be with his sister." Lizzie gets the same puddly look Little Sister had.

"Uh huh," is all I say because I'm afraid she might cry.

Lizzie's changed in a lot of ways. For one, she's taller, prettier, and has bosoms like my mama's. That's what's different on the outside. The inside's a little harder to figure out, but I'd say Lizzie's turned out to be a nice girl, nearly as nice as Peck—with one exception. She still can't stand Hobart any more than Miss Lila can. I've seen the ugly pictures with monster faces that Lizzie's drawn of him. But one of them is not of Hobart's face, it's his future gravestone. On it she's printed: Do Not Rest in Peace! She stacks the pictures in a pile, in the darkest corner of her room near the radiator. She won't let Izear touch them, so the pile is covered with dirt, dust, and mold; almost black, until she tops it with another drawing, worse than the one before. I'll bet Lizzie has as many mean pictures of Hobart as Miss Lila has sweet faces on china plates. One thing about Miss Lila, she never let her dislike of Hobart mess up her love of Art. I wonder if the nurses at the rest home where Miss Lila is now, are nice as Miss Candy. If Miss Lila was at Piney Woods, I know Miss Candy would find her plenty of plates to paint on.

What We Need is a Party!

Lizzie

My brother once said, "Lizzie, you don't see things as they really are. You're *too* content." But that's changed. I'm not at all content now. I'll never be content until Hobart pays for what he's done. Day by day, I watch him build up his real-estate agency next door, tearing down rooms, then adding new ones. Nothing about the McSwain house looks the same either. Sometimes I stand on the other side of his driveway, despising its difference, and wait for him to come out so I can tell him. Once, I took Pearl's just-in-case gun and stood there for hours with the gun in my pocket, just-in-case Hobart—oh, I don't know what, but it doesn't matter because he stayed inside all afternoon. When I do catch a glimpse of him, he never looks at me, never speaks to me. It's getting to be pretty tiring, all my hatred and nothing to show for it except the bunch of drawings I've made of him. But then, I'm not myself without Peck. It's like I'm trying to ride a see-saw without him to balance the other side. Now, I'm the one who wants what I can't have. I want Mama to come home from the hospital and paint fine china faces again. I want Pearl to have another Christmas open-house. I want my brother back! Of course, none of that happens. Highlow is old and stale, and lonely, so I mope around. Naturally, Pearl and Izear notice.

During a particularly rainy week, three years to the day after Peck died, we are all stuck inside. Izear and I are playing Canasta, which he hates, while Pearl sits behind us in the gold tufted, rosewood chair that matches her Victorian rosewood desk, sewing up a hole in her winter coat. More and more, she goes back in time, telling us story after family story. The one she's finishing up now is about a dinner party her grandmother, Grace, was planning when Pearl was a child.

"Before every occasion, Grandmother Grace inspected each piece of the fine china, taking note of the flaws of time; chips, cracks, any sign of unfavorable wear. Always, she repaired it as best she could then returned it to its proper place behind the glass-doors of her mahogany cabinet." She looks over at me, tugging her needle through the air. "There wasn't any Super Glue back then, you know."

"My goodness, Pearl. I'm happy you have some." But I'd be happier if she'd let me concentrate on the Canasta game.

"Yes, except for dancing, reparation was what Grace did best. The china is ours now, along with the cabinet scrolled with flowers, because Grace took care of it."

"Good thing," Izear says, to be nice. He picks up a pile of cards that has several pairs he needs.

"And you should have seen the dining room that night," Pearl continues. " On the table between the candelabras was a large bowl of deep, blue-green ferns interspersed with four kinds of flowers of particular meaning: white myrtles for love and marriage, bronze zinnias for thoughts of absent loved ones, rhododendron for risk, and thistle and golden rod for defiance and precaution. It was Grandfather Joseph who chose myrtles for the table, even drove the wagon thirty miles back into the woods to get them because they were Grace's favorite. The bronze zinnias were only seeds the year before, planted in the side garden of the house within view of their bedroom. In the evening light, Joseph watched Grace sew them, watched her lovely fingers turn the earth. The following fall, when the mass of copper colors prompted by her hands came forth, Joseph called it a miracle. But every flower is a miracle, isn't it, Izear?"

"Yes'um." He counts my Canasta books with two nods of his

head. He has only one.

"Joseph insisted on the rhododendron, packed around the front yard like soldiers guarding the house, just as they are today. Those flowers rise wild, require no real care yet become beautiful without it. At first, Grace questioned their pink rowdiness as too ordinary for her dinner party, 'a flouting against proper taste,' then finally, she agreed with Joseph. The thistle and golden rod were Grace's personal choice for the table. She gathered them herself. The stalks of golden rod were at the edge of the woods; the thistles grew beneath the tall pines. It was an effort for Grace, but Joseph encouraged her."

"I'll bet it was all real pretty, Pearl." Five canasta books, I have now.

"It *was* a lovely party, and extravagant. It was customary then to display some fare of the food that would come." She indicates toward the dining room and the ornate sideboard. "On that very sideboard, there were crabs and oysters, secured by a friend of Joseph's, whose steamboat shipped cotton to Mobile. There were apples and walnuts, sent to Grace by her family in Montgomery, arranged in sterling compotes, embellished with silver grapes. The rest of the food was served later; beef and venison, chicken and wild duck accompanied by beetroot, cabbage and potatoes, pears and stuffed dates."

"I never heard of such!" Izear exclaims, though I'm sure he's been privy to the story many times before.

At once, Pearl stops sewing. Folding her hands over her old repaired coat, she sits back in the tufted chair, as if telling the story has given her an idea. "I think we need some celebration in this house."

"Yes'um, we do."

"We need a party," Pearl says. "Let's have a little tea for Lizzie, and invite some girls her age." Even I like the plan.

The following day, the three of us drive to Crisscross to buy me a new dress and shoes.

"Oh, don't you look like a fine, little lady!" Pearl beams when I step out of the changing room of the new Pizitz Store. The dress I'm wearing is blue as Pearl's Buick Roadmaster, with padded shoulders and a hemline just below my knee, and I have on shiny black heels with little white butterflies on the toes.

"Pretty as a picture!" Izear says, standing behind Pearl who is sitting in a cushioned armchair in the 'Better Dresses' department.

Pearl pays for the dress then buys a tube of pretty pink lipstick, and lots of sponge curlers to do up my hair. "Time to have a party," she chimes. "Let's go back to Highlow.

The next morning, I help Pearl wash the crystal, silver and china. I help Izear make tea cakes, cucumber and watercress sandwiches, and ginger-ale punch. Then we wait for the guests. We wait over two hours for the guests, but no one comes.

"I don't understand it," Pearl says, covering her silver trays with Saran wrap while Izear pours the punch down the sink drain.

I stand there with a lump in my throat—is it me? But I have plenty of friends at school. "Maybe you put the wrong date on the invitations," I say to Pearl, hoping that's the case.

"What invitations? You know I never send invitations, Lizzie." She turns to Izear. "Didn't you tell the postman about our tea, like you do for the Christmas Open House?"

"You know I did. He promised to spread the news, lickety-split."

"Well he didn't, did he? I'll have to talk to The Judge about his sorry government help. And I will talk to him tomorrow."

Izear nods in agreement. "Can't do nothing about it, now."

"I'm sorry about the party, Lizzie,' Pearl says. "Hopefully, we'll have a new postman soon, but we can't control everybody, can we Izear?"

"Nome, just our own selves."

On my way upstairs, in my brand, new butterfly heels, I take a cucumber sandwich from beneath its plastic cover. I don't expect it to taste good, but it does. In my room, I look at myself in the mirror and for a split second I see Peck's face, brooding. But I'm tired of brooding, so I make myself smile. Then I take off my blue dress, hang it up in the closet, and lay on my rosy, flowered bedspread to re-read some of Peck's diary. When I get to the part about Leona, Hobart's so-called kissing cousin, I put the diary down then draw a picture of the slut, wearing my bright blue dress and standing against Pearl's cabinet of fine china. But when I'm finished, I tear it up; the dress looks a lot better on me. And heck, Leona wouldn't know what to do if somebody thought enough of *her* to give a fancy, tea party. I'll bet she's never even bitten into a cucumber sandwich, and I know she's never had anybody like Pearl, or Izear, to love her.

Marriage?

Hobart

"Ooooh Hobart, you are some kind of wounded lover, Shugah!"

"Dammit, get off me, Leona! It's time to open up my office."

"Aaaw, just a little longer. I'm getting used to this big old bed."

"You're just used to D.C.'s supply, but what you just had was the last of it. D.C's drying up, got the Feds on his tail. I won't be a distributor much longer, so you'd better be getting used to going without."

"C'mon Hobart, I know the truth. You're the one that's quitting, not D.C. You're upset because the boy was killed and you feel responsible."

Shut your mouth!"

"Don't you raise your hand to me, Hobart McSwain! I know the Chief of Police from way back."

"Listen you stupid bitch. I'm out of the powdered sugar business. I don't care who's supplying. I've told D.C."

"You think I need you for that? I've got plenty of suppliers, Shugah Bear. But I do love what you've done with your mama's house, and I hear you have other property."

"I'm in real estate. What else would I have?"

"You could have me. We could be partners. Let's run off and get married, Hobart. We belong together. Well, what do you say-- marriage? Hobart!"

"Alright Leona, maybe I'll marry you. But dammit, not today!"

Part Two

A Few Years Later

No Money, but Good Blood

Lizzie

Some say it takes years after a mirror's been broken to get to good fortune again. But Pearl said it's not good fortune a person needs to get to. It's how to forgive whoever broke the mirror in the first place. Pearl said that would take a while, even a trip or two on the wrong bus; but one day, good fortune would come again, if I had the patience to wait.

So I waited. With a child's hope, I waited for Jay to return my ticket to Cincinnati. I waited while Hobart built up his real-estate agency next door, defying him to come within an arm's length of me with Pearl's just-in-case gun in my thoughts, just in case he did. I waited for Mama to come home from the hospital and paint fine china faces again, and for Pearl to have another Christmas open-house. None of the things I waited for ever happened. Now, Pearl says it's time for me to make a new start, to get rid of old images.

The day after I graduate from high school, I burn every picture I drew of Hobart. Little Benedict helps me stuff all the moldy papers in the garbage can out back, on top of a mess of shrimp shells Izear discarded when he was making last night's 'graduation celebration' creole. When I strike the match, I expect a great, raging fire, and satisfaction as Hobart blazes, but there is only smoke and an awful smell that gags us both.

"Is that all?" Little Benedict says, holding his nose as we look down into the can at the puny smoldering. "I think Hobart would be disappointed."

"Well I don't have any more drawings, and I don't intend to

draw his face ever again."

"That's good, Lizzie. You know it wasn't his fault, anyway."

It was! But I don't protest. The smoke and smell finally go away. Only a pile of ashes remains in the bottom of the can, too small a pile to bother with. Anyway, I'll soon be leaving Highlow-- a second bus trip. This time I leave with Pearl's approval and my new monogrammed luggage, crammed with clothes from Pizitz. The bus is going to Mobile. I'm going to college there to study art.

Right off, I meet a boy, Richard Bolding. He's in his last year of a medical residency at the University of South Alabama, earning extra money by playing cab driver to arriving college students. "Need a ride?" he asks, watching me lift my two heavy suitcases from the baggage check. Pearl bought me only two pieces of luggage, in case I didn't like being away from Highlow, so they were crammed full. "I pass right by Rosemont College on my way to USA," Richard said. "Five dollars is all I charge."

"How do you know I'm going to Rosemont?"

Richard laughs. "You look like money in that green dress."

Without waiting for an answer, he squeezes my suitcases into the trunk of an old, faded blue Ford Falcon. A plump, blonde girl from Montgomery is already sitting under the rear view mirror, but she seems happy to move even closer to the driver's seat when I get in. The back seat is crammed with three other nervous freshmen headed for the University of South Alabama.

Richard delivers me to the dormitory steps, helps me with my two suitcases, and wishes me good luck. Then he takes his five dollars and drives away. A week later, he shows up again, turning the old Falcon through the wrought-iron gates of Rosemont College. He opens the door to a vacant front seat and I get in. Then I fall in love with him.

By the end of the semester, I have painted his face, sculpted his body, and drawn his hands and eyes on smooth grey stones, until prints and canvases and fired clay replicas of Richard fill my dormitory room.

Today, he holds up a charcoal drawing of his handsome face. "There's something in these eyes. Something he wants."

"What does he want?"

"He wants you."

He kisses me like he's used to it. I kiss him back as well as I know how, and then daily watch the wrought iron gate to see the Falcon come through it. From my room that overlooks the humble graves of priests, some dead for over a hundred and fifty years, I continue to create replica after replica of Richard. I become so enamored with my imitations of the boy that I don't recognize his lack of authenticity as a man.

Fall break of my senior year, the leaves are still on the live oaks in Highlow, but the pines have discarded their straw. Izear is raking it into piles. A ragged brown patchwork covers Pearl's yard. "Rake the front, too, but keep off the curb," Pearl calls to him from an open window as if it were yesterday.

"I know where to step," Izear says.

By Christmas, I will step into marriage. "A Georgia boy studying to be a doctor sounds promising," Pearl says when I tell her. Still, she has her cousin The Judge check him out, and now, she's saying his name like she's trying it on. "Dr. Richard Bolden. Did you know he's related to the Catholic side of the Pendleton family that moved to Atlanta?"

"Yes, Pearl."

"No money, but good blood."

"Good, Pearl."

"And of course you love him."

"Of course, Pearl."

"Your Mama's painting again. Since she's been home, she's happier than I've seen her since--." Pearl doesn't finish. She taps back into the kitchen where she came from. She has lost the words, and her soup's boiling over. She calls to me from the stove as if she has a second thought about Richard. "Do you think Peck would have liked him, Lizzie?"

"Yes, Pearl." Though I'm not sure of that.

The tea pot starts to whistle, and Pearl goes to take it off the burner. I take a walk down Main to where the pavement still stops at the dirt road that leads to the woods. The primroses aren't blooming, but the bright red pyracantha berries make an archway into the trees. There is a leaning sign that says the City of Highlow will soon begin some asphalt work for a street through the woods; but for now, it's still a dead-end.

"Whatcha doing, Lizzie?" Little Benedict comes out of the afternoon shadows and sits on the curb beside me. He's about the same age, now, as Peck was when he died.

"Hi. Wasting time, I guess."

He's grown a lot. He even takes a handkerchief out of his pocket to wipe his nose now, and I notice that his voice is beginning to crackle like Peck's used to. "I hope they pave this road soon; paved roads are better."

"They do keep dust out of the house."

Little Benedict stuffs the handkerchief back into his pocket. "I got me a girlfriend."

"Who?"

"LaRosa Jackson. Her daddy's the garbage man and her mama works out at Piney Woods." Little Benedict says this proudly, but I have to smile, thinking of what Miss Billie Nana's reaction must be. "Daddy likes her," he adds as if he's read my thoughts.

"Is that where you met her? Piney Woods?"

"Yeah. I think she loves me," Little Benedict laughs." She loves Little Sister, too. She carries her round from room to room when she comes after school to help her mama."

"How is Little Sister?"

"Fine. She's not an idiot child. She smiles all the time." Little Benedict fidgets with his shoestrings. "And she knows she's got a Daddy."

"Does she know she has a big brother, too?"

"Sorta. But I told her to call me 'Mama.' Miss Candy said it's better if Little Sister thinks she has a mama that comes to visit."

"Miss Billie Nana doesn't visit?"

"No. She won't come. Little Sister's never seen her real mama."

"That's too bad, Little Benedict."

"No it's not. Daddy and me got Little Sister thinking she's just like us. If Mama was to come, she'd make Little Sister think she was different."

"I suppose that's true."

"It is," he says, sneezes, and takes out his handkerchief. "Can I be the ring-bearer in your wedding, Lizzie?"

I laugh a little, but Little Benedict seems to take offense so I get serious. "Ring-bearers are usually real young. You're thirteen now. Maybe you could be a groomsman."

He lights up. "Is that what Peck woulda been?"

It takes me a minute to answer. "Probably."

"Then that's what I wanna be."

"Okay, Little Benedict."

"I can be your brother, too, if you want."

I hug him hard. He goes home happy, as if being my brother is all he's ever wanted.

The Muffin Man

Lizzie

Sitting on the top step of Pearl's staircase just outside Mama's room, I'm thinking about my wedding, about Richard, and that I love him. I hear the little clink of a china plate and Mama's humming of *Do You Know the Muffin Man?* She used to sing the song to Peck and me until Peck changed the lyrics to *Do You Know Your Daddy's Name?* She got irritated then and said she'd never sing it again.

Pearl sits downstairs at the dining room table under the fractured light of her crystal chandelier, worrying over the inquiry sheet The Highlow Eagle has sent for me to fill out, except Pearl has taken charge of it. The newspaper will announce my wedding with a picture in black and white, but the blank space beside 'Father of the Bride' has Pearl stumped. She has written and erased and written and erased, until Izear says, "You're gonna put a hole in that paper, Miss Pearl. Just leave the thing blank."

"But Lizzie has a father," Pearl snaps.

"Well, he don't belong at her wedding. You want all kinda trash down here again?"

"He'll probably never see it. It's The Highlow Eagle, after all."

"Don't matter. I was you, I'd let that dog lay."

At once, Pearl has an idea. "Izear, what's your middle name?"

"My name? You gonna print a downright lie in the paper?"

"It's not an actual lie. It would only be a lie if you weren't a real person, but you are."

"But I ain't a real daddy."

"No one will know that. It's only your middle name. Now,

what is it?"

Izear grunts, "It's Elijah."

"Elijah?" Pearl sounds disappointed. "Maybe we could just use your initials. Yes. I.E. Black." And Pearl writes it down over the rubbed-out spot.

"But 'Black' ain't my last name," Izear says quickly.

"That doesn't matter. You're not the daddy either."

"Miss Pearl, if I get to be a thousand years old, I still won't understand what goes on in your little, white head."

"You don't have to understand," Pearl says. "You won't live to be a thousand years old anyway."

A few weeks before the wedding, Pearl abruptly changes her mind about Richard. She says she's seen him, several times, slipping hundred dollar bills from her rose-painted tin box when he didn't know she was watching. "Take off your blinders and look at that boy, Lizzie!"

I deny that Richard would ever steal anything.

"How do you know that he wouldn't steal?" Pearl asks.

"I love him, for God's sake!"

"Remember the boy in the bus station? You told Izear you loved him, too, and look what happened--he stole your money and took the next bus out."

"I was a child then, Pearl!"

"And children are trusting, but now you're grown. I wouldn't put my whole heart in that Georgia boy's hands if I were you. He might decide to tighten his fingers."

I touch her shoulder. "Richard *loves me*."

She appears unconvinced and taps over to sit in the chair beneath her picture of The Sacred Heart. "Are you sure you ought to take this bus, Lizzie?"

I know what she's thinking about: Mama and Cincinnati. "Yes. It's where I want to go." So, we go on with plans for the wedding, my ceremony of deliverance. Richard drives to Highlow in his ancient, blue Ford, a dazzling groom with money in his pocket. He and I drive away in the new, white Thunderbird he bought for a song at D.C.'s car lot in Dixie. On our way out of town, on the river road, an army-green shadow casts itself on the hood of the car in the shape of a great, wide wing. It stays with us until we pass the city limit sign and exit to the highway ahead.

It isn't Love

Hobart

"I don't want this baby, Hobart! Leona yells.

I say she should have thought of that before. It isn't my fault she got pregnant.

"Whose fault is it, then--some farmer working a cabbage patch?"

I said it could have been some farmer for all I know.

"You are the father, Hobart."

"I say I'm not sure of that; she's had plenty of other men.

"Well, you were the first." Leona says in her sweeter voice, snuggling up to me.

"I say, "Really? The first?" But who is she fooling?

"I guess I could have the baby if we get married," Leona says, leading me down the hall to Mama McSwain's old room where she appears to size it up for moving in. She flops on the bed like she's decided to stay, pulling me into her arms as if I belong there. "It will probably look just like you, Shugah;" she whispers, "big, blonde and handsome."

A baby who looked like me? Maybe it wouldn't be so bad.

"Are we going to get married? Leona asks as I lay beside her in my mama's bed. "I could handle all the invoices for your real estate company. I'm good at that, too."

"Maybe, Leona," I say. If it is my baby, I want it to have a father.

"Maybe? I've heard that before. You've put me off for years, sugar bear, and I still want you."

But I don't want her. I want Lila, the only woman I ever really loved-- a woman who'd love to see me dead. Then I think of Lizzie, who looks just like her mother. And of Peck, yearning for some bird I was never able to give him. And even Pearl, who believes I can be "fixed" enough to belong.

"Okay Hobart?" Leona prods. "Are we going to tie the knot?"

"Okay Leona," I say, because Pearl would call it 'right.'

Then Leona and I make something together, but it isn't love.

Little Sister and Truth

Little Benedict

Six years ago, I was a groomsman in Lizzie's wedding. Now, I've gotten married, too. I married the garbage man's daughter, LaRosa. She loves me. She says so all the time. "I love you Little Benedict."

"Well, I need somebody to love me," I always tell her.

Then LaRosa says, "Don't worry, Little Benedict. You've got me and Little Sister."

Today, we're on our way to Piney Woods to bring Little Sister home. I ask LaRosa, "Do you know what Little Sister said when Miss Candy told her that her mama was gone to heaven?"

LaRosa smiles and shakes her head, no.

"Little Sister said, 'No, she's not gone to heaven.' Then she pointed at me. See? There's my mama.'"

LaRosa giggles and squeezes my hand.

"Miss Candy believes in telling the truth no matter what," I say. "Miss Candy's sweet, but truth to Little Sister's not the same as it would be to me or you."

LaRosa nods in agreement.

"It's time to bring home our surprise baby girl. Isn't that right, LaRosa?"

LaRosa kisses my cheek. That's why I love her and why I married her; she's never been shy around surprises. "You know how much Little Sister and I love you?" I ask LaRosa.

She snuggles up, and lays her head on my shoulder. "Yes, I know."

My daddy and mama wouldn't come to our Catholic wedding. Daddy wanted to, but Mama said she'd never set a foot in a church that didn't believe in controlling the birth of the human race. LaRosa told her God was the maker of the human race, so maybe mama oughta let Him control it. She asked Mama to use her head and think about that fact. Just after that, in November, both mama and daddy *lost* their heads. My daddy's new MG-- one he bought down in Dixie--ran under a semi-truck. They never knew what hit them. So, Mama didn't have time to think. Hers was the first head they pulled out from under the semi-truck .When they pulled out Daddy's, all I could think of was how I wish he could've lived long enough to call me "knucklehead" one last time. I miss hearing that. I miss my daddy, too.

Now, LaRosa and me and Little Sister have the big house to ourselves. At Piney Woods, we say goodbye to Miss Candy, and Miss Candy says good luck to us. Then the three of us drive away to our happy life where LaRosa will soon have our own new baby. "We're going to have lots of babies, idiots or not," LaRosa says on the way home kissing me, and then Little Sister, too.

In the kitchen, Little Sister puts her head on LaRosa's tummy and gives it a kiss. LaRosa laughs like she can't stop, then she fixes us all hot dogs and sauerkraut. After we put Little Sister to bed in her new room, LaRosa asks me if Pearl ever hears from Lizzie.

I say she does. Lizzie writes, but she doesn't come home. "She must be having an awful nice life outside of Highlow."

LaRosa gives me a hug and another bowl of sauerkraut. "Well, outside of Highlow might be nice to some people, Little Benedict; but to me, it's not the world."

Back to Where He Came From

Hobart

I've been a daddy for a while. I named my boy Peck Two because he looks a lot like Lila's dead son. Leona didn't want him though. She said she didn't on the day he was born, and she's said it, ever since. When Peck Two was a little baby, he'd just cry and cry for a mama to hang on to. I told Pearl then, I'd give him to Lila, and maybe make-up for what she lost. That made Pearl angry enough to throw her black iron frying pan at me, right through the screen of her back door. Then she hollered, "You haven't gotten very far in fixing yourself, Hobart!"

She still hasn't told Lila I have a green-eyed, copper-haired boy. Hell, he'd be a good boy to keep if he liked us, either me, or Leona. But he doesn't. He's always running over to Pearl's, trying to get in. Pearl treats him sweet, but she won't open her door to him. She's afraid Lila will see him and go crazy again because the boy looks so much like her own Peck. Then she'd have to go back to the hospital for another rest. Pearl said she had to put the welfare of her own child first, so when Peck Two runs over there, she has Izear hurry him back to the servant's quarters. They spend hours up there in conversation, but then Izear's always been on the level of a four-year old. Leona says, "Just leave him up there, if he likes Izear better than his own mother." She acts like she's mad, but she don't really care.

I've got a big business now; bought and sold a lot of houses since I started. I sold 'em quick and made lots of money, and figured I'd invest some of it. I built a subdivision just outside

Highlow, on the opposite side of Dixie. All I did was to pour out six or seven concrete slabs then added some siding for the walls. Every house has a metal fireplace that don't even take wood to make a fire. Maybe they're not built well, but they're all new and that's what the people want. It helps them forget they can't live on Main Street. I called the place, 'Mirage.' Got a big sign on the gate surrounding it that says: *Things Happen When You Buy a Mirage.* Sold every one, and I'm building more.

So now, I got enough money to buy Peck Two anything he wants, and I try to be nice to him. I remember how it was when I was a boy, so I've never once stuck him in a box. But still, he cries. Maybe he wants a mama who don't spin around town with every Tom, Dick and Harry. Who cares if she does? Well, maybe Peck Two cares.

Leona throws some vienna sausage on a paper plate and calls it his supper. After she leaves, I give him a popsicle and he smiles a little. I try to talk to him like Izear does, and wipe off the colored sugar-syrup running down his chin, but he just glares at me and slaps my hand away. I took him hunting once, tried to teach him how to shoot. It looked like he was learning good, 'til he turned the rifle on me. I had to yank it away from him; I got enough holes already. So hell, I don't know what to do with him.

Leona said, "Maybe we oughta just wrap him up and send him back where he came from!" She said that after she'd sucked in some Dixie sugar from her new supplier.

Little Benedict's wife, LaRosa, says Leona's an unfit mother. LaRosa says there's plenty of room at hers and Little Benedict's house for one more. Someday, I might just send him over. Leona would never notice he's gone.

Taking Notes for The Judge

Little Benedict

The Judge is getting old enough to have arthritis. Sometimes he has trouble taking notes, so he says to me, "Little Benedict, will you take some notes for me? I need a history of Peck Two, and you know a lot about him." The Judge still calls me 'Highlow's finest;' so naturally, I say I will.

I start off with myself. The first line I write is: "I love being a daddy." Then I go on: "Me, LaRosa, and Little Sister have two growing kids, LaRosa's expecting another one. Now we have Peck Two." Then comes the part The Judge wants a precise record of, so I give it my best effort:

Three years ago, and three days before Christmas, Hobart brought his boy over for LaRosa and me to babysit. It was Christmas Eve before he came back to get him. He and Leona were busy playing dodge ball; Leona high on the powder, trying to dodge the ball of Hobart's fist. On the holy night that Hobart came to get Peck Two, The Judge happened to be driving down Main Street because he hadn't been able to sleep from his arthritis. He saw me and LaRosa and Little Sister standing on the porch wringing our hands. Then he saw Peck Two dressed in the new Santa Claus pajamas LaRosa bought him, and heard him screaming and hollering while Hobart tried to drag him home. LaRosa and Little Sister were running behind them, crying that since Leona was an unfit mother, Hobart ought to let them keep Peck Two.

The Judge slammed his brakes, rolled down the window, and

asked what in heaven's name was wrong? When the boy heard the Judge's voice, he wriggled away from Hobart, ran back to our porch, and wrapped his skinny arms around LaRosa's leg, begging The Judge to let him stay with us. Since it was Christmas, and The Judge has always been partial to little boys with a mission, The Judge said that looked like a good arrangement to him. So, Hobart went on home without him. Little Sister hauled Peck Two into our house and plopped him on her lap, while the emerald and wine-colored lights on the trees reflected on both their faces. Then she showed him the tiny porcelain Jesus from our manger. 'Look Mama,' she said to me. 'See how Jesus fits just right in his little ole hands.' Little Sister's real attached to him now.

Hobart and Leona were divorced a short time later. Leona ran off and Hobart never asked for his boy back. Peck Two's been with us ever since. LaRosa and Little Sister and I have turned our house into a daycare center. We painted the sign out front while our latest toddler did somersaults in the grass with Peck Two. LaRosa bought red, yellow and blue colors for a sign. Little Sister thought of the name: God's World. And I said, 'Where every child is accepted.' So, that's what we painted on our sign.

-- By Little Benedict Spratling. Taking notes for The Judge."

Today, Peck Two comes down the yard carrying our littlest baby boy on his hip and tickling him with a powder puff from the mimosa tree. The baby's just laughing. LaRosa and I have had no trouble at all with that green-eyed son who used to be Hobart's. We love him like he was born to us.

Pearl taps over from her house, her cane sinking in the just fertilized grass. She has her eyes on Peck Two. She loves him, too, because of his name, and because she thinks he favors her dead grandson. Pearl says to me. "Izear and I thought we might take Peck Two downtown. Izear has some shopping to do and we were going to go by the ice cream store."

"Can I drive, Miss Pearl?" Peck Two asks.

"Well, maybe you can sit on Izear's lap and steer," Pearl says cheerfully.

LaRosa gets nervous when Peck Two is out of her sight. "We're in the middle of painting the sign, Miss Pearl," LaRosa says, "and Peck Two wanted to help."

"Well, now I wanna go, Mama LaRosa," Peck Two whines. "I wanna be the first boy to drive Miss Pearl's car!"

Pearl gives a bubbly laugh. "Peck Two, you do like to be first; don't you?"

He nods, yes, and aims a nice, polite smile at LaRosa. "Can I go?"

"We won't be long," Pearl says.

LaRosa hears pleading in Miss Pearl's voice and gives in, so Miss Pearl walks back across the yard with Peck Two's hand in hers; a scene that could be yesterday, he's so like Lizzie's twin.

"Do you think Peck Two will be alright?" LaRosa asks me, snuggling our newest baby in her arms. "I hear Leona's back from Texas; she might see him."

I kiss the top of her head. "Don't worry. Leona wouldn't know him if she *did* see him."

I Won't Wear Blinders Anymore

Lizzie

We have a leash-law in Mobile where Richard and I live, but we've never had a dog. Early in our marriage, I wanted one. Richard said a dog would take up too much of my time and he wanted it all. So, he took it, but gave none in return; my Richard, my prince, who took his princess out of Highlow when she answered 'yes' to a promise of new life.

Richard delivers new life into the world everyday through his own hands. Sometimes I watch when he doesn't know I'm there. A particular nurse lets me take her place in the delivery room, even suits me up. Richard still isn't able to tell the crucial difference between the nurse and me. The last baby was beautiful. A boy.

I want a baby. Richard doesn't.

"I want you on the pill, Lizzie, until we can build a house," he says in his doctor voice. He hands me a plastic punch-out package of pink and white. "These are the best you can get," he says, princely proud.

We build our first dream house, a castle too big for his salary as a resident, with too many rooms on too little land in a much too-restricted neighborhood for a new life.

"I want a baby."

"A creative distraction is what you need."

He buys me a set of oil paints and some canvas and turns one of the rooms into an artist's studio. I try to paint faces on the canvas. I can't. And when I can't, I tell Richard I'm going out for some fine china plates like Mama uses for her portraits.

Richard says, "Buy plastic; it's cheaper." Then he buys himself a sail boat.

It doesn't matter. I'm not the artist Mama is anyway.

Richard sometimes works night and day at the hospital, so I'm alone a lot. I interview at the newspaper for an editorial job and get it. Richard isn't happy. He says he wants me home, with or without him. He buys me a subscription to Southern Living. He tells me to decorate the big house and then throw a party to advance his career. I do that. Party after party, after trite, stodgy party; every one of them. Still, I want a baby.

"Go join some clubs or something," Richard says. "It'll get my name out there, help build my practice and then maybe we'll think about a baby."

"I won't take these pills anymore!" He doesn't hear me on his way out.

I join a bridge club that meets twice a week; eight young women, mostly beautiful and thoroughly wealthy. On the other days, I meet with the Junior League, with the Art Guild, with the Symphony Association. I lunch with the doctor's wives, brunch with the ladies of the Country Club, and learn tennis from the tennis pro who teaches me to swing a backhand then tries to teach me how to cheat on my husband like he cheats on his wife.

"Who's it gonna hurt?"

"Who wouldn't it hurt?"

The tennis pro looks as if he has a thought, but he keeps pawing until I hit him in the crotch with my racket and tell him, "I don't want any more lessons!"

"You won't tell my wife, will you?" His wife is the daughter of the Country Club's Chairman, one of the beautiful members of my bridge club.

"Why would I hurt your wife?"

Then at our next bridge game, the chairman's daughter—I have told her nothing--breasts her cards and whispers, "You'd better watch Richard. There's a rumor going around about him and a nurse."

Hours later, I go to the hospital to see for myself. I see my husband embrace the nurse who let me pretend to be her so I could watch a life being born. I think maybe it was innocent; after all, he works with her every day. When I tell Richard I saw them, he overreacts, "If you think we're having an affair, you're full of shit!" And so, I know they are.

I try to black out the nurse's name. I read a book on battling infidelity and that's what it said to do. "Remembering her name puts the gun in her hands." Her name is Vicki. Richard calls her Vic. I will not let them get away with it.

Richard has a best friend from childhood who's always around. His name is Anthony, a doctor, too. He is a foot taller than Richard and much better looking. Not that I mean to compare them. I don't mean to do that, but at a hospital party for the new residents, I see how the tips of Anthony's ears hide themselves just under the slight curl of his dark hair, and how his smile caresses the person he's talking to as if he cares about them. Then I watch Richard's cocky grin as he slips his doctor hands around the neck of every low-cut dress in the Red Room of the Hyatt.

Anthony touches my arm gently. "He doesn't mean anything by it," he says of Richard. "I've known him a long time; I know he loves you."

"Oh really?"

Anthony smiles. "Yes, really. And you love him, too, don't you?"

I don't answer.

"Let me get you a drink," Anthony says. "There's no reason why you shouldn't enjoy yourself." He gives my arm a squeeze and goes to the bar. I think he feels sorry for me. Richard would have no trouble finding a ride home if I left now. But I don't leave. When Anthony returns with the drinks, I see more than empathy in his face. "You didn't answer my question," he says. "Do you love Richard?"

"I married him, didn't I?" (I promised something when I did. I made my own bed in spite of Pearl's catching eye and now, I have to lie in it.) "Not that it's any of your business," I say rudely, and Anthony lowers his eyes.

A few weeks after the party for the residents, Richard and I meet Anthony for lunch at a restaurant on the wharf. Anthony rests his elbows on the table and looks at me. "What say we all go to the bay? We should take a color cruise, now that the leaves are turning."

Richard has barely noticed I'm at the table. There is a drip of ketchup on the corner of his mouth which he wipes it away with his wadded-up paper napkin, then says to Anthony, "I thought you'd give up playing sailboat sea-captain after our last trip out." On that trip, we nearly drowned; the three of us, plus Vic. According to Richard, she'd invited herself to keep Anthony company.

"Hell son, you can't appreciate life without near-death experiences," Anthony says.

He smiles and stretches back in his chair and into the sunlight coming through a glass window. I notice how comfortable and kind he appears as the light dapples over his skin, up his right forearm, touches the sleeve of his hospital shirt.

And then I notice Richard, taking four french-fries in his fingers, dragging them all at once through the blood-red pile of ketchup he has squeezed on the paper hamburger wrapper. He crams them into his mouth, barely chewing as he swallows. And when the sun abruptly takes a shot at him, too; Richard closes one eye from the glare and twists in his chair. "Hey!" he shouts to a uniformed teenager at the counter. "Close those damn blinds, will you?"

The girl darts to the window, smiling at the young doctor who's noticed her.

"If the coast-guard hadn't pulled us in we wouldn't be here to appreciate anything," Richard says about our sailing trip. The girl closes the blinds and turns toward Richard to be sure she's accommodated him. He notices her then, and gives her a wink.

"That was just a little squall," Anthony says. "You wouldn't have thought we were in trouble at all if that silly nurse you brought to keep me charmed hadn't bawled on *your* shoulder." He picks up a fry. "Right, Liz?"

"I'm not going sailing again," I say.

Anthony touches my arm. "Come on, you were the brave one! I'll call upstairs about the weather this time, Liz. No more squalls, I promise."

"Well hell," Richard screws his lips into a half smile. "You must have a direct line to the Almighty, just like Lizzie."

I recognize the look Richard throws my way. It is the same look he often throws from our bed, when he finds me gone, when he catches me across the room, praying that Pearl was here to repair him. It grabs at my heart, that look. It squeezes so hard, and conjures up the thought of Vic, and something close to the hatred I have for Hobart.

"Yeah," Richard says, "I think we'll take that cruise. It can't be this weekend, though." His sideways glance at me is cold as Cincinnati. "I'm moonlighting until Monday morning."

Anthony shifts uncomfortably. "The next weekend then. We'll plan on it."

Richard takes a bite of his hamburger, talking as he chews. "I heard O'Connell's taking over orthopedic. Better watch your toes."

"Hey, he's a good surgeon. I watched him do more than a miracle last night. He kept a woman from amputation; a woman who couldn't pay him a dime for what he did."

Richard gives a grunt. "And this morning she knelt at his altar, right?"

"So?" Anthony says. "O'Connell saved her leg, maybe her life."

"All by himself. The all-powerful O'Connell."

"The best bone man in Mobile, Richard."

"And you want to be just like him."

"Don't you want to be the best?"

"I'd rather be the richest."

"Glutton." Anthony shakes his head. "What are we going to do with him, Liz?"

"I'm not going out on that bay again," I say to Richard.

My husband shrugs. "Have it your way. I've got to go to work. I'm back on call at one o'clock." He drinks the last swallow from his paper cup and saunters out of the restaurant. We watch him, Anthony and me and the teenage waitress, through the plate glass window until his white Thunderbird swerves like a misguided bullet into the noontime traffic of the beltline.

"I guess I made him mad," Anthony says.

"Not you. It's me he's upset with."

He moves his hand across the table and stops his fingers inches from my folded arms. "He doesn't mean to hurt you. I've told you before, Liz; Richard loves you." Do I imagine that Anthony sounds sorry about that?

I put my hands in my lap. "Don't make excuses for him."

"Then don't act like his judge."

"I'm not judging him. I'm trying to be his wife. I just can't wear blinders anymore."

Richard invites Vic, the nurse, again; but as Anthony promised, there are no squalls, only a small breeze and a beautiful purple and gold dawn. Vic is impressed. Richard seems happy. Anthony shows me how to keep from going downwind. "A boat with no constraints travels only in the direction of the wind," Anthony says, placing my hand on the tiller. "With this, you move the rudder and you can change directions. Point the bow wherever you want it to go."

But in my hands, the boat turns sideways and the sail begins to flap wildly. "I can't do this," I say. "Let Richard sail it."

"I'm busy," Richard says, grinning at Vic from the bow of the boat.

    Anthony tightens his grip over my hand. "You can do it, Lizzie. Just don't sail directly into the wind. Zigzag a little, a forty-five degree angle. It's called tacking. See? The wind crosses over the bow, not into it." The boat straightens and stays that way as long as Anthony keeps his hand on mine. We have a smooth sail and make it back to shore, but our other passengers hardly notice.

Leona Wants to Bargain

Hobart

"Get off my lap, Pharaoh, I gotta answer the phone. Good dog. You're the only hunting dog I'd let in my house. Hello?"

"Hobart?"

"Yeah Leona; what now?"

"I haven't gotten my alimony check this month."

You ain't gonna get it. I don't owe you nothin' since you got married again."

"How'd you hear about that?"

"I got ears."

Well, I'm not staying married. I'm getting a divorce. That cowboy's as much an idiot as you are. So, you owe me."

"It don't work like that, Leona."

"You owe me, Hobart! I'll take you to court. I'll sue for the boy, so you might as well pay me."

"Hell, take me to court then! You're the one who left me and the boy."

"And you gave our son to that garbage collector's daughter!"

"Oh, you wanted him?"

"That's not the point!"

"What is the point, Leona?"

"The point is that you've made more money than anybody in Highlow, so what's a little check made out to me?"

"I work for my money."

"You and I were married."

"Well, we're not married now."

"The boy's still mine. If you're not going to cooperate; I want him back."

"Peck Two's better off where he is, without either one of us."

"Hobart, I mean it! I'll take him."

"Bye, Leona . . . Dammit Pharoah, don't chew on the phone wire; I'm trying to dial! . . . Hello, LaRosa. How's Peck Two ?"

"I can't talk to you now. I'm getting him ready for bed."

"I don't wanna talk, just how's the boy doin?"

"Fine."

"Leona wants him back . . . LaRosa?"

"You gave him to me and Little Benedict. He's part of our family. She can't have him back!"

"Oh, she don't really want him, but--."

"She can't have him!"

"Well, she's gonna make trouble, I know her. I'm just saying to watch out for the boy, LaRosa; that's all."

He's In There Somewhere.
Yes, He Is!

Little Benedict

Every morning at breakfast, soon as she sits down at our table, Little Sister says to me, "Mama, can I see the Lord Jesus today? I put down my fork and smile at her, broad as I can, because Little Sister says she sees Jesus in anyone who gives her a grin.

It amazes me that some people don't return her smile. Maybe they're too busy, or maybe they're afraid of her affection, like the Highlow Foodliner manager is. He's come up to LaRosa and me in the store, saying that Little Sister is bothering his customers. That's because Little Sister has just kissed the big smiley face imprinted on his toothpaste display, and knocked the whole thing over.

The Foodliner manager tells us we need to take Little Sister back to where she came from, that she would be better off with her own kind. LaRosa has a fiery look. She tells the Foodline manager that Little Sister is already with her own kind.

"Oh?" he says with a smirk. "You mean all ya'll are nuts?" Then he trots off, waving a limp wrist at a stock boy to come pick up the boxes of scattered toothpaste.

LaRosa is so mad she says we'll never shop in the Highlow Foodliner again. But Little Sister doesn't take rudeness personal; she's always looking for Jesus. She tiptoes toward the fruits and vegetables and comes up just behind the Foodliner manager who's absorbed in checking for bruised tomatoes. She taps his shoulder. He turns around to see Little Sister smiling at him, and then she gives him her best kiss, right on the mouth.

The Foodliner manager is stunned. "Jesus!" he shouts, wiping his lips. "Jesus!"

Little Sister tilts up her chin in triumph. "Uh huh!" she says. "I knew He was in there somewhere."

The Image is Mine

Lizzie

Richard is tired of his white Thunderbird. He wants something new, something with more excitement. "You drive the old one," he says. "I've bought a red BMW."

"How are you going to pay for this on a resident's salary?" I ask, standing beside the new car as he cranks it up.

He gives me a boorish smile that turns me cold. "I've got extra work moonlighting at the Baldwin County Clinic, assisting the subsidized poor deliver their babies."

But I don't trust him. Tonight, I drive the old car to the county clinic where Richard is supposed to be helping the poor, because I've heard that Vic lives in Baldwin and I'm thinking that Richard is lying about his moonlighting job. He isn't lying, not about the job. His brand new, blood-red BMW is parked in front of the clinic, but Richard isn't delivering babies inside. Not live ones.

"Have you got the money?" A girl's voice, about fifteen, tumbles from the open window of a pick-up truck.

"Yeah," answers the nervous male voice, barely a man's."

"Seven hundred fifty; you're sure?"

"I got it! C'mon. Let's get it over with."

Seven hundred and fifty dollars a child. Five children already, tonight. Richard will have his new blood-red chariot paid off in no time. I wait several hours in the shadows of the parking lot for Richard to leave. He comes down the clinic steps with Vic. He opens the door to his blood red car and she gets in. I notice that his right hand has a small bandage."

"You'd better see about your hand," she says, settling into the leather interior.

"My hand's fine, but I'd like to sue the damn latex company that made those surgical gloves." He kisses her, not an innocent kiss. Richard backs out of the parking lot and they drive off.

I follow them to Vic's house.

I could get out of the car, walk to the side of the house and look in the window. It wouldn't be hard; I've looked in windows before. But what will I do when I catch them squirming? Then a curtain is pulled back and quickly closed; Richard appears shirtless on the porch. I'm certain he sees my car, but he goes back inside as if I'm of no consequence. So, now what? This is not the trip I wanted to take, not the ticket I bargained for. I think of Pearl, who battles with words, and I think of Mama with the "just-in-case" gun. I'd even like to be Izear, and poke out their eyes, Richard's and Vic's. Instead, I drive to our big house to wait for the next lie. But it will be the last time he'll play me for a fool. On the dark, narrow road home, I make plans for Richard's retribution. He will pay for what he's done.

If you don't want to go to Cincinnati, then don't get on the bus. I was never quite sure what Pearl meant by those words, until now. It took Richard himself to show me. The man I insisted on marrying was a mirage, not at all the man I *thought* I was marrying. On that moonlit night, I waited to catch Richard and throw him out, but he'd already caught himself. He'd aborted the baby of a woman with Aids, scraped the scalpel into his surgical glove, as well as into the child. He'd cut her mother's poisoned blood into his own. He got on the bus, too, and it took him where he didn't want to go. Now, he faces the consequences.

The morning after it happened, Richard had his blood tested and then several times after that until the disease showed up. He fell apart when he read the results. Today, I am Richard's only nurse. The other one is afraid to touch a man with Aids. So,

Richard does not cheat, anymore, and he does not lie, except in the bed he made for himself. He is dying.

I'd wanted to pay Richard back for his affair, but his diagnosis has done that for me. Pearl would say, "Show a little mercy, Lizzie." Well, I'm a good nurse! I haven't slept for weeks. I time out medication every four hours, keep watch that the oxygen hose stays in his nostrils, and the battery works in case of a storm surge; but I resent the stench of his bed pan, the ooze of his lesions, the diapers wrapped around hips so thin that bones show through tissue-paper skin. That requires more medications, bandages administered. I do all of it for the man who betrayed me, who gave me nothing I wanted, except a misguided ticket out of Highlow. I would like to be a saint in this, as Pearl would have it. But a saint has compassion, a saint forgives. I do not. My indignation grows until every assist I give to Richard becomes one more log on the fire of vindictiveness. And it produces a meanness I did not know I could muster.

Richard is captive, now. He cannot run from my questions.

"Why?" "How long did it go on?" "Do you love her?" "Do you wish you'd married her, instead of me?" He doesn't answer my questions and he doesn't say he's sorry. Neither his silence nor his suffering vindicates him.

I want justice. No, I want payback. So, I seduce Anthony.

He is hesitant when I put my arms around him; I'm the wife of his best friend, after all. But he doesn't remove my hand that slides down his chest, to the buckle of his belt. When we begin, I feel no passion, only anger. I am thinking of Richard with Vic. It seems different for Anthony. He is careful, even tender, as if he loves me. He holds me close. "Don't worry. Don't worry," he says. Still the tightness around his mouth says, "I shouldn't be here."

When it's over, I replay Richard and Vic in my mind to erase any remorse. Anthony dresses slowly, guiltily, sadly. Then he goes to Richard's room, opens the door. "See you tomorrow, buddy."

Richard gives a weak nod of acknowledgment.

Anthony turns to me, touches my shoulder as if waiting for me to say something that will make him feel better. I nudge him out of the door and close it, then carry out my nightly nursing routine. In bed, beside my husband, I wait for the gratification I aimed for. It never comes.

The next time he comes, Anthony stops in the doorway, holding a Confederate Rose bleeding to crimson and near the end of its single-day life. "Are we more than this, Lizzie?" he asks.

I take the flower from him. "More than what?"

"Just sex?"

"What's wrong with just sex?" I attempt a smile, but Anthony gives me a blank stare. He goes in to Richard to say hello. They talk until my husband dozes on soiled sheets that ought to be changed. The sheets can wait. Richard can wait. But my vengeance cannot.

A room away, I embrace Anthony again, but there's more remorse than passion in his eyes when he touches me. "It has to be the last time," he whispers.

I press against him. It won't be the last time. By now, I'm certain he loves me. How do I feel about him? I don't let myself think about that.

Afterwards, Richard lies in pain, one ankle over the other as if nailed together. Anthony peeks in to tell him goodbye. Richard smiles. "See you tomorrow, buddy," they say to each other in unison.

When Anthony has left, I go into Richard's room to change the sheets. "Where were you two?" he asks. Why should I answer his questions when he won't answer mine? Instead, I complain about the sheets. I grumble when I bring his medicine. He reaches for my hand. "I'm sorry; I was wrong." Then he starts to confess. "You asked about Vic. She and I--." I put a finger to his lips; if he repents, I'll have to do the same.

It's storming the following day when Anthony returns.

Between bolts of thunder, he and Richard talk about their long friendship, about the hospital, about Anthony finding a woman to settle down with. When Richard's voice becomes too weak, Anthony says he should rest. He follows me to the other bedroom. In the dark, between flashes of lightening, I un-make the bed. And we slip between the sheets. I don't realize that the power has gone off in the house, or that the battery powering Richard's oxygen is not working. I don't know that in the other room, black as an underwater cave, Richard is gasping for air. Later, when I find him dead, the mirror reflects a dragon-like image, crouching over his cold body as if to devour it. I have to look twice to see that the image is mine.

Cut Out of Me, Not You!

Little Benedict

Me and my sweet LaRosa are talking over the fence to Miss Pearl. "Lizzie's doctor husband's died on her," Miss Pearl announces. "She's all broken up about it, so she's coming home."

"She ought to," I say. "It's not good to be all broken up."

LaRosa says, "Don't worry, Miss Pearl. You and Highlow will put her back together."

Then Izear sticks his head out the back door and hollers, "Miss Pearl, where'd you hide the super glue?"

"I did not hide it, Izear. It's where it always is, here in my pocket."

"Well, I need it 'cause I had a teeny weeny accident with the lamp in the living room and Miss Lila's got out and she's walking around there barefoot and she's gonna cut her foot on all those pieces if you don't bring that super glue. Right now!"

Miss Pearl gives a tsk-tsk. "Sweet Jesus; my house is overloaded with pieces. Something's always got to be fixed."

Tonight, in the Spratling house, we're all in one piece; lots more of us than used to be. Little Sister's got her own room down the hall. We put a television in there with an old VCR machine so she can watch the old black and white cassettes of Perry Mason that Miss Candy gave us. When Little Sister was a little kid, she watched all Perry Mason's TV shows at Piney Ridge. It's why she likes to defend the good guy.

The rest of our kids, adopted or born to us, sleep in bunks in the other two bedrooms. LaRosa's snoring. She does that when she's content. I snuggle up to her and hold her hand under the blankets until a baby cries down the hall, then LaRosa gets up, sleep-drugged, bumping her way toward the noise. Soon the rocking chair is creaking and LaRosa is singing about a little lost lamb losing its way and finding it again. And when she finds her way back to our bed, she kisses me hard like she'd really miss me if I ever left. She doesn't have to worry; I'd never leave. Like LaRosa says; Highlow's the world to me.

"Little Benedict?" she whispers. "Leona's gonna try to get our boy and she might have some grounds on account of there's blood between them. But Peck Two's ours now, blood or not. I'm his mama and you're his daddy. Did you hear what I said, Little Benedict?"

"I heard, LaRosa. Peck Two's ours, and I'm his daddy."

"I thank the merciful heart of Jesus that all our children know their daddy." LaRosa says. "They don't have to miss you, or hunt for you like Peck and Lizzie did." She takes a deep breath and starts snoring again.

The next morning, I have two of my smallest boys in the bathtub upstairs when I hear the doorbell, and then LaRosa shouting, "You can't have him!"

I hear Leona's voice. "Pack him a suitcase. Now!"

Peck Two peeks around the bathroom door. "It's my other mother. She wants me."

"Stay with the babies," I tell him, just as Little Sister comes out of her room. I give her a hurried smile on my way down the stairs, hoping she doesn't follow; but she does.

In the living room, Leona's pin-point eyes cut into mine, as high on the powder as I've ever seen her. "I'm taking my son!"

"Now Leona, you know his father gave him to us." I touch her arm, trying to calm her. She slaps at my hand.

LaRosa shouts at Leona, "You're not his mother!"

"I am his mother! I got the goddamn scar to prove it!" Leona begins to unbutton her skirt. "He was cut out of me, not you!" She says to LaRosa and points to the scar running low across her exposed belly. "See what I suffered for that goddamn baby?"

I don't see LaRosa take the poker from the fireplace, but Little Sister does. She's able to grab it before it hits Leona, who crouches under its swing, and then trips on her loose skirt and falls in a heap on the floor.

"Uh oh. What's Little Sister done now?" Peck Two calls from the top of the stairs. He's flanked by two brothers, swaddled in white towels. Little Sister hides the poker behind her back.

"Go take care of your sons," I say to LaRosa. Her eyes strike me like bullets, but she goes up the stairs.

I lift Leona and button her skirt around her. She wobbles like she's spinning. She heads for the door then calls back, "I'll sue. I'll get him back!"

Little Sister steps in front of Leona, waiting for a 'thank you' for saving her from the poker. But Leona has no appreciation. She only glares at Little Sister. So Little Sister gives her own broad smile and when Leona doesn't return it, Little Sister puts a finger on edge of Leona's upper lip and pushes up. "Can I please see the Lord Jesus now?"

Leona shoves Little Sister away like she had the plague. "All you people are idiots!" she says, the corners of her mouth drawn even further down as she marches out.

Upstairs, LaRosa sits on Peck Two's bed, while the smaller ones play on the floor. She kisses Peck Two, then each of the others, and goes down the hall to our new little girl who is calling for her.

Peck Two takes over. He descends into the middle of his brothers. "I'm the first with two mothers," he says, because he likes to be first. "But the second one loves me."

"She loves me, too!" the smallest one says.

Peck Two tousles his hair. "Yes, she does. But not the most."

We All Got To Pass by the Dragon

Lizzie

When we were ten, my twin, Peck, found a raccoon in the woods with an awful cut on its back leg and carried it to Pearl's. Feeling threatened, the animal in his arms bit him all the way home, on his hands and face. Pearl went straight for the First Aid box when she saw the wounds, but Peck wouldn't let her touch him until they doctored the raccoon's leg first. It hissed and twirled, but finally, Peck held him and Pearl bandaged the cut. I swear it I heard it hiss, "Thank you," melting my heart with its lovable, little face.

Pearl wanted it caged, but Peck said, "That will just make it mean, Pearl." So Pearl agreed to let it loose in the house, because she was enamored with it, too. For a while, it was playful and funny to watch. We all laughed at it, even Mama--the first time she'd laughed in a long time. But after its leg healed, it clawed its way up Pearl's skirt and Izear had to swat it with the broom to get it off. Soon, even Peck understood; the raccoon lived by only one set of rules – his own. With its razor sharp teeth and claws, it took over Pearl's house doing whatever it pleased, raking its human-like, five-toed paws over everything it could grab or pull apart. Pearl was continually going for the super glue.

"That thing's got us all fooled. It's keeping us as pets, instead of the other way around," Izear said, nursing numerous scratches on his forearm. "Either it goes, or I'm gonna kill it right here in the kitchen." So Peck wrapped the raccoon in a blanket to keep it from biting him, and tearfully took it back to its home in the woods where it belonged. It took weeks for Pearl to restore her shredded house, yet she did. "It's all repaired now," she said with a tired sigh. "And by the grace of God that little devil's gone, too."

My house--my life--is in shreds today. I no longer look in any mirror. I do not play bridge, or even speak to the beautiful women who wrongly admired me. I have thrown out every sign of Richard's sickness, and sold the bed I laid in with Anthony. But what good is it? There's no First Aid kit, or Super Glue, to repair what I did. Worst of all, I haven't told Anthony about the baby, a baby that ought to have been Richard's.

I try to separate myself from the place I called home, but all I can think of now *is* Highlow. I have to go back. And so like a thief hiding the spoils of her sin under the cover of night, I'm driving the blood red BMW home. I called Pearl to tell her I was coming. She asked, why? I said I'd tell her when I got there, but I'm barely out of Mobile when I realize I can't tell her what really happened. I don't think she has enough Super Glue for it. Of course, I will need some sort of explanation, some lie. I take the cut-off to Gulf Shores to work on that, in the grandiose condominium where Richard and I spent our honeymoon.

I keep my head down when I sign for a Gulf front room, not wanting to face the night clerk. She directs me to the fifth floor; shell-shaped pillows on a king-sized bed, gauzy drapery mimicking crystal green water, and double-paned windows, framing a fire-breathing dragon-like sunset. At home, Pearl quoted St. Cyril. "Beware of the dragon," she once said about Richard.

I stretch out on the king-sized bed and turn on the massage. The pulsing reminds me of his fingers and the expensive bottle of sun block he bought, using all of it on me. Richard liked manipulation, the slip-sliding feel of possession. Maybe he was born that way and couldn't help it. Maybe I could have changed him, then maybe he wouldn't have died.

Before I left Mobile, I telephoned Anthony to say I was leaving. Again, Anthony said, "I love you." He wanted to know if I love him. I gave no answer.

"I think you do love me." An empty pause and then, "Richard's death was an accident, Liz. You didn't create the storm. I'll call your cell tomorrow."

The next morning, a ruthless streak of sunlight wakes me. Beyond the paned window, the sand is sugar, the Gulf, opals. A patch of blue sky births an unblemished sun, so holy in appearance I turn away. I dress and take the elevator down, intentionally leaving my cell phone behind. I go over lies I might tell my family about why I'm coming home. On the beach, I realize how hard it will be to fool them.

"He won't bring out your best," Pearl had said.

Once, we built a castle on this same beach, Richard and I, with delicate turrets of dribbled water thinly mixed with sand. In my palm, the water looked pink and blue, the colors of dreams. I imagined we lived inside, until a wave exploded, and thousands of tiny, silver mirrors turned it back to common sand.

"Let's build another." But Richard walked away.

"Unreliable," Pearl said.

A small crab creeps out of a nearby hole. It peeps up with black dot eyes that judge me, then scuttles sideways across the whiteness, leaving a sketchy trail. Overhead, glides a V-shape of sea gulls, an arrow pointing north. A little girl emerges from behind a dune of sea oats. The beach-child's eyes are bright with marvel. She runs beneath the sailing birds, as if their magical wings are all she ever wanted, as if they might swoop down and carry her away to enchantment. A bikini-clad woman and a fat-bellied man clutching an over-sized Solo cup, follow. He hurls a hairy arm at the gulls. "Here come the shit-bombers!" He pretends to safeguard the woman by tossing a beach towel over her head.

She throws off the towel, "Quit it!" but warns the child, "Look out them birds don't dump on you, Shugah."

The child looks up, grabs the woman's hand, and the three of them break into a run down the beach, away from the fairy-tale.

"He's not the prince you think he is,"

A lone man, pale, bald, and heavy with middle-age, trudges in my direction. He's fair-skinned, like me, at risk for a burn. Already, the sun has blistered the crown of his head. He has a dog on a leash, one of those little ones with the big barks. The man yanks on the leash when the little dog barks at the waves, but the dog continues to bark, and the man continues to yank. Finally, the dog bites the man on his leg. The man doesn't appear angry that his pet turned on him. He gives the dog a forgiving pat, like he'll love him no matter what; and they continue down the beach.

"You'll spend your life forgiving him."

The woman, man, and child, come back up the beach. The child whines, "I wanna 'Co-cola,'" then cries that she's hot and tired and no one will carry her. Neither the man, nor the woman picks her up.

"Gotta get home on your own, Baby Doll," the woman says, wiping sweat off her face. "Hurry up. Looks like a storm."

Back in my room, the phone rings. I don't answer it. From the balcony, a dark cloud covers the sun. Bronzed bodies scramble, hide beneath weak-roofed pavilions, rocking in a storm to be wary of. Lightening smears the sky, thunder cracks wildly, same as the night Richard died.

Around noon, I leave Gulf Shores and take I-10 across the Florida Panhandle, still wondering how I'll explain why I've come home. At Pensacola, the bridge over Escambia Bay is under construction from a recent hurricane, so I inch along with a convoy of others on a two-lane county road, all the way around the bay to get to some useable interstate.

In the tiny town of Vigil, nearly out of gas, I leave the procession to fill up at a run-down gas station buttressed by a rusty, tin-roofed café. But when I try to get back in line, no one will give up space to let me in, so I back up the BMW and go inside the café for a cup of coffee, thinking a little time might produce a Good Samaritan on the road.

Inside, are three Formica-topped tables. The two in front are taken by men speaking Spanish. The third table is empty. It's in the back corner next to a closed door that likely leads to the kitchen. I take that one. There's a napkin dispenser and a clay pot holding a Christmas cactus with four pink buds, just forming.

An old, black waitress in a starched white uniform—she must weigh three hundred pounds—leaves the Hispanics and comes to hand me a one-page, plasticized menu. "Sweet tea, Hon?"

I want coffee, but not words, so I nod yes for the tea and take the menu, except I don't look at it. I look at the Cactus. Richard once gave me a cactus just like it. I thought it would require no care. Not so. It needed water, fertilization two or three times a week, and pruning. It was a delicate plant, requiring a watchful eye. It died during the first November we were married.

"The barbecue's real good; you want a barbecue sammich?" the waitress asks.

I shake my head, no, just as the blast of a radio comes behind me, smacking condemnation. *"Hey you ho, you bitchin' ho; why you try to kill me with yo stankin mojo?"*

The waitress twists toward the kitchen. "Cut that stuff off, Cecil!"

"Aw Grandmaw!" But the radio stops.

The waitress shakes her head in dismay. "Lord, Jesus," she whispers, reaching over me to poke her thumb into the soil of the cactus, as if checking for moisture. I catch the crisp smell of her starched white uniform.

"Honey, what ever happened to sweet Aretha?" she asks, like

she's known both the singer and me all our lives. "Can't nobody spell R-E-S-P-E-C-T, anymore? I love that boy, but I told him and told him; 'Cecil, that kinda music is a recipe for ruin!' He puts his hands over his ears whenever I say it, but he hears me. He ain't a bad boy, he just don't use his brains sometimes. You know how kids are nowadays."

She waits for me to respond. Instead, my eyes fill.

"What's wrong, baby?" The waitress takes a napkin from the dispenser and hands it to me. I can't even say, thank you. "Well, I'm gonna get that barbeque sammich. It'll make you feel better, and the pork's real fresh." As she leaves, she touches my shoulder like she cares. But if she really knew me, she wouldn't bother.

She returns with the tea, and the sandwich is huge, a pickle on top, chips piled round it. She smiles, watching me take a bite. "That's some good ole soul food, ain't it, Hon?"

I glance up and smile, only an attempt to return her kindness. She drops heavily into the opposite chair and reaches for my hand. Her eyes pin me, appear to see right through me. She reins me so close I can't pull back without being rude. The tender buds on the table quiver and the fork clinks against the plastic tea glass. "You need some comfort, doncha Shug? Well, I'm ready to listen."

But I can't handle her now! The image in my mind, when I found Richard dead, is breathing fire and scaring the hell out of me.

"Oh, go on; you know you need to. Like I told Cecil; I ain't gonna judge you." Then she laughs. "Takes somebody even bigger than me to do that."

"We go to the Father of Souls."

In the end, I reveal to the waitress what I meant to hide. I tell her about St. Cyril and the dragon, about Richard and Anthony. She can't have thought much of me afterwards. I have a little breakdown, and I can't eat the sandwich. She calls for Cecil to take it to the kitchen and wrap it up for me.

Then she grasps my hand. "Listen Shugah, we all got to pass by the dragon. That fire-breathing sucker's gonna be there, waiting with his jaws open, 'cause he's gotta be fed. Don't give him nothing else to eat. Go on home and tell 'em the truth."

Cecil comes back with the gold-foiled package and a thick paper napkin. He hands it to the waitress, who hands it to me. I take it to be nice; I'm not a bit hungry; talking about truth has taken my appetite.

Minutes later, back in the red BMW, I wait nearly twenty more minutes for a space in the traffic. A young girl with long brown hair finally lets me in, but she isn't a Good Samaritan; she's dropped her cell phone and has to brake a few seconds to reach for it; so I T-bone in front of her.

The sandwich, a bit of the sauce escaping, is captured in foil beside me, blinking like a yellow caution light on the sunlit seat. Fifty miles from Highlow, I'm hungry, and tear into it; consume every chunk of it, until I'm holding only the crushed gold wrapper as if it's part of the steering wheel.

I notice there's barbecue sauce, thick as blood, on my hands. I wipe it away with the napkin, stuff the trash into the litter bag on the floor of the BMW and take the next exit home. But I don't intend to tell anything close to the truth, as the waitress suggested. I'll lie, as I've come to do, when I'm trapped in the jaws of something I've done.

Buy Now, Pay Later

Hobart

Some time back, I politely told D.C., "No thank you, I plan to give up my powder route." D.C. wasn't happy about it, then, and he ain't happy, now.

We stand on the curve of Cat Alley and the afternoon sun shows every weathered line in his face when he invites me to pimp his powder, again. "It's the purest form of heroine, Hobart, my man. It's Fine China. One hit, they'll chase it forever."

But I tell him, "I got too much money, now, to be somebody else's patsy." Of course, I thank him for the offer.

D.C. says my thank you ain't enough. "You accepted an invitation to the party, you gotta stay and dance with the one that brung ya."

"There're new people you can dance with, D.C. I've already told you about the Cajun lawyer that moved here from Mobile. He's anxious to distribute."

D.C. is chin high to me, but feisty as a Pitt Bulldog. He looks up and pokes a finger into the old scar in my chest. "You oughta know how dangerous it is to quit on me. Remember what happened to that little twerp that tried to leave---the one from Chicago? It was you and me that connected him to the 'Buy Now, Pay Later' sign."

I chuckle in recalling it. "Fun times; but I've got an interest in other things, D.C. Plus, I'm getting to old for this trip."

He reaches up to yank my collar. "You was the first white man I let in my organ-i-zation, because you promised me Main Street. But you didn't deliver. I ain't gonna let you walk without some payback."

It's true, I did promise that. I didn't deliver because nobody in Highlow would let me in, except for Lila. So, D.C. gave me powder to give her, and then a deal on a car with a horn that played Dixie. And look what that cost me in the long run!

I shove D.C's hand away from my throat. "Highlow don't take to new obsessions; they got enough old fine china of their own."

"I don't want Highlow, anymore. I want something new. I want Mirage, *your* Mirage. I want it delivered on a silver platter, every damn powder-sniffin' honky that lives there!" D.C. makes a clicking sound with his tongue against his gold front tooth, "Ya hear me?" Then he twists on his heels and struts off, south on Rebel. He glances back once, before he marches on down to Dixie where old times are not forgotten.

But hell, I don't intend to play second fiddle to D.C. I like being first.

Some Things You're Hungry for Will Eat You Up Instead

Little Benedict

    LaRosa's always saying to me, "Little Benedict, don't talk about the past." Well, I know *some* people don't wanna talk about the past. Like LaRosa, they wanna talk about endings, and moving on. But once a person's lived a while, they're coated inside with the paint of the past. And sometimes all those coats get too heavy to carry around.

    Take Miss Pearl. One summer, years ago, I was waiting on the front porch steps for Peck and Lizzie to finish clearing the china from their supper table when Miss Pearl came out instead. I stood up as she tapped down the first few steps because Miss Pearl likes good manners. "Here, Little Benedict," she said, handing me her lamb's head cane and holding to the porch rail. "I'll sit beside you." So, I helped her down. We sat quietly for several minutes; Miss Pearl reaching over to pick a few yellowed blades off the red Bottle Brush bush stuck between the railing posts. That was just something to do, I could see she was bothered. Then she asked me, "How's your daddy, Little Benedict?"

    "Fine," I said. "My mama's fine, too. She went to the beauty parlor today, so they're both taking a nap."

    "I suppose your father pays you lots of attention?"

    "Yes ma'm. He pays me a nickel every time I take out the garbage." I said, and she smiled. I could feel one of her stories coming on. She'd already told me two or three others, but I don't think she imagined I'd remember them. It was like Miss

Pearl just wanted to get the coated stuff out of her old self and into somebody newer than she was.

"Fathers are important, but they can be disappointing."

"Yes ma'm; like Peck and Lizzie's father.

"No," she said with a little irritation. "They have Izear. He never disappoints. I'm talking about Lila's father, William Crawford."

The story went this way: One night, when Miss Lila was six years old, William Crawford took her to the Highlow Hotel because she cried and cried to go with him. The bartender said William Crawford sat her at the bar, ordered her a Shirley Temple then left her there to go play poker in the back game room. After Lila finished her Shirley Temple and ate all the cherries in the bottom; she tried to get to where her father was, but the game room door was locked. She knocked and knocked, but no one let her in. So--the bartender told Pearl--she sat down on the floor, by the door. He said she looked so sweet and pretty in her little pink pinafore and white patent shoes that he knocked on the door himself. But all he got was, "Go away!"

The bartender decided he ought to telephone Pearl to tell her Lila was alone at the Highlow Hotel, so he went into the kitchen where the phone was. When he got back, Lila was gone. Then Miss Pearl rushed in with her cousin The Judge. They banged on the game room door, too, hollering that Lila was missing. William Crawford finally opened it. He was winning, he said, and he was in the middle of a tedious hand so why didn't Pearl and The Judge just go look for Lila? So they did. They looked and looked, but couldn't find her.

The Judge called out the whole town to help and everyone came, except for the gamblers. Miss Pearl was real mad at William Crawford, but she said, at least he wasn't out hunting with a shot-gun again, and that gave her some solace.

Miss Pearl said she didn't know it at the time, but what

happened was this: When the bartender left to call Miss Pearl, Lila left the hotel to walk home, but it was dark and she took a wrong turn. She ended up at the Dixie Gravel Pit where D.C.'s car lot is today. Back then, it was just a big, wide dip in the earth, surrounded by wiregrass and filled with discarded parts of cars; old wheels like big, empty eyes, a chassis here and there, rims like fat ribs, steering wheels, and useless auto seats. She wandered around in there, going through at all that worthless stuff until just about dawn. Finally, she sat down on one of automobile seats, but the thing was so rotten it caved in and her arm got caught between the springs and she couldn't get it loose. And that was the way the bartender, who hadn't slept a wink from searching all night, found her; crying and trying to remove her bleeding arm from the rotting seat.

    The bartender pried Lila out by using a piece of rusty pipe he'd found, and took her to Miss Pearl who was so thankful she gave the bartender all William Crawford's winnings from the night before--two hundred and fifty dollars, taken from his coat pocket while he was lying exhausted on the bed. After that, Lila wouldn't go anywhere with her father, though she wanted to. She couldn't trust him. "Of course, it all left an empty hole in her heart," Miss Pearl said. "It changed her, made her fragile, and out of balance. Futile longing for what you don't have will do that."

    Then Peck and Lizzie had come out of the house onto the porch. And Miss Pearl got up. I handed back her cane, and she went inside. Lizzie put her ventriloquist hand on the back of my neck then. "What were you and Pearl talking about?"

    "Fathers."

    "My father?" she asked expectantly.

    "No, just everybody's, I guess."

    Then Peck said, "C'mon, Little Benedict. Let's go hunt!" Even then, he was searching the trees for that elusive bird.

    When I think about Peck's death all these years later, I know I learned one big lesson from it: Some things you're hungry for will eat *you* up instead. Having that thing you're chasing after ain't gonna make you happy. Wanting what you have, does that. Like Peck, Miss Lila wanted a father. The one she had craved gambling more than he did her. So, I think Pearl was right; it put her out of balance. That's the paint of a heavy past, and it explains a lot of things—except for one that's still bothering me.

On the night Miss Lila mistook me for Peck--after she'd shot Hobart the second time? That was when she told me who the twins' father was. Sure, what she said was crazy! I promised her not to tell, and I haven't, not even LaRosa. But now, I'm wondering; should I mention it to Lizzie when she gets back to Highlow?

Home is A Piece of Fine China

Lizzie

 A few miles outside Highlow, I'm almost home. River Road is just ahead. It leads to Memory Hill Cemetery. I take the turn, then get out and walk. The shadows of a setting sun define bright, bronzed spaces of bare ground that would have been thick with wiregrass in summer. On both sides of a straw-covered path lined with pine trees, there are graves and the stone shoulders of angels draped in straw. Every now and then, a slight wind from the south exposes the swell of a white marble wing, re-dressing it quickly in russet and brown. It's not quite cold enough for a coat, but I'm wearing one; a dark, blue cashmere I bought last year at The Holiday Shop in Mobile. As soon as I can, I plan to get rid of it. It has bothersome associations.

 The most recent grave in the Todd family plot is my brother, Peck's. He died too soon, only thirteen when we put him in there. Such a short time on earth! And I'll never get over his leaving it. In the silk-lined pocket of my cashmere coat is a fragment of porcelain with the hint of a painted wing. No bigger than a quarter, it is from the only piece of fine china Pearl was unable to repair because Peck and I hid it from her. After he died, I kept it beneath my pillow, touching it throughout the night. I took it to college, and kept it after my marriage. For years it was positioned in my jewelry box next to my wedding rings. (I did not keep the rings. I gave them to a nun from Catholic Social Services in Mobile who said she'd sell them to provide food for the poor. I kept the piece of china.)

"Body a' Christ," my twin had said, a six year-old playing the priest when he held up the small chip like a Eucharistic host, in line with his freckled nose. He'd looked so impressive--one of Pearl's green towels around his shoulders, and over his heart, a silver crucifix, a wedding gift to Pearl from William Crawford--so impressive, I forgot my response.

"Say Amen!" he commanded.

"Amen!" I said, snatching the piece of china to keep it hidden from Pearl who was tapping down the hall. She'd been searching for it for days, her fingers gripping the Super Glue tucked in her pocket. When she saw Peck, pretending to be a priest, she opened my hand to find the little piece of china. She looked at it for quite a while, then closed back my fingers and said, "The Eucharist is the closest you'll ever come to God on Earth. Remember that, Lizzie." And she left the room.

Peck's grave seems more kept than the others, no straw upon the wings of the little boy angel that marks it, no stray grasses or leaves on the slab of granite. Someone has cared for it. At once, a hand touches my shoulder, slipping across the strap of my leather purse that bulges with make-up and combs and money. "I heard you were coming home, Lizzie."

I turn to find Hobart waiting for reception; broad shouldered, blonde and handsome, perfect white teeth showing, a face that still says without words, 'I'll-do-nice-things-for-you-if-you-let-me-belong.'

"What happened to your fancy doctor-husband?".

I don't answer.

"You haven't been to Pearl's yet, have you?"

I don't answer that either.

He wipes his thumbs over his copper belt buckle, the initials so tarnished they don't look like his. "Well, I'd know if you had," he says in the pompous tone I remember. He bends to brush some fresh-fallen straw off the slab with my brother's name. It's close to sacrilege.

"Don't touch his grave!"

A moment of pain crosses his face, then he looks over my shoulder to the car I came in. "Expensive car. You musta done alright to have a car like that."

"I did nothing for it. In fact, I'm going to sell it."

"How much?"

"You're the one who knows about cars. What do *you* think it's worth?" A slight breeze around us releases a hint of his cologne; Curve, I think. The same as Richard wore.

"Don't ever ask a perspective buyer what the thing's worth. It ain't how you play the game."

"I don't want to play games with you."

"Oh, get off your high horse, Lizzie. I know what happened to your uppity husband. You may as well 'fess up."

My fist tightens around the remnant of china in my pocket, and I turn toward the BMW.

He catches the sleeve of my coat, but I wrest it away and hurry to the car. The farther away I get, the higher he raises his voice. "You've always had it wrong. Nobody made you better than me, Alizarin Crimson Todd. You come back here. I know everything about you!"

I turn the key in the ignition and press the accelerator to the floor, framing Hobart McSwain in the rear-view mirror. I picture his primped, blonde head with a rope around his limp neck as he hangs from a tree for what happened those years ago. I hear him plead for mercy. But it's only a mirage. Hobart is stiff-necked in denial.

On the highway, I click on the radio. Pearl's favorite homeboys sing out: *"My home's in Alabama, no matter where I lay my head. My home's in Alabama, Southern born and Southern bred."* Nearing Main Street, the radio skips to static like Pearl's old cabinet radio once did. She first reached for the super glue, then she saw the problem. The light inside had flickered to nothing, so she pried the thing open, tightened the bulb, and plugged it back up. No static, at all. I wish I were like Pearl. I wish I could put my life back into place, and find the light I once had inside me. But the static continues, a worrisome noise with bothersome associations; splintering, shattering like fallen fine china.

In the Arms of Dixie

Hobart

I went to the cemetery because I knew Lizzie would stop there. I wanted to be the first Highlow face she saw, wanted her to see that I'm the one who tends Peck's grave because I cared about him and never intended his death. Hell, she might as well have been blind for all the consideration she gave me. Except for the color of her hair, she looks exactly like her mother, even acts like that woman who hates me. Lila's lost to me, and Peck is gone, but something inside me commands: *Don't lose Lizzie!* A command I don't yet understand, but it sticks to my insides like Pearl's Super Glue.

I've developed some advantageous associations in the real estate business, like that Cajun lawyer from Mobile. He wanted to distribute for D.C. so I sold him a house in Mirage. That Cajun's got a real big mouth. The day we signed the contract, I asked if he knew Lizzie and her doctor husband. He said he did. In fact, he used to play tennis at the Mobile Country Club with the tennis pro who told him all about Dr. Richard Bolding and how he died from Aids. Valuable information. I turn on the truck's radio, because things are looking up.

"I'm in the heart of Dixie, Dixie's in the heart of me."

I had to look up to see out, back in Detroit. A boy stuck in a box learns fast that freedom comes from above. The first time I looked up and saw the white cloth wings of Sister Perpetua was the first time I saw I had a chance. She stroked my face with hands as pure as fine china. "Hello, little fellow!" she said lifting me, wrapping her arms around me. I heard my first heart beat in the breast of a woman with wings. "You may not know it, little fellow, but Jesus loves you. Oh yes, he does," she sang. Then she flew me up, up, and away, to the orphanage where I never wanted to be out of her sight.

But Jesus's love didn't keep me from walking around with my arms raised above my head. The winged-woman said my raised arms were a product of self-preservation, having been in that Detroit box for so long. She said I was reaching up for hope. Then just when I was able to lower my arms enough to wrap them around her waist, she gave me away--to loving parents she said-- and I suppose they were. So, I came South, where I made my fortune in the heart of Dixie, and where I now live high on Main Street and reach for anything I want. *Don't lose Lizzie!* Well, maybe I'll reach for her. She's the picture of her mother. Maybe she'll love me like Lila never did. A mirage? We'll see.

The Mirror Throws Back An Image of Disorder

Lizzie

The streetlights on Main Street flick on as if I'm expected. Beneath umbrellas of live oaks, fragile shadows move across the pavement, finger the walkway to Pearl's house. She taps down the steps, followed by Izear. I hug them both.

"Oh, I've missed you, Lizzie," Pearl says. "You look good, even a little stout."

"Richard fed me well." I don't know why I said that. At once, I regret it. In Pearl's grey eyes there is a familiar speck that catches family, that forces responsibility.

"But did you feed *him*, Lizzie?" she asks. "If you had, he might not have died on you so quick."

"He didn't die of starvation, Pearl. He died of Aids."

"Oh, I think I've heard of that. Haven't we heard of that, Izear?"

"Yes 'um. We heard of that."

"I reckon people have to die for some reason," Pearl says. "Nobody dies for nothing."

"No'm, not for nothing. Always some reason."

Pearl's house appears smaller, squeezed between the Spratling's brightly painted childcare center on the right and Hobart's tacky reconstruction on the left. Pearl glances toward Hobart's. "He turned his mama's house into some kind of business."

"Yes, real estate. He did that before I moved to Mobile."

"Well, Hobart's gone now," she says. "Gone to Florida."

"No, he isn't."

"He is, too. He's gone to Florida. I saw him leave!"

"Oh? To Florida?" I see no sense in upsetting her; not yet.

"He put his mama in a nursing home and then he tore up her house."

"Yes, Mrs. McSwain lost her mind," I say.

"No!" Pearl taps her cane, one hard tap on the walkway. "Hobart *said* she lost her mind, but it wasn't true. He put her in the nursing home, the first nursing home in Highlow."

"Hobart likes to be first."

"Yes, he does," Pearl says, and Izear gives a grunt of disgust. Oddly, Pearl seems proud of her neighbor's alien son. "Hobart built the first real-estate business in Highlow. He's trying to fix himself, you know."

She takes my hand, Izear takes her elbow, and we go up the steps to the porch where there is a clearer view of the sign in front of Little Benedict's house. *'God's World, Where Every Child Is Accepted,*' it says, in dancing red, yellow, and blue colors.

Pearl lifts a hand, points at the house. "Little Benedict and his wife run that. LaRosa's from here, and Little Benedict's the only Spratling left, if you don't count the sister. Third generation."

I give a nod of affirmation.

"You'll have to visit Little Benedict," Pearl says as if she'd never taught me manners.

"I will in a day or two. How is he?"

"Fine. He has a nice family, all of them healthy." Again, the catching grey speck in her eyes. "Wasn't there something unhealthy about that boy you took up with; that Richard. What was his last name?"

"I didn't take up with him. I married him, Pearl. Anyway, his last name was Bolding. That's my last name too, now."

"No, it ain't," Izear says quickly. "He's dead. You're a Todd, again." And Pearl smiles.

The noise of barking dogs comes from Hobart's. A car door slams then a light flashes from the back corner of the McSwain house. Pearl leans on her lamb's head cane, craning her neck toward the light, nearly losing her balance. "Is that boy back from Florida so soon?"

Izear steadies her. "You gonna fall off this porch. Quit worrying 'bout Hobart!" He pushes on the brass handle of the front door and we go inside, closing out the noise of the barking dogs and the artificial flicker of Hobart's light.

Pearl taps across the tiled foyer like a miniature queen. "Izear's making us his oyster stew for supper, aren't you, Izear?"

"Yes'um. Better go start it, too." He heads for the kitchen, then turns back to me. "Sorry about the doctor, but me and Miss Pearl decided a long time ago, we wouldn't cotton up to him noway."

Pearl takes in a breath of surprise. "Izear, we have never talked ill about the dead."

"Yes'um." He gives Pearl a calculated smile. "I reckon I forgot what we *ain't* done." And the door to the kitchen swings shut behind him.

"Don't pay him any attention, Lizzie. We've hardly said anything about your doctor. After all, we didn't know him any better than you did when you married him."

I can't respond. There's nothing truer than what she just said.

In the living room, Pearl sits on the Victorian sofa next to the marble fireplace filled with old ashes, her round white hair-do, glowing in the tangerine light of the tiffany lamp like a warm halo around her face. Southern Living is inborn here, no need for a magazine.

"How's Mama?" I ask.

"She started painting a little girl when I told her you were coming." Pearl balances the lamb's head cane against the satin cording of a pink damask cushion and pats the padding, a signal for me to sit beside her.

Then out of the blue, she returns to the subject of Richard. "Now, tell me about that boy you married," she says as if she'd never met him, as if she hadn't planned the wedding. She was proud, at first, of my choice in a husband, until she determined he was a thief. "Lizzie?" There's impatience in Pearl's voice.

"It doesn't matter, Pearl; he's dead."

"Well, I'm sorry for his family. Who were they?" A wiry line appears between her brows, an attempt to trap recollection.

"He was related to that part of the Pendleton's family that moved to Atlanta. Richard was from Georgia, remember?"

Her face brightens in clarity. "Oh yes. Poor Richard, poor enough to steal my money! Where do you suppose poor, dead Richard is now?" Her eyes move to the picture of the Sacred Heart where the knotted frond of a dried palm sticks out from behind the frame, and then back to me. "Well, God *is* merciful. Heaven is filled with reformed sinners: liars, thieves, even murderers."

Murderers? Air from the attic fan rustles the hair-like strings that have peeled away from the palm, making a slight noise as they brush against the picture of Jesus's heart. Peck and I used to study that picture, wondering what its uplifted eyes could see. We used to touch our hearts like Jesus did, pretending they were pierced with thorns. And like Jesus, we looked up, thinking we might see heaven. But all we saw was the high ceiling of Pearl's parlor.

"You know I've forgiven Hobart," Pearl says.

"Well, I can't."

"You mean you won't."

I rise from the sofa. "I think I'll look around a little."

"You asked about your mother. She's painting again."

"Is she better?"

"Better than who?"

"You wrote she was confused. Will she know who I am?"

"God knows who you are, Lizzie," she says with

condescension. "That's all that matters." Then she calls Izear from the kitchen to bring in my things.

I walk through rooms, the same as the day they were completed, even the same furniture, except for the television in the corner of the music room. In the 1960's, Pearl finally gave in and bought it with some of William Crawford's insurance money. "William Crawford always wanted a television," she says when she sees me looking. "And you know I adored the man."

I take the stairs to the second floor and open the door to my room. Pearl calls up, "You'll see your bedroom hasn't changed. It's just as you left it."

The window is open and a breeze billows the white curtain as if there is someone waiting behind it. On the fancy chintz bedspread are purple and pink flowers like those a girl might pick. The mahogany dresser with its rose-carved pulls, the standing mirror with a Queen Anne pedestal, the intricately sewn needle-point of a peacock on the stool at the end of the bed; all appear the same. But Pearl is wrong. The room has changed. The paint on the window frame is peeling; I can see its scales from here. There is a tear along the ruffle of the pink and purple chintz spread and it hangs unevenly to the floor. The dresser is covered by a film of age, the peacock is unraveling, and the mirror throws back the image of disorder. Pearl has grown accustomed to the room, accustomed to her idea of me. She doesn't see what either has become.

Down the hall is Mama's room. She sits at her table, below four, white shelves of porcelain plates angled against rose-colored walls. From the doorway, she looks to be the center of a multi-colored tapestry of staring faces; children, teenagers, young adults, all with copper-red hair and green-eyes. She is brushing shape into the eyes of a girl, about thirteen. "You are good," the eyes say to any heart. I feel uncomfortable in their view.

Mama looks up. Her mad, dark hair is wild around her face. I bend to kiss her forehead. She lays a stained hand on my cheek.

"You've been gone so long, Lizzie. Your brother and I have missed you." She turns back to the table to dip her brush in the color of copper.

I need a Check

Hobart

The rustle in the top of the tall, thin pine through the pane of my window is only the wind, but the breath on my back is Leona's. I know it without turning.

"That damn freak-of-a-baby-machine next door tried to kill me with a poker!" she shouts.

"LaRosa's nobody to tangle with."

"I need a check, Hobart, or I'll kill her when I take back my boy."

"No check, Leona; and I ain't worried. LaRosa can take care of herself."

"Then just give me some powder I can sell."

"You've got me mixed up with your present provider. I don't have any."

"You've got some! You used to have plenty."

"I'm out of distributing. I haven't used since--."

"Hell, don't start on that again! Maybe I could have stayed here if you hadn't turned droopy--always moping over how you killed that kid."

"I didn't kill him. It was an accident!"

"Yeah, right. Tell that to The Judge. It was manslaughter at the very least; you flying high as eagle with angel dust on its wings. I can testify to that."

I step toward her, my hand raised. She backs up, her chin stuck forward defiantly; a replay as I recall. Then somewhere outside the window I hear a ragged suck of breath; maybe another burst of wind, but it causes me to lower my hand to keep from striking Leona.

Leona recoils. "The powder's inside one of those stuffed birds, isn't it?" She heads for my trophy room in the back of the house. I go after her. She flings open the door. The largest in the line of the mounted, golden-eyed hawks seems to blink when she flips on the light.

"Stay out of there!" I yank her back into the hall.

"Write me a check."

"Get out, Leona."

"Write me a check, or I'll tell it all. I'll tell how you were sniffing china the night that boy was killed, how you lost control of the car and ran it into the woods then blamed it all on a goddamned bird. I'll bring it all up, again, when I sue to get my boy back. And I'll get him, Hobart. I will! Even The Judge says I have a legal chance."

So that was why she was at the Judge's office!

My palm stings as Leona leaves with my check in one hand and the other covering the mark I made on her face. But she'll be back. Leona's the kind that keeps a checklist for life.

I've held the night of Peck's death inside me for years; a scab on my heart that won't heal. Now Leona's picked it to running. She was right; I had used the china. It was my birthday, after all. I was young. Nobody let me belong. Those are my excuses. Excuses for the death of a boy I loved. But it was the Osprey that killed Peck. It was! On the night he died, I shot the hawk that murdered the boy. Didn't matter though; it came back. The bird had a daddy. Hell, it's got more than one! It goes way back; a real family tree. Like a damn legion.

I put on my camouflage jacket and get my rifle. "C'mon Pharoah. We're going hunting." Outside the window, the ragged breath sounds a second time, but when I look, no one is there.

What Richard Kept From Me

Lizzie

It must have been a dream, the sound of gunfire in the distance; or an early hunter making use of the dawn. Now, the sunlight expanding across the tattered bedspread says I ought to get up. In my suitcase are a few outfits, a robe, and toiletries. The suitcase is initialed to prove it's mine, but all else I left behind, except for the computer Richard bought for himself. Somewhere inside it is a diary of all he kept from me. I've been afraid to look at his words, certain they would not be kind. Today, I mean to read them.

Hobart's raucous voice assaults the open window, hollering at his dog. It yelps like it's been kicked. I put on the robe and start downstairs. Through the side window beside the staircase, I see Hobart coming across the yard. He is dressed in green camouflage and appears haggard, as if he's been up all night.

In the turquoise kitchen, Pearl has her back toward me. She is standing in the opened screen door, asking Hobart about Florida.

"I didn't like Florida," he says. "Too much damn sand and too many Yankees that don't belong." He looks behind her, into the kitchen. "Is Lila still asleep?"

"I wouldn't let you in if she wasn't."

Hobart appears relieved and Pearl moves aside for him to enter. I don't want to see him, so I take a step backward into the hall, but Pearl notices me. "Lizzie, get some coffee and come sit. Hobart's here."

"I'm not dressed yet."

"You're dressed enough to sit at the kitchen table," Pearl says.

Hobart acts like he hasn't seen me in years. "How's life been treating you, Lizzie?"

Pearl wipes a damp rag across her white lacquered table. "Hobart said he was surprised you were back." I'd like to tell her that he's lying; it was just yesterday I saw him at Peck's grave, but then Hobart pushes back in his chair. The legs scrape across the floor, making unwanted streaks on the linoleum.

Pearl sighs as if she can expect no better from him. "I thought you were trying to fix yourself. If you'd think before you do, boy, you might not make such a mess of things."

Hobart spits on a napkin and bends to the floor. "Sorry Miss Pearl. It'll wipe up."

"Izear," Pearl calls. "Bring a mop."

Izear lumbers through the swinging kitchen door with the mop, straight for Hobart, flopping it down on top of Hobart's fingers rubbing the floor.

"I can get it!" Hobart grits his straight, white teeth.

Izear shoves the mop with a one hard bump up against Hobart's tooled leather cowboy boot then flings it back over his shoulder. "I done got it!" Hobart wipes his eyes from the spray of mop-water. Izear grins, then goes back to whatever he was called away from.

Pearl puts two cups on the white lacquered table and taps to the stove for the coffee pot. Hobart settles in his chair. "Little lady looks good, huh Miss Pearl?"

Pearl pours. "I told her so, even a little stout."

Hobart laughs. "She needed a little more flesh."

"Better to be stout than thin," Pearls says, replacing the coffee pot on the stove. "Some girls I've seen look like they'd blow away if a big wind came up." She gives me a look of pride and sits beside Hobart.

"Yes ma'm, I like flesh on ladies and copper hair, too."

"Of course a person gets whatever the Lord decides to give, flesh or bone, copper hair or no," Pearl advises.

Hobart gives me a long look of appraisal. "Well, he gave Lizzie a little more than most."

I've had enough. "Sweet Jesus! You talk like I was covered in Saran wrap with a price tag from the Piggly Wiggly."

"Oh, you know we love you, Shugah." Pearl pats my hand.

"We sure do," Hobart rapidly agrees.

Pearl shifts the conversation. "Lizzie's brought a computer, but we don't know where to put it."

"I had the first computer in Highlow. I put it in my office."

"We don't have an office, Hobart," Pearl retorts.

"I got two or three computers. It takes two to run my real estate business. People keep me busy all the time buying and selling. I've got--."

"It's not my computer; it was Richard's," I say, to shut him up.

"Well, it's yours now!" Pearl snaps. She slaps her small hand on the white lacquer. "When a man dies, he leaves you everything that was his; good or bad, like it or not."

"I plan to leave my next wife every good thing I have." Hobart takes a slurp of coffee.

Next wife? I don't remember Pearl telling me that Hobart had married a first time.

"And who is your next wife?" Pearl asks.

"Oh, you'll know her," Hobart smiles at Pearl. "But she hasn't said 'yes,' yet.

"Well, I do know everybody in Highlow," Pearl says to me, as if I'm the visitor in her house and Hobart, the relative.

"Miss Pearl! Miss Pearl!" Izear's voice gets louder as it nears the kitchen. "There's a big old dog in the parlor!" Izear pushes through the swinging door. "It run right in when I opened the door with its big old tongue just slinging spit!" The swinging door swings back and hits Izear in the shoulder. Izear grunts and grabs his arm, aiming a finger at Hobart. "It's his dog, and now, it done hurt my shoulder!"

"Hobart," Pearl warns, "I will not have Izear hurt!"

"Pharoah!" Hobart yells.

Izear flattens himself against the door as Hobart's dog plunges by him into the kitchen, wagging its tail and leaping up to lick Hobart's face. He slaps the dog on its nose and it cowers to the floor, drooling saliva.

"You don't have to be afraid of Pharoah, Miss Pearl; he's a tame dog," Hobart says. "First Golden Retriever in Highlow, you know."

"The first shall be last," Pearl quotes to Hobart.

He grins back at her. "Not in my lifetime."

Then Mama calls down. "What in the world is going on down there?"

"Uh oh. I'll be seeing you, lady girl," Hobart says to me, a hand to his chest as if remembering the old bullet wound. He yanks his dog by its collar to leave. "We'll talk later about me buying your car."

"Why are you buying Lizzie's car?" Pearl asks.

Before he can answer, Mama hollers down, again, "Izear, do not let Hobart McSwain in this house. You know I can't stand the man!" Then Hobart is gone and Pearl has forgotten her question.

Secrets Boomerang Back

Hobart

In the afternoon, I see Lizzie in the yard. So pretty, she could almost be Lila if she had dark hair. I go directly over to talk about the car.

"I don't want much for it, Hobart," Lizzie says. "I just want to get rid of it."

I walk around it, running my hand over the hood, over Lizzie's clear reflection in the blood red paint. "I'll take it to D.C. He'll probably have it sold in a week, nice car like this."

"Fine," she says coldly, and turns to go back into Pearl's house as if she can't wait to get away. I don't want her to go. I want to change her opinion of me.

"Aw come on, lady girl. Can't we be friends?" It is the wrong thing to say. She gives me a frigid glare and I know what she's thinking about. "I'm sorry. Really, it wasn't my fault."

"It *was* your fault. You took him away from me. You put hunting in his head until he chased after that wild bird every chance he got. Then you drove him to his death!"

"I didn't put nothing in his head. Peck chased what he wanted to chase, I never made him do it. He chose it himself, like you chose to leave Highlow."

"He was only a boy. You preyed on his dream and used it to get what you wanted."

"It's the way of the world, lady girl. It ain't like you never used somebody as a ticket to get where you wanted to go, somebody like Dr. Richard Bolding."

"I did not use him!"

I start to say I know the truth about that, but she's in the house before I can. Some people have too much pride to admit their mistakes. They don't realize that most secrets boomerang back to slap them right in the face.

No Daddy

Lizzie

Pearl is still concerned about the computer, that it seems out-of-place on the small table in the corner of the music room. "Izear, put the screen there," Pearl says, "on the desk, by the television."

Izear picks up the monitor and sets it on the television, next to the Pac Man and Donkey Kong games, their covers peeling now.

"I'll bet you still don't know how to play Donkey Kong, do you, Izear?" I tease.

"I'll bet you still don't know how to make this thing work either," he says giving the computer a slight kick.

"Don't worry, we'll ask Hobart," Pearl says. "He has two or three computers."

"No, we won't. I'll figure it out, Pearl." She looks at me, irritated.

"What about this part?" Izear asks.

"The tower? It will have to go underneath the desk so it can talk through the monitor."

"Uh oh," Izear says. "Ain't you heard about the babbling tower? Is this a evil thing?"

"It's just a thing," I tell him, but Izear thinks in clear-cut terms. A thing is high or low, good or evil; there is no in-between.

The monitor sits in place on Pearl's antique Queen Anne desk, looking freakish between the 1903 Chickering quarter grand, and the Hildebrandt pump organ that Pearl had been given by her loving father, a man whose face she never had to wonder about.

"Be careful, Izear, it may be too heavy," Pearl says.

"Evil stuff's always heavy!" He lifts the babbling tower and shoves it under the desk.

"Not too heavy for you, Izear," Pearl smiles and pats him on his arm. "A lot of men couldn't move it at all."

Izear grins back at her. "You're a good little thing, Miss Pearl." He whips a white rag from his back pocket and swishes it over the monitor screen to get rid of the dust. "What are we gonna do with it now?"

"I'm going to use it. It belonged to Richard."

"Richard who?"

"The man I married, Pearl."

"Oh, the doctor? Well, you'll just have to forget him, Lizzie." She taps out of the music room, her voice tingling down the hall, into the kitchen. "I have learned to forget what I don't need to remember. Some days, I even forget William Crawford."

Izear shakes his head, "No, she don't."

"Well, it would be nice to forget what you don't want to remember," I say.

"That ain't easy to do." Izear's eyes are on me, stomach level. "And it ain't gonna be easy for a baby with its daddy gone. Miss Pearl and me done been through that once."

There is no use denying the truth to Izear. "Please don't mention the baby to Pearl. It won't be born for several months. That's a long time."

"Umph! Only young people think time is long."

"But you won't say anything, will you? You'll help me?"

"You belong here, dontcha?" he says as if I'm an imbecile, then he leaves the room.

On the blank screen of the monitor is some dust that Izear didn't notice. I run a finger through it, wondering if it's dust from our house in Mobile. All at once, I feel dizzy. I hear a long whining hum, and then darkness. When I come to consciousness, I am in my room and Mama is there, holding my hand. Beside her are Pearl and Izear. He has a sheepish expression on his face. On the other side of the bed is Dr Lazarus Sharbel, Pearl's old friend, all of ninety and apparently a bit senile because he thinks nothing of making a house call.

"You should have told us about the baby, Lizzie," Pearl says in an admonishing voice that quickly changes to joyful. "Oh, it's been so long since we've had new life in this house."

"Out of the way, Pearl," Dr. Sharbel fans her back with his hand. "Let's have a look at what little Miss Lila's got for us."

"This is Lizzie, not Lila," Pearl corrects him firmly.

Dr. Sharbel ignores her, presses here and there, and then sticks a stethoscope on my stomach. His eyes light up like a blue bulb on a Christmas tree. "Here it is," he says. "Your baby's heart."

"We know it has a heart, Lazi," Pearl says, impatiently. "But what else will it have?"

I think she's concerned the baby will have Aids, but Dr. Sharbel seems to have no clue about what she means.

"Now, now, Pearl." Dr. Sharbel pats her shoulder. "Of course, it will have an artist's talent. Isn't the father an artist, too?"

"Oh, go home, Lazarus Sharbel!" Pearl says, a phrase she uses when she realizes someone has gone in the wrong direction. "The baby's father is a doctor."

He gives her an impish little-boy look, which she returns with a smile that re-attaches them immediately. "Come on down to the kitchen. We'll have our coffee, Lazi-boy."

Dr. Sharbel touches the pulse point on my wrist; a gesture, not a medical procedure. "You'll be fine--uh, uh--Lizzie," he pronounces proudly. "Pearl and I will take care of you and the baby." Their giddy-sounding voices tumble from the stairs.

"New life, Lazi. Isn't it wonderful?"

"Yes, Pearl. My God, yes!"

Saved by a Baby

Hobart

I was the first one to hold Peck Two after he was born. Leona didn't want to. "No, Hobart," she said, and tuned away, but when I looked down at that little thing in my arms, I had two thoughts: Sister Perpetua, the bird woman from Detroit, and the baby Jesus.

The bird woman used to lull me to sleep with a song about how baby Jesus was born in a stable, but he never cried about it. He just grew up the best he could, made a few friends, and a lot of enemies who finally killed him. I used to cry every night at the orphanage because I knew if I did, the bird woman would come, wrap her wings around me, and sing to me. She said when I grew up I oughta try to be like Jesus, because one day I might have a baby of my own and I'd want him to think of me as somebody special.

The first time I held my son was also the first time I thought about giving up my powder route. I even told D.C. I'd had enough of Dixie's sweet stuff; I was turning my life around. D.C. put a finger in his ear like he was clearing it out and asked if he'd heard me right. When I said he certainly had heard me right, he asked why? And when I told him it was because I wanted to be something special, D.C. burst out laughing. "Jesus! You got saved by the Lord?"

"Hell no," I said. "Got saved by a baby."

It didn't last though. Leona saw to that. Soon as we came

home from the hospital, she called D.C. behind my back and had one of his elves bring some more stuff. When I caught her feeding the baby and sniffing at the same time, I hid her sugar in my first, stuffed bird. She tore the house apart before she found it. After that, she forgot we even had a baby. When the boy finally ran away to God's World, and the Judge told LaRosa she could keep him, it was weeks before Leona realized he was gone. Looking back, I'd say maybe I didn't miss him much either. But lately I've been hearing the bird woman's voice, again, and feel the need to visit Peck Two. Besides, I want Lizzie to meet the kid, see that he really likes me, then maybe she'll like me, too.

Truly, Hobart's Child

Lizzie

LaRosa Jackson Spratling stands on the other side of the picket fence separating Pearl's backyard from the one she inherited by marriage. "We'll take care of your baby when it's born, Lizzie," she says. "I mean, if you need to go to work." LaRosa is a heavy, thick-lipped woman with dark, stringy hair.

I shade my eyes from the afternoon sun "Thank you, LaRosa, but I don't plan to go to work."

"Some folks don't have to, I reckon. I myself always need the money."

"Do you? The Spratlings were well off, I thought."

"Everybody thought so," she laughs heartily. "Problem is, it was *only* thought. I catch a whiff of baby lotion and there is a sweat stain on her blouse as she raises her solid arm to push back a strand of hair.

"How much longer you got?" she asks.

"About two months."

"Oh, a Christmas baby! Just in time for Pearl's open-house."

"She hasn't said anything to me about having her open-house."

"Well, she told *me* she was," LaRosa says, proudly. "Soon as she heard you were coming home, she said she was gonna take out all the fine china and have a party."

The back screen door of the Spratling house opens abruptly and a tall, gangly, brown-skinned girl steps out and yells to LaRosa, "There's a mess fell outta Angie's britches, and Mama said to tell you!"

"Be there in a minute." LaRosa turns to the girl, then back to me. "That's Little Sister. She still calls Little Benedict, 'Mama.'"

Never having seen Little Sister, I'm thoroughly surprised. "You mean she's Miss Billie Nana's idiot baby? The one she put away?"

LaRosa bristles. "Little Sister ain't never been an idiot. She's just different."

"Of course. I'm sorry." I smile at Little Sister and she returns a broad grin, sunlight on her maple-colored face as she starts toward me.

"Go on back inside, Little Sister. I'm coming." LaRosa watches the girl go into the house, then says to me. "I'd best go. Little Benedict don't like changing diapers much."

"I'm not surprised! Tell Little Benedict I'll be over to see him, soon."

LaRosa waves to me from the back door of the Spratling house. "Come over anytime."

I like LaRosa's genuineness. It must be why Little Benedict loves her so much. Unlike Miss Billie Nana, the garbage collector's daughter doesn't pretend to be anybody except herself.

Entering the kitchen, Pearl catches my arm. She must have seen me talking to LaRosa. "Did she tell you what Hobart did? I meant to tell you myself, but it slipped my mind."

"I'm not sure what you mean, Pearl." The baby inside me gives its first sudden kick.

"I mean about Peck."

I touch her arm. "Pearl, I was here when he died, remember?"

"For God's sake, I know you were here, then. I'm talking about after you ran off with what's-his-name. Remember Hobart's cousin, Leona from Crisscross? Well, she wasn't really his cousin, you know. And after Mrs. McSwain died, Hobart married her."

"He married Leona?"

"Yes, and they had a baby boy. They named him, Peck Two."

"What?"

"Then out of the blue, Hobart brought that baby over here. He wanted to give him to Lila, to make up for our Peck."

"My God, what did Mama do?"

"For heaven sake, Lizzie, you know she can't stand the man. She still doesn't know about Hobart's child."

"You never told her?"

"No!" Pearl taps her cane emphatically. "And don't you tell her either. The boy's with Little Benedict and LaRosa now, and I thank God your mama can't open her own window to hear LaRosa call his name."

When Pearl leaves the kitchen, I go next door. The back screen door to the Spratling's hangs a little off-balance. I open it a bit. "LaRosa?" From inside comes the smell of something like vegetable soup then the voices of children laughing. A curly blonde head pops from the corner wall of a small alcove. A younger face peeks out from beneath a table where several children are sitting. "Mama!" the child under the table cries. "Bruno's chasing me!"

Then LaRosa barrels in. "Ya'll kids get back up there and eat. Now! You ain't hurt, Angie; get out from under there and sit down. Bruno do not chase your sister. Frankie, use your spoon, not your fingers." Then she turns to me, smiling as if I'm expected. "Ain't they a precious mess?"

"I don't mean to interrupt. I just wanted to say hello to Little Benedict."

"Sure. Come on back to the den."

Little Benedict, pale skin shining through his thinning orange hair, is sitting at a table, playing checkers with Little Sister. He appears genuinely glad to see me. "Look how Little Sister's grown," he says right off.

"She sure has." I turn to the so-called 'idiot child' who appears as normal as anyone here. "How have you been, Little

Sister?" And I give her my biggest smile

At once, she comes up to me. Breast to breast, she plants a kiss on my cheek. "I've been doing fine, Lord Jesus. I'm doing some work for you."

LaRosa notices my bafflement. "Little Sister sees the Lord Jesus in everybody,"

"And she likes to work for the Lord," Little Benedict says, getting up from the table to hug me. "Pearl told us you were expecting. I'm sorry about Richard, but at least you'll have the baby to remember him by."

I take a step backward. I don't want to think about Richard, or the baby that isn't his. Hurriedly, I ask what I came to ask. "Do you have Hobart's child?"

LaRosa's enraged response almost frightens me. "He gave him to us!"

"Pearl told me that Hobart gave him to you," I say cautiously, "and that he was named after my brother." I look toward the kitchen where I came in. "Is he in there with the other children?"

LaRosa grips my arm. "You can't have him!" Little Sister steps up, too. Her smile is gone.

"Of course not. I just want to see him."

LaRosa studies my face, her lips pressed together. "Check on the children, honey," she tells Little Sister.

"But don't you need me?"

"Yes, angel. In the kitchen." Little Sister hesitates a moment, then leaves.

LaRosa takes a breath and sits in a chair at the game table. "We love Peck Two, Lizzie. He may not mean much to those that birthed him, but me and Little Benedict love him to death."

"We do love him," Little Benedict says. "But you need to meet him." He goes to the door, and calls down the hall. "Peck Two, someone wants to meet you!"

"Does Hobart have anything to do with his son?" I ask LaRosa.

"He comes over every now and then, but a kid ain't a puppy dog you can birth one day and give away the next. Far as I'm concerned, Peck Two's ours now. Nobody else's."

A copper-haired boy bolts into the room. "Who wants to meet me?"

I'm caught by his green, almond-shaped eyes. "I do."

"Who are you?"

"I'm Lizzie. I used to live next door."

"You're going to have a baby," he grins, a one-sided smile with perfect white teeth.

"Yes, I am. Would you like to play with my baby after it's born?"

"No thanks. I got plenty 'round here to play with." He turns to LaRosa, "Can I go?" LaRosa nods, yes.

On his way to the kitchen, Peck Two yells to the others. "Listen to this! I'm the first kid here that anybody ever wanted to meet!" Truly, he is Hobart's child.

What Has Little Sister Seen?

Little Benedict

During Lizzie's visit, I thought about the secret her mama told me, that old secret, whispered in my ear many years ago. She never said, *Keep this to yourself, Little Benedict*. But what good would it have done to repeat Miss Lila's crazy words? So, Lizzie and I just had a pleasant conversation, and then she left. Now, five minutes later, Little Sister is calling to me from the porch. "Mama, there's a police car in Hobart's driveway!" Its blue lights flash in the overpowering brightness of noon, and a uniformed policeman is retreating from the locked, side door of Hobart's-Real-Estate-Agency-home where Hobart has hung the sign: "Closed. Gone Hunting." In the front seat of the patrol car, sits Pearl's cousin, The Judge. In the back seat is Leona. Her face has a bandage on it. Little Sister points at Leona, "I saw that."

I assume she means that she saw the patrol car. "I see it, too, but don't tell LaRosa. It might have something to do with Peck Two."

"Okay," she says. "But I saw it."

I hear the boys fighting upstairs and need to go referee. "Come on up, Little Sister. You can watch a Perry Mason tape in your room."

"The truth, the whole truth, and nothing but the truth, so help me God," Little Sister says, like she does every time she watches Perry Mason. I smile and go upstairs. I think she follows me, but later on, I don't hear the television, and when I look, Little Sister is not in her room. LaRosa and I can't find her anywhere.

Truth is Always Right Next Door
but only the Oddballs seem to see it

Hobart

Ray, the taxidermist, takes the hawk by its limp neck and lays it on his preliminary table, then asks me. "How many more of these are you going to have stuffed, Hobart?"

"As many as there are." I have my back to the taxidermist because I'm looking out the storefront window, watching a police car pull up in front of The Judge's office across the street.

"You oughta' have an Osprey museum by now."

"Quit jackin' your jaws. Just tell me when you'll have it finished." I can see Leona getting out of the police car. The Judge follows and goes into his office.

"Not before next week. I'm outta arsenical soap. I'll give you a call."

I'm out on the sidewalk when Leona's voice plummets from across the street. "I've cooked your goose, Hobart McSwain!"

Two well-dressed old ladies of Highlow blood are coming toward me. At Leona's outburst, they cut their questioning eyes my way. I smile, nod politely to acknowledge their presence, then shake my head as if to say, 'what else could anybody expect from a woman like that one?' Each lady gives me a look of agreement, and they totter on.

Leona dodges an oncoming car that honks at her. She shoots the driver a bird then yells to me again, "See this?" She is pointing to a white bandage on her cheek as she comes closer. "I've got you now, for the sexual assault of a spouse!" One of the old ladies who passed, looks back in my direction. I nod and smile, again. She does the same then whispers something to her friend as they round the corner.

Damn Leona! I grip her arm as she reaches me, but not too hard. By all appearances we're just talking. "There was no sex. And you are no longer my spouse."

"It still counts," she says, wrenching away from me. "I've got a witness, too. Your goose is cooked alright!" She starts to cross the traffic. The driver of a van stopped at the red light whistles as she passes between him and another car. She blows him a kiss.

I yell over the acceleration of the vehicles. "I gave you a check! Remember?"

Leona doesn't answer. She's prancing into the beauty shop across the street.

I kick at the tire on my truck and get in only to be jolted by Little Sister, grinning at me from the shotgun side. The first time I saw Little Sister on the day she was brought home to Highlow, I thought, *Well, at least there's one person besides me that Main Street will never accept.* I was dead wrong. Little Sister fastened herself right in. Anybody with a heart just has to like her.

"What are you doing here?" I make my voice gruff as I can.

"I saw what you did." She puts a finger to her flat, coffee-colored cheek. "I saw you hit Leona."

At once, I remember the sucked-in breath I'd heard, before and after I'd slugged the bitch.

"You didn't see anything, Little Sister," I say as if I'm talking to an idiot, but even I know she was never that.

"I saw it. Leona says I'm a witness," Little Sister says proudly. "She's not gonna take Peck from us because I told The Judge the truth."

Which truth? But I know how to deal with Little Sister. I give her my broadest grin. "Jesus knows I never meant to hit her. Leona just pushed me too far." Then I get ready for her sloppy kiss. She doesn't give it, just studies me with her bright, black eyes.

Finally, she says, "I didn't see Leona push."

"Hell, I gave her a check. Didn't you see that?"

"It isn't enough." The same tone, the same exact words Leona had used.

I give Little Sister another smile, the sweetest I can muster. "But Little Sister, I gave her almost everything I had. That is the honest to goodness truth."

She gets right up in my face and stares into my eyes as if, this time, she's going to kiss me. Instead, she asks, "Lord Jesus, do you think Leona wants it all?"

"Yes, Little Sister. Leona wants it all. Tell that to the Judge!"

Little Sister lays her hand over her heart as if she's seen the flag. "I will tell the Judge the truth, the whole truth, and nothing but the truth, so help me God." Immediately, she plants a wet kiss on my lips, gets out of the truck, and canters across the street to the Judge's office.

For a while, I sit in the truck cab with a smile on my face, thinking how Truth is always right next door, but only the oddballs seem to see it.

Please Forgive Me

Lizzie

It's Mama's naptime, so Pearl has called Hobart to come show me how to work Richard's computer that's been sitting for weeks in the music room. "I don't need him, Pearl, I can learn on my own."

"Well, you *haven't* learned, Lizzie. Anyway that would be impolite," Pearl reprimands. "If Hobart is willing to give his time, you should be grateful."

So, Hobart comes over and sits down at the monitor. "I'll take over," he says. I stand behind his broad back as dozens of white sentences fly over the screen. My name is there, disappearing, appearing again. Hobart moves his fingers from the keyboard and the screen is still. The words sit dead center, surrounded by other words from Richard, an obvious letter of apology. My heart sinks when I read, *"I love you, Liz. Please forgive me."*

"You can leave, now, Hobart. Thank you."

He twists in the chair to look up at me and throws me even more off-balance with what he says. "I love you, too lady girl, and I want you to forgive me."

All I can do is stare at him.

He slaps a fist on the keyboard, disrupting the lines. "Hell, that damn doctor never knew you! He gave you nothing but misery."

"You don't know anything about Richard."

"I know more than you think. I know your fancy husband died of Aids. And that your baby isn't his."

I take in an unsteady breath. "Who told you that?"

"I'm in real estate, remember? New people are moving here all the time from Mobile. I got me a lawyer with a big mouth who used to play tennis with the pro at the Mobile Country Club, and even a doctor who wants to set up a practice here in Highlow. In fact, the doctor asked about you. Anthony O'Conner's his name. That ring a bell, lady girl?"

I'm not sure about the lawyer, but I'm sure Hobart is lying. Anthony would never give up his big practice in Mobile and move to Highlow. "Dr. O'Connor is only an acquaintance. He wouldn't know about the baby."

"It wasn't him that told me," Hobart sniggers, enjoying his power over me. "A little birdie, worrying whether the baby will have Aids, let the news slip when she was forgot who she was talking to. Miss Pearl is getting a bit careless with her secrets."

"I'm not worried about Pearl. What have you told Dr. O'Connor?"

"All I told him was how you and I have always been next-door neighbors and very close." He shows his perfect white teeth. "The doctor seemed a little jealous."

"I don't feel well, Hobart. Please leave."

He moves closer. "I could take care of you, Lizzie, and your baby."

"I want you to go!"

"Maybe you've got a follower in that egghead, lady girl, but don't forget I was here first. I belong here. Dr. Anthony O'Connor doesn't."

"It's you who never belonged!"

"Yeah? Well, I've always had my foot in the door, haven't I?"

Damn Yankee from Detroit

Hobart

Women usually screw things up for men. Take Lila, or Leona, or even Lizzie for that matter; which one of them ever gave this man what he deserved? Far as I can tell, Little Sister's the only one appreciates me. But hell, it's not like I'm looking for compliments. It's not like I think I'm God's gift; nothing like that. Still, I ain't the bottom of the barrel neither. If she'd just size up the competition, Lizzie would realize I come out on top. O'Connor might be a doctor, but he wasn't the first of anything in Highlow. Dammit, I want her even more now that she's blown me off. She's back home unattached, so why not? Plus, I already know her laundry.

"Hooobaaart? Open up! I know you're in there. We've got things to discuss."

I push open the door with such force, I almost knock Leona down the steps, but she recuperates quickly, able to walk a razor even when she's on the powder.

"Look out, Hobart," she says, coming in, sloughing her purse on the kitchen table, and straightening the bandage on her face. "It is not going to be pleasant if you're put in jail for assault. Why don't you just come around with the rest of the money, Shugah?"

"The rest? I gave you a hefty check already."

"Well, it's gone," she growls like a bob-cat about to pounce. "And there's something else. Our divorce wasn't legal. I'm still your wife, Hobart."

"Like hell. I've got the papers to prove you're not!"

"You know I was on a high when I signed them. The Judge

says a signature doesn't count if the signer doesn't know what she's doing. So, I'm still your wife." She steps into my space, rubs a shoulder against my chest. "We could start over. I'll even drop the abuse charge."

"I wouldn't start over with you if you were the last mangy feline on earth! Anyway, I plan to marry somebody else."

Leona's face turns pepper red. "Who?"

"Lizzie Todd, that's who."

Leona laughs. "You killed her brother. She hates you!"

"It was an accident. She's forgiven me."

Leona snatches up her purse and flings open the door. "Well, her mother hasn't forgiven you. We'll just see what Lila says about your marrying her daughter."

"You stay away from Lila--and Lizzie! Stay away, you hear?"

Leona marches to a truck in the driveway. Behind the wheel waits the big-mouthed, Cajun lawyer. I sold that turncoat a place in Mirage, my finest subdivision, and put him in touch with D.C. Now he's in cahoots with Leona.

I hear the turncoat ask, "Is he going to co-operate?"

"Hell, no!" Leona says, getting into the car.

"We'll have to force his compliance then, won't we?"

Leona punches a fist into his upper arm. "Oh, be quiet!" Then she sticks her head out of the window and hollers. "You still don't have a clue, do you, Hobart? You'll always be a damn Yankee from Detroit!"

A Sack of Dixie Sugar

Little Benedict

The Judge called me this morning. "Little Benedict," he said, "come pick up Little Sister. She's here at my office. We've had a nice visit, but now, she's ready to go."

LaRosa and I are relieved. We searched over an hour for her.

Soon as I enter the Judge's office, Little Sister says, "Mama, I told The Judge about Leona. She wants everything, but she won't get it. Leona's not smart like Perry Mason. She has thrown out the truth."

The Judge looks at Little Sister with the pride of a daddy and lays a palm on the top of her head. "Now remember what I said, Little Sister. The truth boomerangs."

"Uh huh," she says. "Even if it takes years and years, the truth will come on back."

"That's right, Little Sister, but it can smack you right in the face if you're not ready for it." He gives her a big smile. She gives him a big old kiss

"I wasn't born an idiot, Judge. I'll be ready."

When we get in the car, Little Sister turns to me. "Mama?"

"Hum?"

"The Judge thinks Leona's stupid. He says she's traded off the sense she was born with for a sack of Dixie sugar."

"Well, The Judge is right. Leona got rid of Peck Two, but now she wants him back."

"No Mama," she says. "That's not true. It's not Peck Two she wants, its Hobart's money. But The Judge says she won't get either one."

When we get home, Little Sister hunts for Peck Two and hugs him hard. Then she sticks an old, battered-looking tape of Perry Mason into the VCR player and they watch it together. "The truth and nothing but the truth," Little Sister says, her mouth full of the popcorn LaRosa has fixed.

You Were His Friend.
I Was His Wife!

Lizzie

Apparently Hobart wasn't lying; Anthony called this morning. "Let me help you set things straight," Anthony said, as if I was a broken bone. "Let me love you, Liz." I told him neither was possible, but he said he was coming over anyway.

I stay in my robe to cover the pregnancy; he'd know at once the baby was his. Then I watch the wide-faced clock on Pearl's mantle. The time is always wrong, yet it continues to tick, the only sound I hear until the doorbell rings.

"This is Anthony, a friend of Richard's," I say to Pearl who taps into her living room because she has heard the bell and it would be impolite not to greet a visitor to her house.

"Richard? The baby doctor? Then I'm glad you're here. I think Lazi's losing his marbles and we're going to need another baby doctor before too long." Anthony looks puzzled as Pearl taps out. I am afraid he will ask me what she meant, but he doesn't. He sits beside me on the damask-covered sofa, extends his arm across the back of it, his fingers brushing my neck.

"I'm opening up a practice here in Highlow."

"I know. Hobart McSwain told me." He looks at me as if there's more I should say. "Hobart's a neighbor," I explain.

"I've met him," he says dryly. "I'm opening the practice to be near you, Liz."

"Everything I did was wrong."

"You didn't intend it."

"If I hadn't been so quick to pay him back, I'd have known about the battery failure and Richard wouldn't have died. I killed him!" I try not to cry, but it's no use.

"Sh...sh..." Anthony turns my face toward his with his doctor hands.

"You were right, Richard did love me. I saw the words in his computer. Remember how he was always typing into it?"

"I remember."

"You were his friend."

"Yes."

"And I was his wife, but look what I did to him!"

"It was my fault, not yours."

"Was it? He cheated on me, I cheated on him. I used you to get back at him."

"That doesn't matter, I knew you loved me, and I know you love me now."

"No, I don't."

Of course, it's a lie, but he rises from the pink damask as if he's been stung. "When you decide you want me, I'll be living on Willow Street." He's gone in an instant.

A voice inside me says, "Go after him!" I ignore it.

Only What Belongs to Her

Little Benedict

There're some people in this world who like to make trouble for everybody, even happy families. Leona's one of them. Give her an inch and she wants a mile. Now, she's back, wanting even more than that.

Through the closed front door she hollers that she's come to see Peck Two. "Don't let her in, Little Benedict," LaRosa says, but I say we ought to let her in because she's his blood mother, after all. So, Little Sister goes and opens the door.

"You want everything," Little Sister says to Leona who stands on the porch with a dark-skinned, white man. "But you can't have everything you want." Leona ignores her.

"The lady only wants what belongs to her," the man says. He steers himself and Leona inside our house. But LaRosa steps in front of them, and pokes a finger into the man's chest. "Take one more step and I'll slice out your heart."

"Look here, LaRosa," Leona says, "this man is my lawyer and he's got a paper. Show her the paper, Cletus." The man pulls a document from the pocket of his suit.

LaRosa grabs it and rips it apart. "Well, he don't have a paper, anymore!"

"Look," Leona says, "ya'll work with me and you can have the boy." She's purring like a kitten, now, but her spinning eyes show she's on the powder. She turns to me. "Little Benedict, just help me get rid of Hobart."

"Get rid of him?"

"Oh, I don't mean kill him, though God knows I'd like to after all he's done to me!" She glances at Little Sister, giving her a fleeting smile of appreciation. "All I want you to do is testify to the Judge like Little Sister did. Tell him how Hobart abused me when I was the one helped him start the first real estate agency in Highlow. Just remind the Judge that I'm Hobart's wife, so his money is my money. Tell him, like Little Sister did."

Little Sister edges close to Leona, and says, "The Judge knows the truth, the whole truth and nothing but the truth."

Leona takes a backward step. "I sure do appreciate it, too, Little Sister."

Little Sister points a finger at Leona. "I told the Judge you can't have everything. And he said that's right 'cause the truth boomerangs."

"Whatever!" Leona says, exasperated. Then she and Cletus sit on our sofa like they came to stay awhile.

"All you have to do, Little Benedict," Cletus says, pinning me down with his eyes, "is to say that Leona was a good and dutiful wife, abused by her husband. Just say that Hobart gave you the boy against her wishes."

"But that's not true!" LaRosa yells.

"That is not true!" Little Sister mimics.

At once, our youngest boys run laughing through the living room, chased by Peck Two. All eyes land on him. "What's going on in here?" Peck Two asks, when he notices he's the center of attention.

Leona looks at the boy like she's never seen him before, which is practically true. "My goodness, you've grown."

"Uh huh. I'm the tallest one in my class; first on the basketball team, too."

"You take after your daddy," Leona says sourly.

"Naw, I take after my granddaddy. He was the first garbage collector in Highlow, over six feet four inches tall."

LaRosa looks proud. Then she swats Peck playfully on the

seat of his pants. "Take your brothers out in the back yard or you'll never see close to six feet."

Peck grabs my smallest boy and throws him, giggling, over his shoulder. The other one follows through the kitchen and outside.

Cletus seizes the moment. "Can't you see the love of a mother in Leona's eyes?" He elbows Leona who comes to attention, taking on the sad look of a hound dog. "She only wants the boy she adores."

I can tell LaRosa's had enough by the way her jaw is set and the way her shoulders rise to her ears. She moves toward the sofa where Leona and Cletus are sitting. Just in case, I step in front of the fireplace poker, but LaRosa doesn't need a weapon besides her own hands if she's angry enough. She grabs Cletus by the throat. Leona scrambles for the door.

"Yeah, you'd better get out, and take your boyfriend with you!" LaRosa hisses, loosening her grip on Cletus.

Cletus coughs, catches his breath then wags his finger at us. "Ya'll are gonna have a hard time explaining an assault on innocent people." He accidentally steps on Leona's foot as he hurries to catch up with her.

"Ooow, you sonofabitch!" Leona yells and kicks him in the shin.

"I reckon we'll have this whole neighborhood in court!" Cletus calls back, limping down the walkway.

"Yeah! Hobart and his whole damn neighborhood!" Leona shouts from the truck window as they take off down Main. I think about Leona's statement and how it would please Hobart to hear that somebody has finally connected him to Main Street.

When Hobart Comes

Little Benedict

Soon, Hobart's back again to see Peck Two; he sits on the sofa, waiting. LaRosa ushers the boy across the room and sits him at a distance, in the straight-back chair. She asks me to come help her pour some Coca-Cola, so we go into the kitchen; but I can see through the open door. Hobart spits on his thumb and wipes a speck off the toe of his cowboy boot. Peck Two is gripping the sides of the chair, swinging his legs, not looking at Hobart. Yet, there's something between them now, almost like a father and son connection. Little Sister is standing behind Peck Two, her arms wrapped around her chest, her dark eyes glued on Hobart as if she's trying to catch him in a smile. It's the same every time, always the same when Hobart comes.

Two Letters

Lizzie

In her room, surrounded by porcelain faces, my mother asks, "Would you like tea, Lizzie?" I lift my empty cup from its saucer and extend it in her direction. She pours in tea from a mended china pot, its former fracture barely visible because Pearl has glued it back together. I take a sip and smile as if I'm her guest. "It's very good."

Izear brings in two letters addressed to Mama, but he seems hesitant to give them to her. The first is postmarked Crisscross, Georgia. I think immediately of Leona, but why would she be writing Mama? Just as surprising, the second letter is from Cincinnati; Mama opens that one first. While she reads it, Izear runs a finger around the window he has boarded up as if checking for cracks. Every so often, he glances over at Mama.

"Who is the letter from?" I ask her, hoping to sound sufficiently indifferent.

"Someone I invited to the open-house. But he can't come."

Izear gives a huff. "Lord God! Ain't you had enough of that blind man?"

Unruffled, Mama then reaches for the Crisscross letter. "I'm sure I don't know what you're talking about, Izear." At once, Izear seems to reconsider having given her the letters. He's probably wondering, too, whether the one she's holding now is from Leona. He tries to take it back, but she won't let him have it. He turns to me then. "I think Miss Pearl needs your help," he says, an order to leave the room as if I were still a child and the letter would reveal something I should not be exposed to.

Actually, I'm anxious to leave. I care nothing about what Leona might have to say. But I have taken note of the Cincinnati address. After all these years, it presents an opportunity to finally go there, and perhaps meet my father.

In the hall, I dial Pearl's phone--no push-buttons, only a rotary dial that makes too loud a noise when it ticks a lagging connection. I ask for a Peckham Corley on East Blackburn, and the operator gives me a number. Then she asks, "Would you like me to connect you?"

Connect me? Am I ready for that? "No, thank you," I say, and hang up, thinking I should let it go, that it no longer matters who my father is. Except, I can't let it go because it mattered to Peck. The missing piece that kept the broken cup of our childhood from ever being whole, was our father. And though Pearl tried, only one man could have fixed that. The fact that he didn't, that he never acknowledged us, infuriates me enough to reach for the phone again. I want to confront him more than I want to connect with him. Oh, how I relish the confrontation! Until the child within me makes an unexpected move, constricting in my belly to a hardened knot, and reminds me that I'm as much a fraud as my father is. Then I hear Mama crying in her room.

Izear comes out, slams the door closed, and locks it. He whizzes past me with the letter from Crisscross in his hand, hustling down the stairs, and into the kitchen. Immediately, there is a clattering sound of something fallen. So, I rush down, too. Pearl has dropped a pan of boiling peas onto the kitchen floor.

"You're gonna burn your hand. Move out the way," Izear is saying as Pearl backs away from the stove. The hot liquid from the pan seeps toward her shoes. Izear gets on his knees to wipe the floor around Pearl's feet with a dishrag. "I should never have shown you Leona's letter while you was holding that pot! Don't you worry though; I'm gonna fix it for you."

"Lizzie," Pearl cries when she notices me. "Hobart is not our kind. I will not have it!"

"Have what, Pearl?"

"Leona wrote your mother that--" she stops, distracted by an awful thought. "My God, Lila will try to kill Hobart, again!"

"Yes'um, but I locked her in," Izear says, still wiping the floor.

"The Judge is getting tired of it."

"Yes'um. Gonna fix that, too." Izear pats her shoe and rises.

Pearl turns to me. "You know your mother can't stand the man! You wouldn't do that to her, would you, Lizzie?"

"Do what?"

"Marry Hobart."

I am astounded. "Whatever gave you that idea?"

"Leona sent your mother a letter. She said Hobart told her that you and he were getting married."

Before I can speak to the absurdity, I hear Mama violently banging on her locked door. "Izear, bring me back that letter!"

The three of us go upstairs. Izear opens the locked door, and Mama demands, "I need to speak to Hobart. Call him!"

Izear brushes back a strand of her hair. "Sometime when you're feeling better."

"Call him, now!" She glares at me, her hands knotted into fists. I move toward her, to console her; but she backs away.

"It's not true, Mama. I'd never marry Hobart. I can't stand him anymore that you can. Leona's lying."

Her eyes are cold as an old winter moon on my full belly. "Well, aren't you lying, too?

I don't have to answer her. No one expects it. Mama's always been irrational.

One More Hawk Falls Dead

Hobart

"Where're you going, Hobart?" Little Sister asks. She's trotted happily across the yard to my driveway where I'm loading some gear in the cab of my truck.

"What did you tell The Judge, Little Sister?" I'm wondering if she's put The Judge on the right track--after Leona, and not me.

"I told him the truth, the whole truth, and nothing but the truth."

Why did I expect a straight answer from someone who's been called a fool?

"So, where're you going, Hobart?"

"Hunting."

"For what?"

"Some kinda peace away from all of ya'll. And I ain't in the mood to talk, so just go on back to where you came from."

"I can't. Somebody tore it down.'

"Tore what down?"

"Piney Woods."

I start to explain that I didn't mean go back to Piney Woods, but I don't feel like finishing. She gets up in my face. "Somebody said it was you that tore Piney Woods down."

"Well, now I'm rebuilding it. I'm turning it into a pizza joint."

"The kids will like having pizza. They never served us any as I recall."

"I gotta go, Little Sister."

"Back to where you came from?"

"I'm from here! I own property here, and I'll be here 'til the day I die." I go to plug my rifle into the gun rack above the rear window of the cab and notice a lumpy-looking tarp in the back of my truck. I start to lift it, wondering if I've left a stuffed bird underneath, but Little Sister distracts me.

"Highlow's your home sweet home, and home is where the heart is, right Hobart?"

I don't know why her illogical words suddenly make sense to me. "Damn right!" I say. Then I get in the cab, crank up, and leave Little Sister behind.

Near the river, in an open field, I'm scanning the tops of pines for the glimpse of a bird of prey, and thinking about what she said. "Home is where the heart is." Just as I raise my rifle, and catch in its sight the lighting of an Osprey on the limb of a Hemlock, I hear the rustle of the tarp in my truck. When I turn, I am face to face with the boy I gave away.

His bullet eyes aim directly at me. "Are you going to kill that one, too?"

I've heard some people say that history repeats itself. I think of that now, struck at once by the resemblance between this green-eyed, copper-haired son and the first Peck, the Peck who is dead. I'd like to tell them both how sorry I am for . . . being me. That's what comes from the home in my heart, but the words in my mouth say, "Hell boy, it's just a hawk, just a goddamn bird. What's one more or less? C'mere and I'll show you how to take it down."

I offer him my rifle. He takes it in his hands just like the first Peck used to do, except that Peck Two aims and fires. And one more hawk falls dead.

A Secret Revealed

Little Benedict

Peck Two says Hobart took him hunting today. "It was Little Sister's idea," Peck Two says when he catches La Rosa's discerning eyes upon him.

LaRosa says, "Hunting is not a good sport."

I say, "It's okay if you don't waste what you shoot. Did you bring home anything dead?"

Peck Two holds out his empty palms. "Not me."

LaRosa says, "Good."

I ask Peck Two if he's starting to love his father. I mean Hobart, but Peck Two says he's always loved me. He knows who's who. He knows where he came from, too, but he likes to think he came from our house. LaRosa says, "Good."

I get a little nervous about Hobart taking Peck Two anywhere. I know he's taken him down to Dixie, at least once, because there's one of D.C.'s "Buy Now, Pay Later" brochures hanging on the bulletin board in Peck Two's room. Now seems the time to ask our boy about it.

Peck Two says when he's sixteen, he'll need a car. He says Hobart's going to buy him one. LaRosa says, "Over my dead body he will!"

At night, I snuggle up to LaRosa in our big bed. It's when we talk. "We haven't heard from Leona lately, or Cletus," I say. "But I know Leona; she's still stewing, and not dead yet."

"Leona *will* be dead if she sets a foot in our house again." LaRosa says. "I can put up with an obvious Highlow carpetbagger, like Hobart, if I have to; but never a scalawag such as Leona."

I say her assessment is the second time Hobart's been accepted in Highlow without forcing it. LaRosa traces my nose with her finger and uses her mother-voice. "Well, you can't force friends and influence, and you can't keep a fact from being a fact."

I use Little Sister's words to answer. "That's the truth, the whole truth, and nothing but the truth, even if some people try to hide it."

LaRosa hugs me in agreement. God, I love my woman's good sense!

When LaRosa starts to snore, I start to think about Hobart, and his attention to us when we were children, especially his attention to Lizzie and Peck. It was like he wanted them to accept him, even to love him, when we all knew he didn't belong in Highlow. Then all at once, I recall the secret Miss Lila told me those years ago, an unreliable revelation I'd almost forgotten. Except if what she said is true, then Hobart might belong here after all. More than that, our Peck Two may have a blood brother, and a sister. One of them, dead. The other back in Highlow.

I nudge LaRosa awake and tell her the secret. She doesn't bat an eye before she says, "Lizzie needs to know." Then she raises her thick black eyebrows as if she's just had a thought. "Oh no, Little Benedict! Lizzie is his next closest relative. What if she's not like Hobart? What if she wants Peck Two, and takes him?"

I try to assure her that Lizzie wouldn't do that, but LaRosa tosses and turns all night.

Hobart Isn't My Father!

Lizzie

"C'mon in Lizzie." LaRosa greets me with a smile. She wraps a heavy arm around my shoulders and hugs me tight. "Little Benedict's in the living room, waiting for the cookies to finish baking. You know how he loves cookies!" She guides me through the ginger smell of her kitchen, past the stairway echoing children's chatter from the bedrooms above, and into the living room where Little Benedict rises at once from the blue chintz sofa. At first he says nothing, so I give him a look of questioning. "I was just thinking about you, Lizzie," he says. "It's why LaRosa called."

"Were you?"

"Come sit."

"Ya'll go on and talk," LaRosa says. "I better check the oven."

Little Benedict seems ill at ease, like he has something important to say but he's bothered about saying it. Finally, he sniffs, wipes his nose on his sleeve, and comes right to the point. "What would you do if you had two children, Lizzie?"

"What do you mean?"

"I mean, wouldn't it be hard for you to raise two children with your husband gone? You wouldn't want that, would you?"

"Two? I don't expect to have twins."

I can see my answer frustrates him. "I don't mean twins. What if you had another little brother, maybe a little half-brother, and what if The Judge found out about that and said you oughta be the one to raise him since his parents didn't want him and you were his next blood-kin---would you want him?"

"What are you talking about?"

Little Benedict leans toward me and whispers. "Peck Two, in there? He might be your half-brother, but please say you *don't* want him because LaRosa and me couldn't stand being without him."

"I don't understand. Pearl said he was Hobart's child."

"He is, Lizzie," he says, squinting at me, his voice barely audible. "You might be, too."

I can't get my head around what he's said. Why is everything suddenly about Hobart? He's an intruder in Highlow. He doesn't belong here and never did. Not a word of it makes any sense. First, Hobart says he loves me, and then Leona says he's going to marry me, and now Little Benedict says Hobart is my father. All, ridiculous lies. "Have you gone nuts? Hobart isn't my father! Who told you such a lie?"

"Your mother told me, after the second time she shot Hobart. I'd thought she was making it up, but now, I realize I can't be the judge of that."

"Of course, she made it up! My father is from Cincinnati."

Little Benedict leans close to my ear, "Are you sure? Or did she make that up, too?"

Customized Cravings

Hobart

Years ago, I promised Lizzie's twin what he wanted most in the world; something a daddy might do. I could have gotten him that bird, except he didn't want it on my terms. "Don't shoot it; I don't want it dead," he said often enough—unlike his mother who pulls the trigger in a heartbeat. I don't understand her, but I understood her son. I understood the hunger that comes when a person of high blood, or low, is boxed into a life he has no control over, a life without the love of a father, and a mother. If Lila would stop and think before she shoots, she'd understand, too.

We all got our customized cravings, our particular drugs you might say; habits, traditions, our routine ways of coping. Even Pearl has strong inclinations. Take *her* Fine China, restored with Super Glue to keep up her Highlow family, yet Pearl was powerless to fix the genuine break in her grandson's heart. I like to think it's fixed now. I like to think that Sister Perpetua flew down from heaven, took Peck back up with her, and told him what she told me, "You may not know it, little fellow, but Jesus loves you. Oh yes, He does!"

Then I think about *my* Fine China and how I used to crave it. Lila thinks I killed her son, but the thing that took Peck was the simple narcotic need for a father. It was his own craving that killed him. Not me. No, not me.

The Bus to Cincinnati

Lizzie

There is only one thing for me to do after Little Benedict tells me the crazy secret he's kept all these years. I have to go to Cincinnati to prove it's not true. I'd like to take a plane, but regulations don't allow an eight-and-a-half-month-pregnant woman to fly. Instead, I buy a bus ticket. I tell Pearl and Izear I need to go to Mobile to take care of some final things. They accept the lie, until Izear and I are in the car, ready to drive to the bus depot.

"You shouldn't take a bus," Pearl says through the side window of the old Roadmaster. "Izear should drive you to Mobile."

"Yes 'um, I tol' her that," Izear says.

"I'll be fine, Pearl. Izear should stay here with you."

"You'll have that baby on the bus if you don't look out!"

"Don't worry, Pearl. I have a few weeks to go."

"Then just be sure you get on the *right* bus, Lizzie, or you'll end up where you don't want to go." As we back out, she calls down the driveway to Izear. "Don't forget to pick up milk and oysters on the way home for the oyster stew!"

We drive down Main to Dixie and stop at a traffic light, a few blocks from the depot. D.C.'s car lot and its "Buy Now, Pay Later" sign are just ahead. "Hobart wants to buy my BMW," I say to Izear.

"I ain't never liked that red car from the first time I saw it. Looks like it came from evil." He has no idea how right he is.

"I'd like to get rid of it, and Hobart wants the car. So, will you sell it to him while I'm gone? Get D.C. to give you a price and take less than that from Hobart, then put the money in Pearl's tin box for the open house."

"Put money from an evil thing in our pretty box?"

"Let's just say I'd be paying it back with something good. I owe that box some money, remember?"

He gives a condescending smile. "Keep up with your bus ticket, this time."

At the bus depot, Izear notices a schedule on the wall. "Lookathere, the bus to Mobile don't leave for another two hours."

"I must have misunderstood. You don't have to wait with me."

"Well, I'm goin' to. You don't do well in bus stations."

"For heaven's sake, that was years ago. And what about the milk and oysters? Pearl's counting on your making the oyster stew."

Pearl comes first, so he finally leaves.

Cincinnati is ominous; concrete, tall, and different from Highlow, but the people look pretty much the same. In the hotel where I've made a reservation, I notice a stone block planter with plastic flowers, reminding me of Jay, who took my ticket and my trip so many years ago. The woman at the hotel desk sizes me up like she thinks I might deliver on her shift. "When are you due?" she asks in a nasal tone.

"Oh, a good while." I can tell she does not believe me. She motions for a bell boy.

In the hotel room, I make the telephone call. A man answers, "Peckham Corely." His voice sounds kind.

I take a breath and tell him I'm Lila. (I've always been told that I sound like my mother.) I tell him I'd like to see him. Immediately, he says he'll come to the hotel.

In less than an hour, the man who is likely my father stands before me--the tall, blind man in an eagle jacket, from Pearl's long ago, open-house. I take his arm to lead him in.

His sightless eyes fix on a motel chair behind me. "You're not Lila," he says, shrugging away as if by touch he knew.

"No, but I think we're related."

"Jesus Christ, I don't need any relations!" He turns to leave.

I grab his elbow. "Please, sit down for a minute."

He feels his way through the small hall into the open room. His hand touches the top of a dresser, the arm of a sofa, and then sits. "If you're not Lila, who are you?"

"Lila's daughter."

There is a small twitch of his lower lip, a pensive expression on his face, and he becomes quite defensive. "Lila was pregnant when I met her. She told me that was why she'd come to art school in the first place, all the way up to Cincinnati so nobody would know about the baby. But it wasn't my baby. So if you're here to make any claim to my fortune, forget it. I don't have a dime and I am not your father."

"You came to Highlow those years ago, to the open house. How did you know to come?"

"Lila sent me a ticket. I was a blind artist who didn't know how to do anything else. I thought maybe Lila could help, maybe even loan me some money. So I came--just once. I'm not stupid enough to take that trip again. I've sent back her ticket every year since. I was blinded for no reason. God, I was an artist!"

I feel compassion for him, sickened by what Izear did. Still, I don't think he's being honest. "Mama says you're our father, Peck's and mine."

"Peck?"

"Peck was my twin brother." I wait to let in sink in then touch his arm. "Mr. Corley, all I want is the truth."

"I've already told you the truth. I'm nobody's father. I'm just a blind man who shouldn't have been blind"

"You came here thinking you would see Lila. Why did you want to come if you didn't care anything for her?"

His face grows red with emotion. "I did care! I loved her, but she loved that blonde kid from Detroit. She said she couldn't help herself, like he was some kind of drug or something. Then one day, the kid came up here with a black man to take her back to Alabama. The kid wanted me to persuade her to go with them. He said he'd hurt me if I didn't, but I wouldn't lie to her. I said I wouldn't advise her to go anywhere with a homeless-looking mongrel, like him. I turned my back on him. A big mistake. He threw something at me, maybe a wooden chair that hit me hard in the back of my head, then somebody pushed me face-down to the floor and started beating me and wouldn't quit."

"Which one beat you?"

"I'm almost certain it was the kid, but I couldn't see. By then, I was blind."

"Well, it was the black man who went to jail for it," I say, but he isn't listening.

"Lila was screaming. She said if they'd leave me alone, she'd go back with them. The beating stopped then. And that's all I can tell you, except after I knew they were gone, I called the police. Of course, the police couldn't give me back my eyes." He rises from his chair, feels his way to the door, and stops in the threshold. "Why would you want a blind father anyway? I'm only a worthless artist." Then he's gone.

On the bus ride home, the cold, brown vinyl is so uncomfortable I have to shift several times to ease the cramping in my legs. The growing baby inside me constricts to a knot as if there's no more room in the miniscule space that remains, no room in the world for one more replication of a fatherless child who will crave and seek, but will not find. I can no longer blame my mother, or my father whoever he may be. This time, the fault is mine.

Then something snaps underneath me, and the seat lowers abruptly on the side closest to the aisle. I go to the front of the bus, steadying my steps by holding on to the tops of the rocking rows of seats until I get to the driver. "My seat is broken," I tell him, accidentally bumping into his sweaty shoulder.

"Uh huh," he says, his eyes on the road. "Had trouble with that seat for over a month. Ain't nobody in charge even tried to change it out. "

"Who's in charge?"

"Damned if I know," he says. "But it ain't me. Go look for another seat."

"There isn't one. The rest are taken."

Then I suppose you'll have to ride in the one you bought."

I go back to my seat and try to sit straight, but I keep sliding to one side. I take a book I brought with me and try to stuff it up under the hanging side. It stays fine until we get to Birmingham, then the book falls out because it is misshapen and bent. I spend the rest of the trip with one foot extended to keep me from slipping. I have quite a cramp in that foot when Izear helps me down the steps.

"The sign on that bus don't say Mobile. It says Cincinnati. That where you been?"

"If it's what the bus says, then it's where I went."

He wrinkles up his nose and walks doggedly to the baggage trough to get my suitcase. When he returns, he snatches my heavy purse from my shoulder and slings it on his. "Well, did you find the father you were looking for?" No condemnation, just the question.

"Do you mean the man *you* blinded?"

"Is that what he said?

"No. He thought Hobart blinded him."

Izear smiles. "Didn't I tell you before? I wouldn't poke out nobody's eyes 'less they was blind to start with."

"But you went to jail for Hobart. You let him get away with it. Why?"

"All that stuff's water under the bridge. I ain't gonna dive down and stir it up."

But I'm not as forgiving as Izear. On the ride home, I determine to dive for the truth on my own, fearing what I may discover. All I know for certain is that the bus to Cincinnati runs both ways, and either way, it runs broken.

Only a Couple of Times

Hobart

I'm drinking a cup of coffee in my kitchen when Lizzie bursts in. I get all hopeful. Has she forgiven me for Peck's death? Has she reconsidered my offer to take care of her? Then she asks the question with un-moving expression, as if her face is a painting on a flat, china plate. "Hobart, are you my father?

The question steals my breath; I nearly choke on the coffee. What did she say? How could she think such a thing?

"Answer me!"

"No!"

"You mean you won't tell me?"

"I mean I'm not your father. Did Leona put you up to this?"

"I haven't talked to Leona, only to Little Benedict."

"How in the hell would he know who your father is?"

"Mama told him a long time ago. He's kept her secret."

"And you believe her? She got pregnant in Cincinnati. It was that damn artist." I'm practically shouting. She glares back at me as if she's suddenly Lila, gun in hand, aiming another shot.

"I went to Cincinnati. I talked with the artist. He said Mother was pregnant when he met her."

"Well, he's lying and so is your mama. I'm not your father!"

She stiffens then. Her lips tremble and her eyes wash in worry, but her voice is still cold as the barrel of a gun. "Then go ask her about it, Hobart."

"Maybe I would if she'd let me near her."

"She's told Izear that she wants to talk to you. If you think

Mama's lying, then go ask why she is."

"I'll go, but not now." Is it relief I see in her face, or defeat as she turns toward the door? "Izear gave me a price on your car," I say, to keep her from leaving.

"Take it then."

"It's a little expensive."

"Then don't take it, Hobart. Either way, I don't care!" There is so much vindictiveness in her face that I'm sure she'd kill me if she had the opportunity.

I think about what Little Benedict told Lizzie. No way! I don't believe it. Her mother's a liar, always has been; Lizzie knows that. Anyway, I only touched Lila a couple of times.

A Better One Than Richard

Lizzie

Mama remains locked in her room. Izear gives me the key to go sit with her, but when I go in, she won't talk to me. She keeps asking to see Hobart. Izear's not about to let that happen. Then Pearl calls me downstairs, sits me at the table, and gives me raisins to chop. She is shelling pecans for the lane cake while Izear beats the butter and sugar together for his sour cream pound cake. He's already finished his rum balls. When it's all done, they will freeze what they have created.

The open house is in two weeks, the first in many years. I wonder who will come; so many Pearl knew are dead. But there are those she doesn't know, those who will somehow hear and come to try for the Baby Jesus.

Halfway through a cup of raisins, I have to stand up; there's a cramp in my leg from the heavy weight I carry. Izear notices and turns off the mixmaster. "Are you okay?"

Pearl looks up from chopping pecans. "Is it time?"

"No, I'm fine."

"I need know when it's time so I can call Lazi," Pearl says nervously.

"It's not time Pearl, but when it is, I think maybe I should go to the hospital. What if Dr. Sharbel can't come?"

"Oh, he'll come if he knows what's good for him."

"What if something happens, something out of the ordinary?"

"Like what? You said it couldn't have Aids."

"I don't mean Aids."

"Then what do you mean?"

"I mean I've never had a baby before so I don't know what ordinary is."

"There's nothing ordinary about it. It's a miracle; isn't that right, Izear?"

"Sure is," Izear says, holding a measuring cup up to the light to check the cake flour.

Pearl cracks open a coconut with a hammer, pours out the milk and grates it, never catching a finger. "Long as it won't have Aids, what's to worry? Lazi can handle it. And if Lazi can't come, we'll call that new baby doctor--the one that came to see you, and keeps calling.

Anthony has called three times this week. Each time, I refused to see him and I've told him nothing about the baby. "Go back to Mobile," I'd said. "There's nothing for you here."

"Yes, there is."

"You won't have a big practice. People in Highlow don't break too many bones.

"I don't care about a big practice. I don't want everything; I only want you."

"Anthony, don't call, again."

"Quit running away. Admit that you love me." But all I can admit is that it's gotten harder and harder to hang up on him.

Now, Pearl asks, "What was that baby doctor's name again?"

"Anthony O'Connor, but he's not an obstetrician. He's an orthopedic surgeon."

"Well, I hope he's a better one than Richard was." She looks at the cup of raisins I've chopped. "You'll have to do those again, Lizzie. They're not cut fine enough for the lane cake."

*If He'd Been Mine,
I'd Have Known It*

Hobart

It's Sunday morning. Izear has driven Lizzie and Pearl to the church in Crisscross, so Lila will be alone, and Pearl never locks her kitchen door. I take the stairs and stand outside the closed door to Lila's room. The knob will not turn. The door is bolted.

"Izear?" her voice calls from inside.

I don't answer. She tries to open the door and can't.

"Izear, please let me out; I won't try to kill Hobart again."

The old wound in my chest suddenly aches. Off the powder for years and she still wants to kill me, even though I tried to make-up for Peck. I loved the kid, too, but if he'd been mine, I'd have known it.

Lila beats on her side of the door. "Izear, answer me! You blinded the wrong man! I need to talk to Hobart. Do you understand, Izear? Hobart is their father!"

For several minutes, I'm too stunned to move. And then I remember that Lila is nuts. She says all kind of things that aren't true. I leave their Highlow house, grateful for the first time that the door has been locked to me.

A Most Unfortunate Mistake

Lizzie

December twenty-third, Pearl's first open house since my twin brother died. Besides The Judge, I don't know a soul except for Little Benedict, LaRosa, and Hobart. Pearl invited Hobart to help. So he's doing as he used to do, helping himself to wine and cake, helping himself to charming Pearl's guests then trying to sell them a place in his new subdivision, Mirage.

Izear says Mama is anxious to come to the party, but Pearl tells him to keep a watch on Hobart when Mama makes her usual arrival just after the Baby Jesus is found. Izear never takes his eyes off him.

The third-generation Spratlings have all their over-flowing, fourth generation with them, Peck Two included. They add to the noise with their laughter, overlapping the words of lively conversations and the clinking of cut-glass treasures filled with wine.

A slender lady, with hair the color of a pineapple, has LaRosa by the arm, talking about a woman she'd seen at the recent Highlow Chamber of Commerce banquet she'd attended with her husband. "Honey, you should have seen what she was wearing!" the slender lady says. "Cut down to heaven knows where and not a thing on underneath! Well, I told hubby--keep your eyes where they belong, hon, or you'll never see one more penny of my daddy's money!"

"I declare," LaRosa politely comments, her black eyebrows knit together as she scans the room until she's found Peck Two. Her eyes continuously dart back to him; watching, watching for any danger.

Pearl is letting Peck Two pour the wine. "You're the best wine-pourer in the house," she says and Peck Two beams. "I told you so, Miss Pearl."

"Hell!" shouts a bald-headed man with square shoulders and a tweed jacket. He's in conversation with Little Benedict and another man, who looks just like him, except he's not bald. The bald-headed man lights a cigar, blows smoke into the room as he speaks. "They played like crap all season. How do those sons of bitches think they gonna win the Shugah?"

"Better win. I got a hun'erd on it!" Little Benedict sniffs and wipes the corner of his mouth. Then he notices Izear is trying to get the wine bottle away from Peck Two, so Little Benedict calls across the room to his adopted son, "Let it go, boy!"

The bald-headed man laughs, "Son, you better hope you find Jesus tonight, else you go'n have one big, syrupy loss on your hands."

"Miss Pearl," Peck Two whines. "Izear won't let me pour the wine, and I'm the best pourer!"

Pearl taps over to Peck Two. "You must learn to take turns. It's Izear's turn, now."

Hobart watches, watches the staircase, as he moves toward the table where Peck Two waits for his turn. LaRosa swoops between them, steering the boy away. "But it's fixing to be my turn to pour, Mama LaRosa!"

Hobart whispers to the boy, "Come back in a minute, I'll let you pour."

LaRosa glares at Hobart. "You are not in charge of him, anymore. We are." She aims Peck toward Little Benedict, calling out, "See to your son that's misbehavin'!"

Hobart looks unusually regretful when he sees Peck Two

standing sullenly in the corner where Little Benedict has stuck him; as if he'd like to take him back from the Spratlings.

"I just wanted to pour the wine," Peck Two says, a tear running down his cheek when he sees me coming toward him.

I smooth his copper-colored hair. He doesn't resist, so I put my arms around him as if he belonged to me, his little-boy smell, so familiar.

"I might wanna play with your baby sometime." he says sweetly.

"You can play with the baby anytime you'd like."

"Can I be the first one to hold it?"

"Mamas hold babies first."

"No, I want to hold it first, before you." Then he twists from my arms and darts off, calling back an after-thought. "So you call me when you know it's coming." And he disappears into the mass of strangers.

Hobart keeps watching the stairs, just in case. Watching, watching, for Mama. The party goes on with the taking of coats, the serving of cake on fine china plates, the pouring of wine, the reflections of red and green lights swirling within cut-glass goblets, the redemption of lost children, the search for missing fathers. Then everything pauses. Mama is coming down. Too early.

"Who has found Jesus?" Pearl asks, nervously.

Izear takes a step forward. "Ain't nobody found him yet."

Mama looks over the faces in the room until she sees Hobart's. She smiles. She lifts a hand. She is holding William Crawford's gun. Another replay of the past.

"Lila!" Pearl shrieks.

"Mama!"

"Lord have mercy!" Izear plunges toward the staircase.

There is a shattering noise. Hobart falls to the floor. Plaster from the ceiling where the bullet hit, falls like snow around him.

"Jesus!" Hobart cries, looking up at Mama. "It's been twenty years! Will you ever quit trying?"

Pearl sinks onto her pink damask sofa.

Izear hustles Mama back upstairs.

Peck Two calls out," Can I pour the wine now, Miss Pearl?"

Buzzing, buzzing voices: "For heaven's sake, what went wrong with sweet Lila?"

"She's always been a little off, but my God!"

"Did anybody win the hundred dollars?"

"Remember when that blind foreigner came and won it?"

"No prize this year; it's time to go home."

So, nobody found the baby Jesus at the open house, the first time that ever happened. In fact, most people left before half the lane cake was gone. Pearl rewrapped the porcelain baby until next year. And despite her pleading with him not to do it, Hobart—his shimmery suit coat covered in ceiling plaster—went straight for The Judge and shook a finger in his face. "You saw her try to kill me with your own eyes. It's time you put Lila in jail!"

Later, Pearl said that confronting The Judge was a most unfortunate mistake on Hobart's part.

Mama and I are Not Like Pearl

Lizzie

Making Hobart pay for the death of her child is Mama's way of coping. It's been my way, too. Pearl would say it's the wrong way, because Pearl is forgiving, a caretaker, and a fixer. And most of all, Pearl tries to trust. She stayed married to a man who paid little attention to their daughter, who gambled away her house, and also killed her sister, accident or not. Who else could do that? Pearl says trust is a ladder she climbs day by day. Mama and I? We don't climb. We don't even try to. We're not like Pearl.

I am due tomorrow, but Dr. Sharbel says the baby won't be born then. I sit across from him at his office desk. He has his medical notes in front of him, yet he continues to confuse me with Mama. "Last time, Lila," he says, "you were late, so you will probably be late again."

"Dr. Sharbel, I'm Liz!"

"Well, whoever you are, the baby will not be here tomorrow. Come back next week."

Outside the doctor's office, Izear is waiting in the old, but ever-sparkling, Roadmaster. Pearl still says she'll never buy a new car when the old one still runs, and Izear agrees; Miss Pearl and him don't need nothing new when they already got a good thing they can polish up.

"It won't be tomorrow," I say to Izear when I reach the car.

He stretches across the front seat to open the door for me. "Are you sure?"

"No, I'm not sure," I say, laughing. "I'm not even sure who I am with Dr. Sharbel."

"Ain't he a card?"

"Izear, there's someplace I'd like to go."

"Where?"

"Willow Street." I haven't heard from Anthony in weeks, not since I denied that I love him. Except, I do love him, but I can't fathom how he could love *me* after my hand in Richard's death.

"Who do we know on Willow Street?"

"No one, it's just a drive."

"Uh huh."

The house is small and neat, two large live oaks in the front yard, and no car in the driveway. "Who lives in that house you're craning to see?" Izear asks.

"Nobody you know; just go on home to Pearl's now."

"I got more sense than you give me credit for."

"What do you mean?'

"I'm adding it up, that's all. Nine months since the funeral of man who was real sick for more than the nine months it takes to make a baby that ain't gonna have Aids."

"Quit adding, Izear. Whatever your answer, it won't do anybody any good."

"Except the daddy. He might have some feelin' about being a father."

"I want to go home, Izear. I'm worn out."

"I reckon so. Keeping a lie going is tiring, ain't it? So tell the truth. You ain't perfect. Nobody's perfect, not even the saints. Miss Pearl says the only difference between us and them is that the saints made their amends by fixing up what they broke, and then they just carried on by the grace a' God." He looks over at me. "Alright now, what are you smiling about?"

"Pearl, and a waitress I once met in Vigil."

He shakes his head as if I've lost my mind, then heads home.

Little Sister's Visit with The Judge

Little Benedict

Today is Monday and every Monday afternoon, by standing invitation, Little Sister visits The Judge, so we're all waiting for her return in Pearl's kitchen—LaRosa and me, Lizzie, Miss Pearl and Izear. Izear's making oyster stew and Miss Pearl's dipping in a spoon to taste it every few minutes to see if he's put in everything he ought to have put in.

Pearl has spoken to The Judge about Hobart's wanting Lila arrested. She said The Judge was anxious to change Hobart's mind because Pearl was his own blood-kin, so she asked him to. Nobody's sure if The Judge was successful because nobody's seen hide nor hair of Hobart for several days.

The screen door springs open and Little Sister rushes in. "The Judge told me everything!"

Miss Pearl drops the spoon in the oyster stew and says, "Tell it all, Little Sister."

So she does.

The Judge was driving around early one morning last week because he hadn't been able to sleep," Little Sister says. "And he saw Hobart hanging by his belt buckle from the *Buy Now Pay Later* sign at D.C.'s car lot. He was just a' waving, so The Judge stopped and got out and went over to see what happened.

"Cut me down!" Hobart hollered, but The Judge was in no particular hurry. He liked seeing Hobart wiggle.

"How'd you get up there in the first place?" he asked Hobart.

"Damn D.C. done it. Now, cut me down!"

"I'll cut you down, if you cut me a deal." The Judge said because he saw an opportunity.

Hobart musta thought he meant a deal on Dixie's powdered sugar because he told The Judge the whole story about how he'd quit D.C. and how he didn't have any sugar anymore, not even to bribe a judge. Then he said D.C. might have some Highlow Fine China, if The Judge wanted that kind of thing.

The Judge said he was tickled pink to hear Hobart had quit D.C., but the deal he wanted wasn't Dixie's sugar, or Highlow's Fine China. The deal he wanted was for Hobart to drop the charges against Miss Lila, and The Judge said he wasn't cutting him down until he did. So sure enough, Hobart said, "I'll drop them then!"

Of course, The Judge wanted proof Hobart wasn't lying. He went back to his car and got his notebook and wrote down what Hobart promised, then he got a new ladder out of his truck—he meant to take the ladder back to the hardware store that day because it was missing a rung—and he climbed up it and held out his notebook to Hobart, along with the pen he always keeps in his inside coat pocket, and said, "Sign this paper!" And Hobart did.

"I'll bet nobody else in Highlow *ever* got such sorry treatment!" Hobart told The Judge when he handed back his signature.

"I felt like you'd want a chance to be the first, Hobart," The Judge said, and put the paper in his pocket. "Now, before I cut you down, I'm gonna give you a second chance."

Little Sister ties it up then, just like Perry Mason would. "Ya'll know how The Judge likes to give second chances? Well, he led Hobart to see how he and D.C. could either leave Highlow--and take Leona with them--or enjoy a long rest together as a threesome in the state prison for selling Dixie sugar, among other things."

Little Sister gives a big sigh when she's finished with all those details about what happened to Hobart. Then she asks, "Guess where they all three went?" Naturally, she doesn't wait for a guess. She opens up her pink, patent leather purse and pulls out a flier The Judge gave her. The headline reads: *THE FIRST REAL ESTATE BUY NOW PAY LATER CAR LOT EVER KNOWN IN FLORIDA.*

"Well, I declare," Pearl says. "I knew that boy went to Florida."

Little Sister laughs. "The Judge said as long as the only thing they sell that looks like sugar is the sand, then that's just fine as china with him."

So, according to Little Sister, the three of them--Hobart, Leona and D.C.--are down there now, starting all over in Florida and surely making waves. Little Sister says she feels a little sorry for Hobart though. She says she agrees with The Judge; all Hobart ever wanted was for one single person to love him.

Carry On

Lizzie

The morning after my appointment with Dr. Sharbel, my water breaks. Pearl calls him to say he's gone in the wrong direction again, this time with my due date. "Oh go home, Lazi!" I hear her say into the phone. "But come over here first!"

I am in the middle of a contraction when Pearl asks me if I know why Izear would want to call somebody who lives on Willow Street. "Don't let him do it, Pearl!" But by the time the contraction is over, she's left to open the door for Dr. Sharbel.

"Should we take her to the hospital, Lazi?"

"Now, now Pearl. She'll be fine. Won't you, Lila?"

Mama has come to stand in the doorway. "Yes, I'm fine," she says. "You worry about Lizzie."

Dr. Sharbel looks as if he is having a moment of uncertainty, but it passes quickly when Pearl pokes him with her lambs head cane. "Lazarus Sharbel, I'm counting on you!"

"Who else would you count on?" he answers and slaps a wad of something sharp-smelling under my nose.

Far-away, I hear Izear's voice. "We ain't had a baby born here in nearly thirty years."

Even farther away, Dr. Sharbel responds, "Oh, it hasn't been that long, has it, uh-Rufus?"

In the darkening room, I'm a child, again, opening the china cabinet in Pearl's Highlow house while a crowd of people stand behind me, watching. I take out a fine china plate with its birds of prey and hold it up to a stream of light from the arched, dining room window. Part of a wing has faded, there are scratches and patched cracks, but the fragile china is still in one piece, until I let go. The plate falls. It shatters. I turn to look at the people behind me to see if I will be blamed; great grandmothers and grandfathers, my mother, my brothers, and Pearl. Pearl smiles and steps back to motion Anthony forward. He picks up each broken fragment. Just before I open my eyes, Pearl hands him the super glue and says, "Carry on." And Anthony says, "I mean to do just that, Miss Pearl."

Then, in the distance I hear Dr. Sharbel say, "It's a girl."

"And a boy!" Pearls chimes in.

"And Lila's just fine!" Dr. Sharbel says, patting my forehead.

"Oh, go on home Lazi!" Pearls turns to me. "Your Mama almost fainted. We had to send her out of the room."

One baby starts to cry, then the other. I kiss their silky heads, nestled in the hollows of my arms like a pair of gentle crutches.

"It's party time, Pearl!" Dr. Sharbel sings. "Will you join us, Dr. O'Connor?"

A familiar hand touches mine. "I'll stay here with Liz."

"It's not that Lazarus really needed help, you know," Pearl says to me on her way out. "It's just Izear said two babies ought to have two baby doctors, so he called Dr. O'Connor."

"Miss Pearl, you know good and well you're the one called him," Izear says, following her out.

"Hush," Pearl says from the hall. "Go open the wine, I'll get out the fine china, and then we'll cut some of your sour cream pound cake. What a party we'll have!"

All Kind of Good Sense

Little Benedict

Miss Pearl gave Lizzie and Anthony a real, nice wedding this past spring. She didn't put it in the paper though, because Izear refused to let her use his name again, and since the postman was out sick, it was a small wedding; but Miss Pearl said she thought it would last. Anthony moved out of the house on Willow Street and into Miss Pearl's house on Main because Lizzie said she'd never leave home again. From the start, Lizzie's babies fit right into Highlow. The little boy's starting to walk and Miss Pearl says the little girl crawls right after him, just like Lizzie used to follow Peck. And Izear smiles all day long, just like he's a real daddy.

Tonight, LaRosa and I are talking on the porch of God's World before we go next door to Pearl's Christmas Open House. "I don't imagine there'll be a shooting this year since Hobart's left Highlow," I say. LaRosa's all dressed up and feeling philosophical.

"You know, Little Benedict, I've never once wanted to leave Highlow, but I can see why Lizzie wanted to. I'm glad she changed her mind and came home."

"Some things you don't forget."

"Uh huh," LaRosa agrees. "Home is part of you, kinda like the painted birds on one of Miss Pearl's fine china plates. Scrape it, chip it, or even break that plate into little bitty pieces, but you won't get rid of all those birds. Parts of them will always be there. And you know what, Little Benedict? I think it's supposed to be that way, just in case somebody with Super Glue shows up to put it back together."

"Woman, that makes all kind of good sense!"

LaRosa smiles, then calls inside for Little Sister and the rest, "Time to go!" And we head over to Miss Pearl's party.

In The Distance Between High and Low

Lizzie

  The doorbell is still ringing for the Christmas Open House. Lots of laughter, lots of voices downstairs. But up in Peck's old room, there is quiet. My twins remain sleeping, moonlight from the window baptizing their faces. There is a fresh smell of wax on the furniture and a single Confederate rose in a cut-glass vase. Its origin is a bush filled with flowers, brushing softly against the glass of the window pane. Before this short night is over, its flowers will be blood-red, and dead. A characteristic of Nature that no one can keep from happening.
  Once I'd picked a perfectly white bloom for Peck, and pressed it inside his diary. Is the flower is still there? I tiptoe to his closet and move to the back of it where four drawers fit into the wall. The bottom drawer sticks as it always did, but finally pulls out. I push my hand underneath the pile of old National Geographic magazines, beneath the studied weight of a puzzling world, where the diary is still hidden. It opens naturally, bookmarked by the flattened flower, burnt red. There is a picture I'd drawn of Peck, folded into a square. Now, a cross-shape creases his penciled face. His high cheekbones were just coming into prominence then. His almond-shaped eyes were green like the bottom of the spring. His copper hair brushed like a fan of sea oats over his forehead. "You got all the talent," Peck had said when he first saw it. "You're the artist."

"But you can write, Peck. You're talented with words."

"How do you know?" he'd asked. "Have you read my diary?"

I smile thinking about that, until a slant of fresh moonlight washes through the pane and brightens the brittle pages holding our memories; Peck's and mine. The light falls on a page I've never seen. A poem by William Blake is centered on the paper. It's written in Peck's hand on the day before he died. I whisper the words with tears in my eyes.

"Father! father! where are you going?
O do not walk so fast.
Speak, father, speak to your little boy,
Or else I shall be lost."

The night was dark, no father was there;
The child was wet with dew;
The mire was deep, & the child did weep,
And away the vapour flew.

I close the diary, hold it to my heart, then return it to its place between slick magazines attempting to clarify an inexplicable world, a world that can only be explained by one who has left it. Then I hear the door open. Anthony's warm, strong hand touches my shoulder. He wipes a tear from my cheek, and together, we take the stairs down.

*From The Official 1960's Archives of Pearl's Cousin, The Judge,
On a single, stained page
Discovered many years later under a tea napkin
by Little Sister
And left just where she found it.*

Lila's twins were born today. She named the boy, Peck, and the girl, Lizzie. Their father is just another Highlow secret, best left untold. Pearl says she and Izear will see to it that Lizzie and Peck don't feel the lack of him, but I say those twins will search the distance between high and low for their father's love. It's just natural.

Made in the USA
Monee, IL
05 February 2020